CRISTINA IN CAMPANIA

CRISTINA IN CAMPANIA

ALESSIA SAINT

Maria DeKoning

Alessia Saint

ISBN-13: 979-8-9855067-3-0
Cover design by: Alessia Saint
Edited by: Maria DeKoning
Printed in the United States of America

CRISTINA IN CAMPANIA

La semplicità è la suprema sofisticazione.
Simplicity is the highest form of sophistication.

Leonardo Da Vinci

This book is dedicated to the people of the town Sant'Angelo dei Lombardi, in Avellino—a town special to me since it is where my family is from. This is for all of the hard-working people of this town, who take care of the land with passion and keep traditions alive, even here in the U.S.

This is also for all of the lives lost in the devastating earthquake in this area in 1980, especially for my aunt, Giuseppina. The strength and resilience of the people of Sant'Angelo continue to shine as the town was rebuilt into the beautiful town you see today.

In loving memory of my Grandma Filomena

1932-2022

I

Uno

una decisione - a decision

"No!" I said out loud as I crossed my leg against my knee and leaned against a building. I held my soy chai latte carefully making sure it didn't spill and I looked at the bottom of my shoe to see my nightmare confirmed. A wad of gum. On the sole of my brand new red-bottoms. This cannot be happening right now.

I frantically wiped the sole against the sidewalk but got more disgusted as I saw it mix in with the gravel and filth of a New York City sidewalk. I desperately searched around for anything to scrape it off with but gave up and scuffed my shoe against the curb instead. I could not ruin these shoes—not today, not ever. In the midst of my own personal hell, I felt my phone vibrate in my bag. I took it out and saw a message from my boss.

ANNOYING TOM: **Late again Cris?**

It was the third time this week he'd texted me about my tardiness at work. Didn't he know how long it took me this morning to pick out an outfit to wear for the meeting today? I refused to text him back, and instead took a sip of my drink, letting the one pump of sugar-free caramel do the trick of relaxing me. Instead of dealing with him, I texted my step dad, figuring that going above my boss and straight to him would send a message.

CRISTINA: **I'll be right there. Crisis on 5th ave.**

When I finally reached the building, I waved to my favorite doorman, Paul, and stood in front of the elevators as he punched the button to the eighteenth floor. I took a deep breath once the doors opened, and politely smiled at two other men entering after me and talking on their phones as I stepped inside. They were each dressed in business suits and holding sturdy briefcases. I smoothed down the hem of my pencil skirt and adjusted my blouse before I felt my phone vibrate again in my hand.

FIONA: **Tom is pissed.**

Fiona, one of the financial analysts, is usually the one to warn me when my boss is going on another tirade. I scrolled through our messages and realized that most of them were about Tom's different mental states and realized they were mostly directed towards me.

CRISTINA: **Be right there.**

I figured I would wait to tell her about the nasty orange gum under my shoe and how I had to turn my entire closet inside out to find something suitable to meet with DeLouise Financial. But I knew if anyone would understand me, it would be Laila, my best friend.

CRISTINA: **Tough morning. Stepped on gum with my new black Pigalle Louboutins. Not happy.**

I felt relieved texting her. She always understood fashion fails and would sympathize with me. There was never a time when Laila was not quick to respond.

LAILA: **Not the Louboutins! That's TRAGIC.**

CRISTINA: **I know! Meet me for lunch at 12. I can take two-hours, Michael won't care.**

Speaking of which, my step dad texted back.

MICHAEL: **You need to be in here now. Tom is really upset and was counting on you to talk about the proposal.**

I took another sip, wondering why he was texting instead of calling me like he normally does when I'm running late. He was never this stern when I lived at home with him and my mom. He had always spoiled me, stepping in to take my dad's place when he started visiting us less.

The year I turned 17, Michael made a deal with me that if I did well in school, he would let me borrow whatever car he leased that month to drive around. On my 18th birthday he gifted me a brand new white Range Rover—the same that Laila's dad had gotten her. He never bothered me about anything, and my mom was always too busy with my two little twin sisters to follow up on schoolwork or anything else that was going on in my life.

CRISTINA: **I'm in the office. I can see Tom's bald spot from here.**

I texted as fast as my fingers could move, then walked towards my desk, re-arranging the flowers Josh had given me on Monday and filling the vase up with more water.

"Love the new sweater, Darlene! The blue is just perfect on you!" I said to Tom's secretary as I passed her desk on the way to the sink.

"Thanks, sweetie!" She said back with a smile across her face as she looked up from her computer at me. "Tom has been looking for you, but later I need to show you my daughter's prom pictures. You really saved the day stepping in after that makeup artist canceled on her—I owe you!"

"You don't owe me, I was more than happy to help," I said as I watched her smile reach her eyes before she turned back to her computer.

I obviously knew I needed to see Tom, but my flowers would not last through the meeting if I didn't take care of them. I put the vase back on my desk next to the picture of me and Josh of our ski trip three months ago in Utah. It had been a last minute decision to go. Josh had surprised me with a ticket for one week with a few of his friends and their significant others. My step dad had argued with me that I shouldn't take off after starting only six months previous, but how could I say no to a trip like that? It was practically our 2-year meet-aversary anyway, so we had to celebrate somehow.

I picked up my tablet, opened the documents I had put together for the meeting, and headed towards the board room, where I could still see Tom's bald spot and his hand waving in the air.

"Well, look who decides to show up." He turned to me as I walked into the conference room, "Cristina, you are late. Really late. And you know how important this deal is. Did you prepare the second-quarter financial report I asked for?"

"Yes, I have it here. I just shared the doc with you."

"The what? The doc?" He looked miffed as he said that.

"Yes, I shared the Google doc with you. I wrote down all of the numbers you gave me and then I put them next to the other numbers you gave me. I figured that was what you wanted."

"Cristina," His thumb and index finger were now spread across his forehead while his eyes closed. "Please tell me you met with Fiona on how to do this report."

Did I? Sure, I met with her when she explained how Tom was mad at me. She kept insisting I meet her for coffee, but I was convinced that it was to go over some gossip in the office. I remember it not being important.

"Um, yes, I did." I replied back, feeling that was the safest answer. I looked over at Fiona, who now had her head down and was refusing to make eye contact with me.

"Fiona, you are telling me you sat down and helped her with the report?" Tom turned to her, making her look like a baby lamb in front of a butcher.

"Well, she was, um, very busy. We tried to meet, but she had, she was..." Her voice was barely audible and her eyes wide. I felt guilty entangling her in this mess.

"Actually, we never met. But it was my fault. Don't worry, Tom—I will take the blame for this one."

"Unbelievable!" Tom stared at me with an ice-cold glare that made me jump back a few inches. He paced for a second rubbing his forehead making it red. After a minute he sat down defeated. "Cristina, I *really* can't deal with this today. Go home. Now." I couldn't believe he was talking to *me*, the daughter of the CEO, like this.

I met his glare, took my tablet from the table, and turned back towards the door. No use staying when Tom was in another one of his moods anyway. I walked straight to Michael's office, prepared to fill him in on another one of Tom's dramatic meltdowns, but his door was closed and when I peered in, it looked like he was shouting through the phone.

I looked down at mine and noticed it was 10:15. Maybe I could hang out with Laila earlier then. Even though it was too early for lunch, we could definitely meet for a little snack at our favorite French cafe on 5th.

My mouth watered when I smelled the baked goods that Antoine, the owner of the cafe, put in the display case. I eyed a raspberry cream cheese tart, but then quickly shifted my gaze to Laila as she waltzed in.

"Okay, so I have something very important to tell you!" I squealed as soon as she reached me. We did a quick hug before sitting down and Laila motioned to the waiter to bring our usual. Laila was dressed head to toe in Chanel, and her shiny, jet-black hair was pin-straight. She looked as though she could have been cast in the movie, *Crazy, Rich Asians* as one of the main characters. I had no idea what her parents did, but from how she spent money, it must be impressive. "I think that Josh went ring shopping!" I continued once we both got situated at the table.

"Ohh, fun. Where do you think he went? To that new jewelry store in Park Slope? Did Blake see him there? By the way, I do love your skirt—is it Dolce and Gabbana?" She asked, placing her orange Birkin bag on the stool next to her.

A feeling of satisfaction comes over me every time Laila compliments my outfits. I always tried to emulate her style.

"Thank you, it is, and no, I haven't spoken to Blake in a few weeks. Ever since she's been hanging out with Matt, Mitch, Max, or whatever his name is from Franklin Square." I inched out of my heels under the table, relieving my feet from the pain they've caused me.

"Tell me about it. It's like the suburbs have already sucked her in. Next thing you know, she's moving out to Long Island and then buying a high ranch and getting a dog." We both laughed as the waiter brought our gluten free croissants to the table. Laila picked at hers with a fork while I reluctantly took a bite of mine. I still eyed the raspberry cream cheese tart in the display case wishing it would miraculously turn calorie free.

I quickly broke out of my trance and thought again about Josh. "I can feel it. It's been over two years since we've met and he'd always said that once he finished his residency, we would get married. He hinted at it a few weeks ago that he has two years of residency left. The perfect amount of time to plan a wedding!

"No way, this *is* big! So, have you mentioned the type of ring you want? Did you talk into Siri on his phone so ads could mysteriously pop up?"

We both started laughing, picking more on our croissants before switching subjects to her love life and how she had started seeing Pablo but her ex Jeff kept calling her. Since I had known her, she had always juggled more than two guys at once effortlessly, with neither of them ever finding out. She was adamant that she would never settle down or have kids, never wanting to be tied down.

Laila and Blake had been the first friends I made when I moved into my new school in 9th grade. Blake, who had stopped me in the hall, noticed I had tears streaming down my face because I couldn't find my next class and she introduced me to Laila. We had been inseparable ever since.

"Ugh, Michael is calling me. I'll let it go to voicemail, but I should probably call him back in five minutes."

"How's your mom doing? Are they still fighting, or are they better?"

"No, they're fine. They always fight before he goes away for one of his business meetings, but as soon as he comes back, they're all over each other. I'm so happy I moved out so I don't need to see the disgusting amount of PDA they display. I get the info instead from the two little pests."

"Those two little pests are about 7 years old, right?" Laila asked while typing a response to a text she had received at the same time.

"Actually, almost 9. And my mom claims that they are getting more and more sassy." I laughed, thinking about how the twins were definitely a handful. "Alright, let me go call Michael back so I can complain about ridiculous, dramatic Tom."

We quick-hugged goodbye and I walked out of the cafe. I absolutely loved June in New York. The perfect amount of warmth and sun, without the oppressive humidity that July and August tended to bring. More parents with babies in strollers, people riding their bikes, and street vendors happily selling their food in the 70 degree weather. It made me wonder why I would want to be in an office today anyway. I walked towards Central Park, looking at the trees in full bloom all around me, and taking in the smell of the roasted peanuts from one of the food carts parked along the street. I felt my phone vibrating and looked down to see Michael calling again.

"Hi, Michael. So, I guess you heard how crazy Tom..."

"What is the matter with you, Cristina?" He spat into the phone, cutting me off. "I trusted you with this! You were supposed to help Tom secure the account!"

My cheeks heated because I've never heard Michael this angry at me before.

"I will do the report, I'm sorry. It won't happen again."

"It sure as *hell* won't happen again. You are coming over to our house at 6 pm tonight. You will not be a minute late. Do you understand this?" He did not wait for me to respond before saying, "Your mom and I want to talk to you. It is very important."

A feeling of dread came over me. What could they possibly want to talk about? I said goodbye, hung up, and suddenly the world looked less happy than before. The birds seemed to stop chirping, the sun creeped behind a cloud, darkening the sky, and suddenly I just wanted to lay down in my apartment. I opened the Uber app, requested a ride, and nervously chewed on my finger, not wanting to walk another block.

"So, my parents want to see me tonight, Josh. They said they need to talk to me about something." I put him on speaker while I searched through my closet for something to wear. "I messed up a little at work and now I'm probably getting the speech about how I have to work harder and blah, blah, you know the rest."

"Babe, don't worry. You know he has to pretend he's mad at you, but he'll probably let it go, give you a warning, and then you can pretend to work again at his company. Just make sure you look hot tonight—I've been thinking about our night together all day."

I laughed a little, still sifting through my outfits to find the perfect outfit for our date tonight.

"Josh, I'm being serious. First of all, I really *was* working there. Or at least *trying* to. And second, he sounded very serious about it. He actually *texted* me this morning about running late—not called, but texted! Then he finally *did* call me, and what he said genuinely made me very nervous."

"It'll be fine. I didn't realize you were serious about the job. I thought it was just so you could take your time and figure out what you wanted to do. You didn't like your first job either right?"

"No, my first job was a joke. They seriously wanted me to stay after hours and treated me like I was their assistant." I thought about all of the coffee runs they sent me on in the freezing winter weather.

"Just make sure you are out of there by seven," Josh continued. "It took a lot of persuasion to get a table at Atera tonight."

"Don't worry, I'll be on time. I'm sure there is not much to talk about with Michael and my mom. Can you swing by their apartment to pick me up? Love you."

"Okay, love you, babe."

I clicked my phone off, tossed it on my bed, and continued rifling through my closet. I figured a quick FaceTime with Laila would help me choose exactly what to wear.

"Hey Laila," I said when she picked up. "You always seem to know exactly what outfits of mine Josh likes. Is this good?" I asked, pointing to my Stella McCartney off-the-shoulder pink mini dress.

"No. The pink washes out your olive skin. And besides, you already wore that last time you went out."

I was amazed she remembered that. I barely remembered what I wore the day before.

"Ugh, nothing is right for tonight." I muttered, already defeated from the day's events. I kept moving each outfit over, my camera still pointed towards my closet, when Laila stopped me.

"The Valentino black and white one! That's perfect, Josh will love it. Alright, I have to go, *au revoir!*"

I slipped into the dress quickly after noticing it was already close to four. I sat in front of my vanity, lining my eyes delicately with my charcoal-black pencil and adding a hint of purple eyeshadow to my lids, trying to make my brown eyes stand out more. I ran the flat iron through my hair one more time and smiled at how the strands now reached well past my shoulders. I'd been trying to grow it out for a few months now after reading an article that said guys like girls' hair better long. I put on the diamond studs Josh had gifted me for my birthday and slipped into my 5" Louboutin black heels, which instantly slimmed my legs more than my spinning classes could ever do.

Since Josh was picking me up for the date at my parents' house, I decided to uber there so I wouldn't have to go through the trouble of getting my car out of the garage. The driver pulled up to their apartment, and the doorman walked me to the elevator. When I reached their apartment, a duplex on the fourth and fifth floors, I instantly heard the shrill voices of the twins Samantha and Stella through the door. I took a deep breath, pulled down the hem of my dress, and knocked. The voices died down and the door swung open.

"Oh, it's you. Dad has had a stick up his butt all day and it's definitely because of you." Samantha said, holding her iPad as she held the door for me.

"Hello to you too, Samantha. I heard the both of you through the door. Where's the other one?"

"Oh, she went back to her room—probably texting this new *boy* she's been talking to. She is utterly obsessed with him and it's honestly kind of pathetic."

Samantha went back to her iPad, her fingers moving furiously on the screen. I couldn't make out if she was writing or drawing something. Her gorgeous tight black curls framed her delicate face. We both had brown eyes, but our similarities stopped there. The twins took mostly after Michael, their skin a few shades darker than mine and their lips fuller, making me envious that they would never need fillers that I had already planned on getting. My deep-brown hair was curly too, but I usually wore it straight, thanks to relaxers that I religiously got every three months. My mother refused to touch my sisters' hair, saying that they were even more gorgeous when it was natural, and I had to agree. They already had more confidence than me at their age than I have now at 24.

I walked through the apartment, to the kitchen, and said hi to Maria, my parents' housekeeper.

"Oh, look at how beautiful you are, Cristina!" She said, stopping what she was doing to smile at me. "I think your parents—I mean your mom and Michael are in the study." I gave her a quick hug and went off to find them.

"Hi, honey." My mom greeted me with a squeeze, but I could tell from her face that she was upset. I was starting to get nervous that this was something bigger than just getting mad at me for today. My nerves started settling in as I sat down next to her.

She always had a look of sophistication, even when we had less money and were all living in an apartment in Brooklyn. We were basically living paycheck to paycheck, but her nails were always painted, her hair was always done nicely, usually pulled back in a bun, and a string of pearls were always around her neck. *Taking care of yourself never costs anything,* she would always say, as she smoothed on her lipstick and lined her sharp blue eyes, something I would have killed to have in the genetic lottery.

Michael walked in a few minutes after talking on the phone. He sat down directly across from me.

"Yes, I have a meeting with John at nine tomorrow. I know...I know. I need to go. I will talk to you later." He hung up and stared at me from his chair.

"What's going on guys? You're both kinda scaring me. Is Nonna okay?"

Michael took a deep breath before leaning back in his chair and folding his arms across his chest. "Cristina, do you know how important that meeting was today and how many people had to scramble at the last minute to come up with the report you failed to produce?"

"I said sorry so many times. Plus, if Tom wasn't such a dick all of the time..."

"Language!" My mother said abruptly, afraid that the twins would pick it up. I wanted to remind her that she used worse language when yelling at my dad right before their separation.

"Sorry..." I said, half-rolling my eyes. "If Tom hadn't been so...*annoying*...I would have known what to do."

Michael shifted in his chair before he spoke. "Your mother and

I have been talking. We have given everything to you, but it might not have been what was good for you. You know I came from nothing and struggled to build what I have. I had to put myself through college on my own and start from basically nothing. I believe that it is because of that, I am able to appreciate having a company, and making enough money to provide for my family. I didn't realize though, when things are just handed to someone without working for it, it could, essentially, *ruin* them."

My eyebrows pinched together as he was saying this. I was not sure where he was going with this—but I didn't like the sound of it. He stood up from the chair, one hand resting on the back of it, while the other still holding his phone. He looked at my mom, who nodded her head at him, and then looked at me again before he continued.

"We are giving you an ultimatum, Cristina. Either you go to Italy, spend time at your nonna's house for two months or..."

"What!" I interrupted, my mouth dropping open as I remembered that he said *either,* implying there was still another choice. I looked over at my mom, who was refusing to look back at me, and then I turned my attention back to Michael, who started speaking again.

"...*Or,* you could stay here, but all of our financial help will be cut off, you would have to afford rent and car payments on your own, and you would have to find another job to help keep up with your lifestyle."

My body froze and I could almost feel my lunch from a few hours ago starting to come up again. I opened my mouth, trying to force something out, but I couldn't. There was no way he was this angry at me over one missing report.

"This doesn't make sense at all. For just one mistake? I promise I will be better. I'll make it up to you. I'll even apologize to Tom." I looked at him desperately trying to get him to change his mind. He stared back at me with no emotion. I had no choice but to turn to my mother. She had to know he was out of his mind. "This is crazy. Mom, you can't let him do this!"

"Cristina, it was my idea. Nonna broke her arm and could use the extra help on the farm. It would be good for you to get out of the city for a while and get some fresh air. It's a simpler life out there. You will be able to find yourself outside of all the outfits and lattes and drama. Plus, it's been years since you've even gone to Italy."

"Nine years, Mom. And it's because there is nothing to *do* there! Nonna visits us here, why do we even need to go there! Plus, she's *your* mom, why aren't you going?"

My mom gave me a cold look, one that I knew very well. It used to scare me into doing whatever chore she wanted when I was younger. It still sent a small shiver down my spine now.

"I wanted to go, but the girls need me, and I can't take them out of their activities for the summer. Between piano lessons, ballet, and summer science classes, they would fall behind their classmates if they missed them. Plus, Michael is right, you need to learn how to work and earn your money."

I glared at her, almost wanting to acknowledge that *she's* never worked. She walked right into this life of glamor when she met Michael. Everything she had was all paid for. I pressed my lips hard together, tears starting to form in my eyes, and I clenched my fists to stop them so I wouldn't ruin my makeup before my date with Josh.

"Take tonight to think about it. If you decide to go to Italy, we have a ticket for a flight on Saturday." Michael then went back to his phone and left the study.

I sat there and looked over at my mom whose face became more sympathetic.

"Honey, I love you, you know that, right? You used to have fun in Italy, remember?"

"Mom, I have a life and boyfriend here. How am I supposed to leave that?"

"Michael says two months, but he told me it was just to scare you. Maybe, at most, a month is all you have to stay. This might be good for you. Josh loves you, your friends have been next to you for years. No one is leaving you, Cristina."

My tears were starting to escape. It was still at least four weeks. I got up and walked to the kitchen, filled up a glass of water, and noticed my fingers trembling hard. I didn't need his money. I could afford it. I could tell Josh all about it and move in with him, he wouldn't mind. That would show Michael. Maybe Josh will propose even sooner, and I wouldn't have to worry about any of this.

My phone vibrated and I saw a text from Josh saying that he was here. I shouted 'bye to Stella and Samantha, refusing to say anything else to Michael or my mom, and went down to meet Josh.

"It's like they want to hurt me or something." I said, after filling him in. I looked at several of the dishes around and scrunched my nose at half of them. I tried really hard to like caviar and duck and would push myself to eat it in front of Josh, but it was really unenjoyable for me. I always stomached it because everyone else loved it, and therefore I should too. I found the plate with what resembled two dumplings on it and grabbed one to fill my stomach with as much appetizing food as I could.

"Yes, I know" Josh said, and I looked at him with a puzzled expression since it didn't really follow what I had said. "Excuse me, waiter, I will take the Blanc de Noirs Grand Cru Brut, please."

He ordered the wine with an impeccable pronunciation. He spent a lot of time in France with his family, often going for at least one month every summer. The waiter commended his choice and went off to retrieve the bottle of sparkling white wine.

"Dr. Lettino complimented me on the last surgery I did with

him, can you believe that? He said he wants Dr. Hasselman from Mount Sinai to check out my next surgery. This could be good for me. I could get accepted into the fellowship that I've been dying to get!" I grabbed his hand from across the table, avoiding the caviar dish, and squeezed his fingers.

I forced a smile, trying to hide the fact that I was still thinking about the ultimatum. "I am so proud of you. You've been working hard for this." I tugged down my dress and slipped out of my shoes under the table. "I wish I could be happier, but I keep thinking about..."

"Dr. Lettino congratulated only me in front of the others. Babe, this is big. I need to focus on getting this fellowship and learn as much as I can." I sunk into my chair, realizing now was not a good time to bring my problems onto him. He needed to focus on his future and not worry about me moving into his apartment.

"What's wrong, babe? You have been moody the whole night."

"I told you, they want me to make a decision by tomorrow. I'm still not sure what to do."

"Oh, that. You said it'll be a month tops—right? You can do that. I need time to focus, and then when you come back, we will plan our future together." He took my hand, lifted it to his mouth, and kissed the back of it. I smiled back at him but couldn't deny that I was shocked by his response. I thought he would insist on having me move in with him immediately. Instead, here he was giving me his blessing to go.

I stayed quiet for the rest of the night, listening and reminding myself to smile as he went on about the fellowship. I played with the cheesecake in front of me, taking the tiniest bites and trying to enjoy it, but also picturing Laila's face warning me to never leave the table with my belly full, or else I would pay when I looked at the scale. She was more disciplined than I was about dieting. I knew for a fact that she probably wouldn't even touch the cheesecake, and here I was forcing myself not to eat the other half remaining on my plate.

We headed back to his apartment after dinner, with him leading me down the hallway, holding my hand as I admired him from behind. His dirty blond hair was always cut neat, the sides faded, and the top long enough to style with gel. His body and muscles were tight even though I had never seen him work out.

We headed into the elevator and the doors had not even closed before he pulled me into him.

"You look hot in this—but it needs to come off now." His voice was low next to my ear, sending racing shivers through my body. When the doors opened again, we walked quickly into his apartment, barely making it through the door before my shoes came off and my dress was hitched up.

"Wait, Josh. Let me take this dress off." I said with a sultry smile across my lips, as his hands were already under my dress, ready to remove it.

"You have two seconds, Cristina." He said, his eyes fiery, showing me exactly what he wanted. "One, two."

I laughed, running away from him as he chased me, threatening to rip the dress off. I finally removed it, showing him my favorite matching bra and undies underneath. He shook his head and lunged at me, throwing me on the bed.

"Are you more relaxed now?" Josh said, turning towards me afterwards. We were both panting and laying in bed, with sweat gleaming off both of us.

"Yes, but I didn't realize you liked my dress that much." I said, my eyes playfully teasing him. He got up, still without clothes revealing his toned legs and backside, and quickly put on a pair of shorts and a t-shirt. I was a little sad that he didn't stay in bed. I wanted to cuddle next to him and feel better from the miserable day I had. I got up too, found my dress, bra, and undies, and quickly put them on before I followed him into the kitchen.

"So, I guess I'm leaving two days from now." It hit me that I had made my choice, or rather Josh did.

"Oh, that soon? Don't worry babe, we will FaceTime. Plus, Italy is gorgeous, I remember visiting Venice and the Alps with my family. What's there not to like?"

"Well, it's different where my grandmother lives. First of all, she's on a farm, near Avellino, in the middle of nowhere, and I'm expected to help her. It won't really be a vacation."

"Where's Avellino?

"It's in Campania, it's about an hour inland from Naples."

"Oh. But yeah, I can't see you *actually* working on a farm." He said, chuckling to himself as he poured some granola over the bowl of yogurt he had on the table. My stomach rumbled as I watched him shovel 500 calories-worth of granola into his mouth and I wished I had eaten more at dinner. "Listen, keep remembering it's only for a month and you will be back here before you know it." He reached over, gave me a peck on my lips, and then took another spoonful.

I followed him to the couch, sat down next to him as he turned on the TV to watch the sports highlights of the day. All of a sudden I realized that my life was going to change and that I needed to start packing. Panic rose up inside me as tears began to trickle down my cheeks in pairs. I squeezed my eyes and turned away so he wouldn't notice.

"I'm going to go, Josh." I said, softly. I gave him a quick kiss on his lips while he was mid-bite. I headed out before he would notice my tears. I couldn't show him I was weak when he kept acting like it was no big deal.

"Bye babe—I will see you tomorrow night. Love you."

"Love you too." I said back, my lips trembling.

I barely slept that night, tossing around, and not able to make myself comfortable, as images of Italy and Nonna's farm came to my head. I suddenly thought about my dad, living out on Long Island with his girlfriend. I couldn't ask him for help because he could barely make it on his own. Plus, I'd rather go to Italy than stay with him. It's not like we didn't get along, but I cringed remembering a time when I had to share his one bathroom and how torturous the train ride would be to see Josh. I needed to brave up, go to Italy for a month, and come back home to pick up where I left off.

***

"Someone will pick you up at the airport, dear. Nonna knows all of the information about your flight and what time you should get there. Please give her a hug from me and the girls too. I love you." I hugged my mom, somewhat forgiving her for making me go through this. I hugged Michael too. I wanted to stay mad at him but couldn't deny the fact that he had been good to me all of these years, treating me like his own daughter. The tears started flowing when I faced Josh.

"Don't cry babe, seriously. You will be back in a month." He said to me, as he kissed the top of my head.

"A month? Two months, Cristina." Michael said, and then I noticed my mom elbowing him. I waved to them goodbye one last time and went through security. My heart hurt so bad that it reminded me of the day my dad had moved out, the day my family had officially broken apart. I took a deep breath and walked to my gate.

Eleven hours later, and one connecting flight in Milan, I finally arrived at Naples airport. My stomach was twisted in a giant knot, and I couldn't stomach eating anything. My bags were being carted by an older Italian gentleman whom I gave ten Euros to as I exited the sliding doors that were dividing the baggage area and the families waiting for arrivals.

"*Signorina, ha bisogno di un taxi?*" A man said, asking if I needed a taxi after noticing me looking around for a familiar face. I shook my head, happy to realize I still understood some Italian and looked for a sign with my name.

"*Signorina De Rosa! De Rosa!*" My ears perked up when I heard my last name in Italian, only ever hearing that after my dad kept teaching me the correct pronunciation and not the American "Dee -Rosa" that everyone would say.

"*Sono io.*" I said, reaching the short, bald-ish man holding the sign with my last name.

"*Prego, signorina. Venga.*" He said, ushering me outside of the airport. He took the luggage cart from the guy that had been following me out and led me to a red van that reminded me of those horror movies that kidnap girls in foreign countries.

My heart was beating in my chest as I looked around for an escape. I needed to get out of here—I could not do this. I couldn't miss summer in the Hamptons, or lunch dates with Laila, or my apartment. I touched my forehead and wiped away the cold sweat that was forming, even though it was more than 100 degrees outside.

"*Signorina, si sente bene?*" The man asked, with a look of worry after seeing panic in my eyes.

I reminded myself to get a grip. If he is asking how I am feeling, there is a good chance he won't murder me. Plus, he didn't even reach my shoulders, that defense class I took with Laila would be of good use if he even tried anything.

"*No, sto bene…sto bene.*" I replied, letting a deep breath out and proceeding to the red van.

I stared out the window the whole ride, refusing to look down at my phone, and instead focusing on the view. I recognized Mt.

Vesuvius as we passed it, laughing quietly to myself as I imagined it choosing this summer to erupt again while I was staying about an hour away from it. We went further inland, moving away from the densely populated cities and into smaller towns, where wheat fields and vineyards dominated the landscape. I looked down from the van's window and saw the road was more narrow than the highway we were on before, with no marks dividing the lanes. There seemed to be no clear curb either. The road just blended into the grass with a crooked asphalt border being the only demarcation between the two. Then it hit me. The memories came flooding back.

2

Due

l'inizio - the beginning

10 years old...

"Nonna!" I shouted, running up to her and giving her a hug after stepping out of the car. She took me in, and I could smell fresh tomato sauce and something fried—and I prayed it was the fried peppers and potato dish she made that I loved.

My mom and dad took the luggage out of the trunk, and then gave my nonna a hug. They hadn't fought that much in the car, and I was praying it would be like that for the rest of the trip. If they started fighting badly again, I'd have put my huge headphones on that I wore whenever I'd hear my mom's voice start to rise.

I settled right into my bedroom, remembering it from two years before when I had last visited. I quickly got my book out from my backpack, *Harry Potter and the Sorcerer's Stone,* and placed it on my bed, ready to read it later. I slipped into my sneakers, changed into the first shorts I could find from my suitcase, and sprinted outside, excited to help my nonna on the farm.

"I pulcini, Nonna!" I squealed, when I saw all of the baby chicks in the little barn that housed the hens. I chased after one, being careful to gently pick it up with two hands, and tried to pet it before it protested enough to be let loose again.

"Attenta, Cristina." My nonna said to be careful. I followed her around the farm, helping her clean up the different cages, and then placing down fresh grass for the animals. I looked over and spied on Alessandro working in the garden with his parents over on his property. Alessandro was the boy who lived in the house next to my nonna's. He was just a year older than me. I had met him for the first time two years prior when we spent the whole summer playing soccer and building clay houses in the dirt. He was funny and sweet, always eager to talk to the American girl who showed up in sparkly Converse and pink frilly tops.

"Nonna, I'm going to Alessandro's." I ran full speed over to his yard with my new backpack containing my book thumping against my back.

"Ciao!" I shouted as I approached Alessandro. He looked up and smiled when he saw me. His brown hair was wild from running around and his green t-shirt had a rip on the side probably from climbing the trees in the field. I ran up to give him a hug. His parents looked over at me and waved hello.

"Cristina!" He shouted, hugging me back. *"Mamma, possiamo andare a giocare?"* Alessandro turned to ask his mom if we could go play.

"Certo." She said back, using the back of her hand to brush her dark hair that had fallen onto her face. She gave me a warm smile, the lines on her face reminded me of my nonna's—revealing how much time she had spent outside under the blazing sun. She went

back to tying the tomato plants and we both ran off towards the vineyards, our favorite hiding spot away from our families.

***

"Puoi leggere questo per me, Cristina?" Alessandro said, asking me to read my Harry Potter book out loud to him. We were both laying down on the grass, under an olive tree, trying to soak up as much shade as we could after running around all day in the strong sun.

"Okay." I said, scooting closer to him. We laid belly-down on the grass, and I propped the book in front of both of us so he could follow along. This had been a sort of new routine we had developed together, me reading him some pages from Harry Potter and trying to act out the scenes so he would understand. Sometimes I had been able to throw in an Italian word I knew, but for the most part I looked like a flailing bird trying to recreate what we had just read.

"Cosa significa, owl?" Every once in a while he would stop me and point to a word, wanting to know what it meant.

"Umm...*uccello?* Hoo-hoo!" I tried to mimic the noise an owl made and used the closest word I knew in Italian which was *bird.* He doubled over laughing when I widened my eyes as much as I could and turned my head to the side, trying to impersonate one to him. I smiled to myself too realizing he had become a best friend in just the short time I was there.

***

"Nonna, posso?" I said, motioning to the string beans and asking for permission to help her pick them. I started to become more comfortable speaking in Italian by imitating the words I heard Alessandro use. I wanted to learn everything I could before I left.

My nonna's eyes smiled as she handed me a smaller bucket and motioned for me to kneel down next to her.

"Gentle, Cristina. Do not break the plant, just take the *fagiolino* and pinch it off." She explained, while demonstrating. I moved the leaves around and found a string bean that was ready and pulled it gently from the plant. She always treated the plants delicately, careful not to take more from it than needed, and made sure that the dirt around the garden was free of any weeds. It was as if she saw each plant individually and wanted each to fulfill their fullest potential. I always idolized how my nonna seemed to find happiness in the smallest of tasks. Her face was always at peace when she was gardening because she knew she was giving life to the ground around her.

I looked up at her after plucking a few more and a huge smile splayed across my face as I saw her stand up with both of her hands on her hips, watching me work in the garden.

"*Va bene, basta,* that's enough for today." She said, while gathering all of the buckets of vegetables we had filled.

"Nonna, be careful! That's too heavy!" I saw her carrying two buckets in each hand and a basket of grass the size of my suitcase on top of her head. I stared at her with my mouth agape as she balanced better than an acrobat at a circus.

She smiled, "Don't worry Cristina, Italian women can do anything they put their mind to."

I shook my head and smiled as I collected the smaller bucket of string beans and followed her back to the house. I skipped along the gravel path, reaching the steps, and admired how the house perfectly fit on the land. It was covered in a rich cream color that reminded me of the wheat fields, with a thick, blue-striped outline around the border of it. I swung the bucket of string beans, a few falling out, and ran up the stairs excited for more adventures that the day would bring.

3

Tre

arrivare - to arrive

Now

The driver turned off the main road and pulled onto a gravel side street that would bring us straight to my nonna's house. I recognized it instantly. The house was still the same rich cream and blue stucco color I remembered, but both time and sun had caused the once vibrant colors to soften. I looked to the right and noticed the wine cellar and grain house were still there, older looking too, just like the house. The property had a fence lining the farm where the animals were, and some clothes were hanging on a line that was connected from the terrace to a tree. I prayed silently that she invested in a dryer. Tears threatened to form again as a feeling of panic overwhelmed me. The driver placed my bags at the steps to my nonna's house and dipped his head before getting back in the van and leaving. I realized too late that I forgot to tip him, but then remembered that they don't tip here. I grabbed my bag, started walking up the stairs, spotting my nonna standing at the door.

"Cristina, look at you!" She wrapped me in a big hug with one arm, taking care not to press her broken arm in the cast, against me. I did miss her; she was always much calmer than my mom and I could usually get away with anything when she visited. It had been years since I had seen her because it was harder for her to travel now that she was getting older.

"Cristina, don't cry. Come here, I have pasta for you." She brushed my tears away that were trickling down because of fear, loneliness, and jet-lag all mixed together. I walked with her towards the front door and stared at the beaded curtain hanging from the door frame, the one she used to keep the flies and mosquitoes out of the house. I pushed it aside, took a deep breath, and absorbed everything around me.

The kitchen looked exactly the same as I remembered it—like it was stuck in the 80's. There were the same beige cabinets with brown handles, and a dark, wooden table with four matching chairs topped with straw cushions. There was a narrow hallway in the center, with my nonna's bedroom to the left closest to the entrance and a guest bedroom further down the hall.

I excused myself to the bathroom at the end of the hall and closed the door behind me. The bathroom was covered from floor to ceiling with the same beige tile throughout. I looked over to the tub and my shoulders dropped when I saw there was no real shower— just a hose attached on a bracket halfway up the wall, not even high enough for a five-year-old to properly stand up and wash their hair. I turned to the sink, turned on the faucet praying for warm water, and splashed my blotchy, red face. There was no way I could stay here. I missed my nonna, but I had to take a flight back tomorrow. I couldn't do this. I reached for my phone and started looking up flights. I figured I'd spend the day with my nonna, and then take the latest flight tomorrow. I would have to come up with an excuse for leaving though. I took out my credit card and punched in the numbers.

Denied?! I took another credit card out and punched it in as fast as I could. That one was denied as well, telling me they couldn't complete the transaction. Unbelievable. I was genuinely stuck here.

Anger took over my body, causing my blood to boil. I couldn't believe they were doing this to me. I called Josh, not caring about what time it was there, but instantly felt regret when I heard his groggy voice.

"Sorry, Josh. But can you believe they cut off my credit cards already? It's like they absolutely don't trust me at all."

"Babe, it's not even seven yet. I had a little more time to sleep. It'll be fine, just stop worrying. It's seriously not a big deal."

Not a big deal?! Of course it wasn't for him! He was home, sleeping soundly in his bed!

"You're right. I guess I'm just tired from the jet lag. Okay, love you, I'll call you later."

"Love you."

I walked back to the kitchen, trying to hide my sadness, hurt, and anger, and I sat down in front of a huge bowl of carbs.

"*Mangia*, Cristina. Make sure you eat. You are tired, with no energy."

Great. How do I tell her that I haven't touched gluten in two years? I pushed the dish to the side, explaining I wasn't that hungry and picked on the roasted chicken that was also there.

We talked for a little, my nonna asking all about the girls and how Michael had been. I noticed she didn't ask about my mom but instead about my dad.

"Dad is okay. He is living with his girlfriend on Long Island.

I haven't seen him in a few months, but I talked to him a few days ago."

"Tell him I said hi. He is such a good man."

"I will, Nonna." I picked on my chicken a little more, and then excused myself to the guest bedroom.

I laid down on the bed, letting my tears fall down. My chest kept rising and dropping rapidly, hiccups now blending into my tears, and I pulled the blanket up over me, wishing I could miraculously be transported back home, and drifted off into sleep.

"Cristina. *Cristina.* You need to wake up or you will never be on Italian time."

I looked up, pulled the hair from my face that was caught in my mouth, and saw my nonna over me.

"*Scusa*, Nonna. Sorry. I'm up. I'm up." I pulled myself up on the bed and saw that she was staring at me with her eyebrows knitted close together.

"*Tutto bene?* Everything okay, Cristina?"

"*Sì*, yes. *Sono stanca.* I'm tired." For some reason, I was speaking Italian with ease, remembering all of the expressions I used.

"Okay, I'm going outside to feed the animals. Do you want to come?"

"In a bit, Nonna. I'm just going to make some coffee." I felt bad saying no to her, since her arm was in a cast and she looked fragile. But I would not be fooled. These old Italian ladies were stronger than any of the girls I went to the gym with. I once witnessed my nonna carry a basket five times her weight on top of her head. She headed out, and I pushed myself off the bed and headed to the kitchen. I stifled another yawn that was coming and reached for my phone when it started ringing. My mom was calling. Great. Now she will rub it in that I look like a disaster. I clicked on accept for FaceTime.

"How was the flight, Cristina? How's Nonna? Are you okay?"

"Yes, everything is good. She's fine. She's outside working on the farm, or something." I said, quickly trying to interrupt the other fifty questions she probably had prepared. I opened the cupboard, looking for the coffee maker, and tried to remember how to make a cup of coffee.

"You have to put water in the bottom part first." My mom said, noticing my confused face. "Then put the coffee in the funnel, and you screw it back together." I nodded my head, still tired of making conversation, and put it on the stove.

"Michael is really proud that you are doing this, and well, so am I." I turned the phone sideways as I rolled my eyes, not wanting to start another lecture.

"Yes, Mom. I know. Why did you guys cancel my credit cards? How am I supposed to live here? It's as if I am in jail."

"You are getting an allowance. Michael already set it up with Nonna, don't worry. Anyway, Stella and Samantha wanted to say hi. Let me go find them."

I sat down at the kitchen table, looking out of the window and taking in the view. It was stunning. It bothered me to admit it, but the rolling hills, the distant houses, and the cut wheat fields, made me feel serene. I pictured this scene in a commercial for fabric softener where the woman ran through the fields in a white flowy dress with her arms outstretched. I heard my mom yelling my sisters' names through the phone as I looked outside and noticed someone familiar driving past my house on a tractor.

He had the same tousled brown hair, the same dark, serious expression in his eyes, but a much bigger build. I saw him stop, jump off the tractor, and talk to my nonna, his serious expression softened as they began laughing about something together.

"Cristina!" I heard my nonna calling me from outside. I started panicking, I couldn't have Alessandro see me like this. I looked down at my phone, to see an empty living room and I hung up, figuring I'd call her later. I checked my reflection in my phone's camera, and patted my hair down, trying not to look like the mess I was.

"Cristina, come outside." My nonna was now in the doorway to the kitchen. "You remember Alessandro, right?"

I followed her outside, the sun's rays were so strong that I had to shield my eyes with my hand as I made my way closer to him. The skin on my arms prickled as his eyes caught mine. The same dark, mysterious stare that I was so familiar with when I was younger now showed a maturity I didn't recognize. I was so caught up in his stare that I realized I had yet to say hello. I offered my hand to shake his, but quickly pulled it back when I noticed his were full of dirt. Had he been planting with his *bare* hands? He looked at me, his eyes closing slightly and his lips now pursed before he gave a quick scoff, shaking his head. He muttered *ciao* before jumping onto his tractor and he rode away without so much as looking back at me.

"*Allora*, he remembers *you*." My nonna said, laughing at how the scene played out.

I stared at the tractor getting further away, the wheels crunching over the graveled path. I inhaled the dry, hot air, my lungs filling with smells of the surrounding countryside. I knew he hated me. And I knew I was the one to blame.

4

Quattro

un ricordo - a memory

12 years old...

"Here they are!" I said, finding two eggs in a little bucket behind a small haystack. The chicken clucked loudly as if congratulating me on my find, and I put them in the basket with the six other eggs I had found before.

"Papà look, I found another hiding spot!" My dad smiled at me, his eyes beaming, before turning around to continue collecting grass for the rabbits.

"I can help—let me try!" I said, dropping the bucket of eggs gently and moving closer to him. I reached for the scythe, trying to take it away from his hands.

"Be careful, Cristina. Here, let me show you, and then you can give it a try." He positioned the handles in my hands correctly and helped me practice the sweeping motion of the scythe across the fields, while I watched the blades of tall grass topple over into a pile near my feet.

"Papà! I did it!" I kept going, now on my own, careful the blade wouldn't cut into my leg.

"Seriously, Antonio, you are making her do that? Her shoes will get dirty and she will hurt herself!" My mom yelled at my dad. I was afraid they would get into another fight, but luckily he just looked back at me, rolled his eyes halfway, and nodded his head for me to keep going.

My mom had not looked happy the whole time we'd been here. I wondered how she could be so hostile towards the place where she was born. My nonna moved to Brooklyn when my mom was only seven years old and spent most of her life in New York.

"She's okay, Giovanna." My dad replied, calling her by her real Italian name. As soon they moved and she started school there, my mom wanted to fit in as much as possible with the other girls, so she insisted that everyone called her Joanna, choosing the closest sounding American name she could find. My dad, however, always insisted on calling her Giovanna, which aggravated her every time.

"You honestly never listen anyway. What's the point of me saying anything?" My mom sounded exasperated as she hung up the clothes to dry. "And can we get a dryer here? How is it possible my mother still does not have a dryer?"

To say she was miserable here was putting it lightly. My dad turned back at me, shrugged his shoulders, and continued to coach me on the scythe.

"Ma, I'm going to Alessandro's! I'll be back later!" I sprinted to his house, my legs not pumping as fast as I wanted them to go. I didn't want to waste a second of the adventures we had planned. Even though he was only a year older than me, he was probably already one of the smartest people I knew.

"*Andiamo*, Cristina." Alessandro said, as I tried to catch my breath. He motioned with his hand to follow him quietly through the vineyards, putting his finger to his mouth so I wouldn't say a word.

"*Gli uccellini*...umm..the birds? Baby?" He said, flapping his hands as if to imitate what he was trying to say. It was common for us to speak to each other in a mixture of Italian and English, sometimes both of us making up our own words in either language, but always knowing exactly what the other meant.

He moved a few grape leaves over to reveal three baby birds chirping and looking up at us as if we were their mom and we had food for them.

"Alessandro, they are so cute—*sono carini!*"

He carefully covered the baby birds again. I could tell he was excited that he could share this with me. There weren't any other houses around, besides his sister's. She was much older than him, lived with her new husband down a gravel road, but still on the same property. His parents were older than mine and let him do anything he wanted to on the farm. I was extremely jealous of him, but I promised myself that I would one day learn everything he knew.

"*Prendo il trattore, ehm, come si dice?*" He asked me how to say *tractor*, and I reminded him. He nodded his head and took my hand as we headed towards it.

I felt free up on his tractor, high enough to see more of the Apennine hills that surrounded us, and feel a gentle, cool breeze blow through my hair. I gripped the handles tightly. I was a little bit nervous but knew I could trust Alessandro. He wasn't like the other 13-year-old kids I knew back home—he was more responsible in my eyes. I knew Alessandro would never do anything dangerous or silly just for attention. He was confident in everything he did.

His expression was serious as he drove the tractor, only turning to catch a glimpse of me for a few seconds before quickly turning back and shaking his head, laughing at how excited I got for tractor rides.

We spent the whole summer together, going on adventures around his farm where he taught me how to take care of all of the animals, and playing games of hide and seek on his property. He always found me right away and made me jump when he snuck up from behind. My nonna loved Alessandro's family too. Since they were our neighbors, they came over a lot and helped her grow her garden when she came back to live in Italy full time.

My nonna had lived in Brooklyn for almost twenty years, but after my mom got married and moved out, she sold her brownstone and moved back into her family house. We had only been to Italy a few times because my mom would start coming up with excuses of why she couldn't go. My nonna, tired of not seeing us often enough, would come to us for a month or two in the winter so she could spend as much time with me as possible.

"*Cristina, prova a guidare il trattore.*" Alessandro said one day, acting like he was holding onto a steering wheel.

"Drive the tractor? *Sei pazzo!*" I told him that he was crazy.

"*Vieni*, Cristina." He grabbed my hand and led me towards it.

I sat down, my hands clammy and my feet not sure of what to do, but I was determined to try. At least for Alessandro.

"Okay, Cristina. Foot—*qui*." He said, indicating my foot should go on the brake pedal.

"Brava. Ok, *l'altro* foot—*lì*." He pointed to my other foot and where it should be placed. He grabbed my hand, put it on the gear shifter, and rested his on top. My other hand was on the steering wheel while he looked me in the eyes before turning on the ignition.

"*Sei pronta?*" He asked if I was ready, and then explained what I should do next. The tractor sputtered forward before immediately dying, causing both of us to laugh until our bellies hurt.

"Aspetta." He told me to wait, he nudged me over to the side, and he made me hold on to the wheel as his feet controlled the pedals. "Like this, we try."

We drove down his field, past the vineyards, with me steering and him shifting gears. We were laughing the whole way down and decided to park the tractor near a little stream that flowed at the bottom of the valley.

"Facciamo un picnic qui." Alessandro said, pulling out a little basket from the back of the tractor. He set out some bread, cheese, and meat, and we made sandwiches before sitting down, listening to the nature surrounding us.

"You leave in four days?" He asked, his English was getting better with each day and so was my Italian.

"Quattro giorni, sì. But I will email you." A sad feeling came over my body as I realized this adventure would be over soon. I looked over to him and noticed he was looking down, playing with a blade of grass next to him.

"Mi mancherai." He was now looking intensely at me, telling me he would miss me. The feelings I had in my stomach felt like sparkling bubbles popping in my belly.

We both stared at each other, and he leaned over and gave me the sweetest kiss—the first one I had ever had.

5

Cinque

abituarsi - to get used to something

Now

Alessandro's tractor was further down the road. I could faintly hear the humming of its engine and my shoulders slumped thinking of his reaction when he saw me. I couldn't blame him for reacting like that. I turned away and met my nonna's stare as a smile crossed her face. She let out a laugh, walked back towards the house, while I followed, trying to forget the scene ever happened.

My phone buzzed again, I pressed the "accept" button and Stella and Samantha both appeared on the screen.

"You look like a mess, Cristina. Brush your hair and put on some makeup. Your eyes are all puffy."

"Thanks, Samantha. I love you too. How's dance going?"

"It's fine. Mom, come grab the phone Cristina wants to talk to you!"

"Wait, what? No, I don't..."

Before I could stop them, my mom appeared on the screen with a smiling face. "Hi honey, so Nonna is okay? Were you able to help out much so far?" She turned her head to the side to respond to an unclear voice calling her in the background. "What, Michael? Sorry, honey. I'm going to go, Michael is asking me something. Love you!"

I hung up, confused by the flurry of conversations on the phone, and went back to my bedroom to dial Josh, wanting to hear his voice.

"Hi babe. I miss you." He said in a low voice which made me want to be near him even more.

"I miss you so much. I'm miserable here, but I promise that's the last time I will tell you that." I didn't want to seem like a depressing girlfriend. It's the last thing he wanted to hear after long hours at the hospital.

"It'll be fine, Cristina. Just think of how nice it will be when we see each other again after all of this time apart."

I let out a sigh, forced a smile on my face and continued to ask how everything was going. We talked a few minutes more before he hung up and I closed my fists, trying to control my emotions.

My stomach started rumbling and I realized I hadn't eaten yet and never finished making that espresso from before. What was I going to eat here? I was surrounded by carbs and oil. I shuffled back to the kitchen, looked through the fridge, and grabbed a plate with raw chicken breasts on it.

I can definitely cook this, I thought, as I rifled through the cabinets in search of a pan. After several attempts, I figured out how to turn on the stove by positioning the knob correctly to ignite the flame. I never made anything myself before and didn't even know how to get started. I opened up Google and typed in *healthy chicken recipes*.

"Garlic? Rosemary? Spray oil?" I said to myself as I searched for some of the ingredients. The cabinets didn't have any of the ingredients I needed so I let out a defeated sigh. I would have to just cook the chicken in the pan and eat it plain. As soon as the pan got up to heat, I placed a slice of chicken breast directly on it. The chicken immediately started to smoke, so I took a fork and tried to flip it over, but pieces were stuck to the pan.

"Ugggghhhhhh....." I let out a grunt, peeling off the stuck pieces. The chicken was now in shreds, half stuck on the pan and the other slightly singed.

I closed my eyes, trying to stop the tears that were threatening to flow down, and left it alone, figuring I would just put a salad together.

"Cristina?" My nonna said, coming up from behind me and putting her hand on my shoulder. *"Hai fame?"* She continued, asking if I was hungry.

"No, no. Sto bene." I replied, saying I was well. I quickly wiped away the tears that reached my cheek, determined not to show her my weakness. Here she was, all alone and in a cast, still working on a farm, and I couldn't even manage to cook a piece of chicken.

"Dai, mangiamo." She said, encouraging me to eat. She walked over to the fridge, pulled out the leftover pasta and started to heat it up.

"Nonna, do you have salad? I think I'm just going to make some salad."

"Si. What do you want? I will make it for you." She opened the fridge, pulling out cucumbers, tomatoes, and lettuce, while I nodded meekly. She started to wash and cut them, and I ran over to the sink, offering to help. She shushed me back down, and I sat in my chair, feeling even more helpless as I watched my nonna prepare a salad with only one good arm.

Nighttime was always the worst for me because my emotions

bubbled up to the surface. I always felt that it magnified whatever negative feelings I had during the day and made them seem as if they could overwhelm me, suck me in, and spit me out after devouring every part of my being. This may have been an exaggerated version of how I felt, but I wasn't sure.

CRISTINA: **This is the worst. Remember that time when my bikini strap undid itself in front of all of our high school friends? This makes that look like the highlight of my 11th grade.**

LAILA: **Cris, it's that bad? I'm sorry, girl. Josh said it's only for a month, so try to have fun.**

At least Josh talked to Laila, probably sharing my misery with her.

CRISTINA: **I know. I feel bad bothering him. Everything here is just dirty. My parents canceled all of my cards, and I have an allowance. Can you believe this? It's like I'm 13 again.**

LAILA: **Yeah, def don't bother Josh. He seems really focused on impressing Dr. Hasselman. Do you need money? I can send some.**

CRISTINA: **No, it's fine. Okay, love you!**

LAILA: **Love you too!**

I hovered over Blake's contact info. There was a part of me that wanted to message her, but I kept thinking about how I hadn't heard from her in a month. What would we even talk about? The time had caused us to drift apart, and I knew Laila would disapprove if I told her anything. Laila always brought up how Blake's boyfriend works in a restaurant and has lived in the suburbs his whole life. Apparently, that meant a lot to her, since she cut Blake off completely after she found out. It sort of confused me though because he seemed nice when we met him, but I couldn't get Laila's words out of my head. Sadly, it caused us to text less often to catch up and for the invites to parties to become sparse. Now, we just stopped talking altogether. I did miss her. She was my balance to Laila, someone who understood me more.

I locked my phone and set my hand down on the bed, still clutching it, almost as if I were magically waiting for some type of update that my life would go back to normal. Eventually, I finally fell asleep.

I heard birds chirping and felt the sun against my closed lids as I stretched my arms out the next morning. I picked up my phone and was surprised to see it was almost 10 o'clock. Jet lag. I always hated this part of traveling east. You would waste most of the day, groggy and still feeling like it was 4 am, but instead it was already halfway through the morning. I got up, headed over to the kitchen, and noticed a small cup of espresso and a note attached to it.

Buongiorno Cristina. Bevi e mangia i biscotti. My nonna had told me to drink and eat the cookies that were next to the espresso cup on the table.

There was no way I was eating those. I didn't even want to look at the sugar and calorie count on the bag. I sipped the espresso, happy to have some type of caffeine in my body, and headed to the bathroom to try and wake myself up more. I looked at myself in the mirror at the dark circles under my eyes becoming more pronounced. I went back to my room, looked through my clothes and got angry at myself that I didn't bring anything to go outside with. I hesitated as I grabbed my Golden Goose sneakers, a pair of shorts that I wouldn't mind dirtying, and a t-shirt.

I walked towards the farm and found my nonna sprinkling some corn around the ground for the chickens to eat.

"*Ciao*, Cristina!" She shouted out to me, waving me over to her. I had stopped, not sure if I was ready to venture into the farm just yet, and shuddered thinking what insects or snakes could lie in the tall grass that surrounded it. The farm was more run-down than the last time I was here. The wire and wood fencing were more weathered and sticking out haphazardly, looking like it was ready to give tetanus to the next unknowing victim that walked by.

"*Vieni!*" She continued to shout, gesturing for me to come over. I walked slowly to the gate, eyeing between every blade of grass, and silently wished she had a landscaper that would take care of the property. Here, when they cut the grass, they do it to feed the animals, not to make their property look pretty like Michael did with his second house in Connecticut.

I reached the wooden gate and tried to open it with the makeshift contraption my nonna had put together, but gave up. How could anyone get by like this?

"*Arrivo.*" She said, easily opening the gate. I made a mental note of how she did it and stepped inside. My nonna gave me a smile and headed back to feeding the chickens on the other side of the fenced area. I stopped in place and took it all in.

A memory flashed back to when I was younger and enjoyed taking care of the animals and collecting the eggs. I saw two ducks waddling by, something I never remembered my nonna having, and then heard the pigs grunting in the distance. I walked over to the bunny cages under a covered awning. I watched them scurry around, twitching their noses. I went to lift up the hatch on the cage, when I noticed my foot stepping into something squishy.

"Oh no!" I said in horror as I saw my beautiful white sneakers full of rabbit poop. My face pulled back in disgust and a dry heave reached my throat. I silently thanked myself for not eating anything because I would've thrown everything up. I searched frantically for something to clean my shoe off with, and ran out of the farm into the field, trying to wipe my shoe against the grass.

"You need to close the gate." A deep voice grunted, as I turned around to see Alessandro closing the gate behind me. "The chickens can escape, and the foxes will eat them at night if they don't go back to the coop."

I stared at him, surprised at how well he spoke English, even despite a slight accent that came through. He looked back at me, his eyes narrowing slightly, and then looked down at my sneakers. He looked as if he couldn't help but laugh. His laughter made me angry.

"If you're not going to help, then just leave me alone." I said, scowling back at him.

He grabbed something from the ground and started heading off when a girl with long brown hair ran up to him, giving him a hug hello. She looked over at me and then said something to Alessandro in Italian that was too fast for me to pick up. After he didn't respond, she walked over to me and gave me a kiss on both cheeks to say hello. I had forgotten that Italians greet each other that way and was taken mildly by surprise, jolting my head back a little.

"*Ciao, sono Arianna. Abito qui vicino.* Do you speak Italian?" I picked up that she lived nearby but was grateful when she spoke in English.

"Yes, a little. I'm Cristina. Do you speak English?"

"Yes, but not the best. It's nice to meet you, Cristina. It's good to see a girl my age around here! Most of my friends are married and boring or have already moved up North to search for a job."

I noticed Alessandro's face softened as he looked at Arianna and wondered if they were dating. Arianna seemed bright and bubbly which probably balanced out Alessandro's moody and gloomy disposition. Arianna was wearing a pair of sneakers that looked perfect for working on the farm and it made me realize that I needed new clothes. I refused to ruin all of my nice clothes here. I had a feeling that Michael wouldn't give me any more money when I got back so I needed to make sure my clothes stayed in good condition.

She asked me how long I was planning on staying and if I liked it so far. I saw Alessandro look away and mutter something, but I didn't want to hurt her feelings, so I told her I was happy to be here.

"Arianna, where do you go shopping? I need clothes to work here, and I have nothing."

"Tomorrow, there is a market. Every week we have one. I will pick you up and we can go together. I sell your nonna's eggs at the market too, that's why I came here, so I could collect them."

I nodded my head and thanked her as her eyes twinkled at our planned date. Alessandro had stared at us the whole time, shook his head, and walked off to his tractor.

I started walking back to the house when I noticed the view from where I was standing. The one from the kitchen was beautiful but could never compare to this. From this elevation, I could see everything, and it was breathtaking. As I turned around, I took in the soft, rolling hills with these little towns planted into them. The yellows, browns, and greens of the fields interlaced together as tiny clusters of houses popped up from them with the spires of churches standing out in the center. Behind these towns stood these rough, jagged mountains as if they were safeguarding everyone. Nothing was obstructing my view as I turned all the way around and took a deep breath in.

I wasn't used to all of the open space. The air was crisp and clean. It filled my lungs as I absorbed the quietness around me. There were no cars and trucks honking their horns and stopping short on the road. Just nature—in its purest and most simple form.

The feeling was short-lived though. I took a deep breath and got a whiff of the smudge on the bottom of my shoes. Another dry heave was sent through my body.

I was laying in bed after lunch scrolling through my feed when my nonna walked into my room. I prayed that there would be some type of news article showing how a teletransporter had just been invented so I could just use it to go home.

"Cristina, come on, you can't stay inside all day. The sun is out, the animals need food, let's go."

"Nonna, I'm tired. I don't have the right clothes. I'm just going to stay here."

She moved closer to the bed and placed her hand on her hip. Her eyebrows were drawn as she stared at me for a few seconds, trying to understand why I would choose to stay in.

"You can use my shoes. We can wash your clothes if they get dirty."

I did not want to tell her that I didn't trust her washing machine to clean my clothes, so I let out a huff, and put down my phone.

"I'll go out to the market with Arianna tomorrow and buy new clothes to use. Then I'll come out."

She stared at me for a few moments more before shaking her head and walking out. I picked up my phone and opened the calendar app to count the days I had left to stay.

The next morning, I woke up at nine, still struggling to get over the jet lag. I found my favorite sundress, paired it with brown sandals, and took my time applying makeup so I could try to hide the dark circles that were still under my eyes. I might as well try to look good while I am here. I was still refusing to fully give in that I was okay with being here.

Arianna picked me up as promised, in a tiny little Fiat Panda that made me nervous. It was old, with rust cracking the white paint around the wheel wells and made a roaring sound that was way too loud for a car of that size. She laughed when she saw my expression and patted the dashboard before announcing that this drove better than any other car out there.

We headed to the main part of town, which was on the highest peak of one of the mountains. I noticed a lot of scattered houses in the distance, and I tried to find my nonna's house, but I had no idea where to even look. Most towns and cities in Italy were like this, the main part was more densely constructed, with houses next to each other, a church in the center, and a main piazza with a fountain. Farmlands and vineyards made up the outskirts, with houses scattered around, much further apart.

We reached the main part of town where white, cream, and light orange stuccoed buildings surrounded a square piazza that was lined with light gray stone. Arianna maneuvered her car into a tiny parking spot that I would never be able to get my Range Rover into. We stepped out and walked towards the piazza. I took in a quick breath, taking in the scene in front of me.

Stand after stand of clothes that looked cheaply made were placed on headless mannequins lining the piazza. There is no way I could wear any of this. Arianna led the way with her bubbly personality.

"What do you need?" She asked, looking at me with a wide smile across her face and hair covering her eyes. She was pretty, in a simple way, and I knew that if Carlos, my hairdresser from back home, got a hold of her hair, he would turn her into a stunning brunette. She had pretty almond-shaped eyes that seemed to get lost under her heavy bangs.

"I'm not sure." I answered, touching the fabric of a shirt and quickly letting it go, my nose scrunched up. I looked over and noticed small stores lining the piazza behind the stands that were set up.

"What stores are those?"

"Those are expensive. You can buy five shirts at the market but only get one hat there."

I squinted my eyes, trying to make out what they sold from the window displays.

"Let's go check them out." I pulled Arianna's hand and walked towards a store.

The interior of the shop was more my speed. An elegant display of folded shirts lined one side of the store, while the other show-cased different accessories. It reminded me of the smaller boutiques I would shop in, and I dropped my shoulders in relief. I looked through the clothes and felt the richer fabric between my fingers. I picked up a few shirts and a shop assistant walked over, asking if I needed help.

"*Scarpe da ginnastica, per favore.*" I said, remembering how to say sneakers in Italian. She walked back with a pair of sneakers that seemed nice until I had spotted a pair of Gucci's on display.

"*Quelle.*" I said to the shop assistant, pointing them out in the middle of the shop.

She pulled her head back, looked at Arianna who shrugged her shoulders, and then went to get my size as I sat down ready to try them on.

I was happy to finally buy something Italian in Italy, instead of at a boutique in Manhattan. I slipped them on, admired how they looked and felt, and took them back off to buy them. I reached into my wallet and dread came over me. I didn't have enough money. I looked in and saw the crisp 100 Euro bill my nonna had given me before leaving and bit my lip. Embarrassment flooded through my body. I dug my nails into my palms so I wouldn't cry and came up with an excuse as to why I couldn't buy them. I walked with Arianna over to the stands in agony. Arianna's face changed to one of worry.

"It's okay, Cristina. Let's find a nice pair of sneakers that are good

to get dirty. Besides, those were too beautiful to wear on the farm."
I appreciated how she was trying to make me feel better.

She was still trying to cheer me up as she showed me all of the
stands that sold sneakers. I needed to become stronger. I could not
let the fact that I can't buy a pair of sneakers make me sad. I took a
deep breath in, let it out slowly, and concentrated on picking a pair
of shoes that seemed the most stylish, but inexpensive.

I was getting my change back from the vendor, after Arianna
haggled the price down even further, when I spied Alessandro across
the piazza, handing over crates of vegetables to an older woman.
Gone was his moody disposition. He was laughing with her, and
then shaking his head when she offered him money. I watched for a
bit longer, wondering what that was about.

From beside me I heard Arianna yell, *"Alessandro, vieni qui!"* I
wasn't still sure if they were dating but thought whatever their
relationship was odd.

He spotted Arianna, turned back to the old lady and patted her
arm before walking towards us. He greeted Arianna with a kiss on
both cheeks, and me with an expression of annoyed amusement.

"I didn't think you would shop here." He said, looking at me up
and down, and then at the shoes I had in my hand. "I didn't even
think you would come out of your house." He smirked, his intense
eyes staring into me.

"What is your problem?" I said right back, my eyebrows furrowed
and my expression serious.

He let out a laugh, nodded to Arianna and then said something
fast in Italian that sounded like he had to go back home.

After he left, Arianna turned to face me. "I'm sorry, I don't know
why he was like that." Arianna said, a puzzled expression crossed
her face before she turned back around. "Let's check out the rest of
the market."

That smirk on his face as he said that made my fists close. Who did he think he was? Did he think he was better than me because I was a rich American girl and not used to this? I will show him. Determination came over me and made me want to prove I could also do what he did. I wasn't some prissy girl that wouldn't work.

I kept shopping with Arianna and ended up finding two pairs of shorts and a few shirts. I was surprised when I realized I still had five Euros left.

"Do you want a gelato?" She asked, seeing the bill in my hand.

"No, I haven't eaten sugar in years," I said. Laila's personal trainer constantly yelled at us to avoid sugar at all costs if we wanted our legs to look envious.

"No sugar? Wow, Cristina. I wish I was strong like you. The way Angela makes the gelato here— it is impossible to avoid. Anyway, we can go back home."

I did miss ice cream though. Italy was known for the gelato, making American ice cream practically inedible after you've had theirs. Maybe at some point I will allow myself just one scoop before I go back to NY.

We got back in her car and made the trek back. Arianna told me all about who lived in each of the houses we drove past, and I nodded my head, half-listening and half-imagining what Josh was doing back home.

She dropped me off and I walked in to see my nonna putting lunch on the table.

"What did you buy?" She asked, gesturing to the bags I was holding. I pulled out the clothes and sneakers, and watched her raise her eyebrows and slowly nod her head in approval.

"*Mangiamo.*" She then said, pulling out a chair for me with her good arm, and then walking over to get a bowl of salad she had prepared for me. I thanked her, grateful she remembered that I didn't want to eat pasta, and then saw her try to scoop the spaghetti from the pot, when I ran over to help.

"Nonna, I can do it. Let me help."

She smiled and stepped back, and I scooped the spaghetti on her plate and brought it over to the table. She poured her own wine, grabbed some bread, and ate quietly next to me as I admired how she wasn't worried about how many carbs or calories she ate. My nonna wasn't thin, but definitely not overweight. She enjoyed the bowl of spaghetti in front of her and even added grated cheese on top of it.

My stomach grumbled. I was not satisfied with the measly salad and chicken I had as I watched my nonna eat spaghetti in her home-made sauce.

After lunch, I was washing the dishes when my phone rang. I reached over and saw Josh FaceTiming me. I answered it, happy to finally see his face.

"Hey." I said, my body warming up when I realized he was FaceTiming me from bed. I decided to walk to my bedroom, down the hall, so I could lay down and talk to him.

"How old is that house?" Josh asked, as I closed my bedroom door behind me.

My cheeks flushed and I looked around, noticing how run down everything was. The walls were a bare white stucco with cracks running down from the ceiling. The furniture looked like it came from a 1990's garage sale—shiny brown lacquer with curved edges. I framed the camera so that he could see only me and some of the headboard of the bed.

"It's pretty old. I think my nonna is in the process of painting and changing everything, so that's why it looks like this." I came up with an excuse even though I knew my nonna would never *waste* money on a renovation when everything worked completely fine.

"Babe, you look rough. What is going on? Are you sleeping at all?"

I checked myself on the small insert on my phone and made the picture larger. My shoulders slumped as I stared back at a ghostly version of myself. I was sad I couldn't hide it from Josh.

"Listen, my sister is using this new cream she swears by. Do you want me to give you the name of it so you can find it? I think it's French, so they have to have it in Italy. Or should I overnight it?"

My face felt like it was on fire. I was mortified that I was getting advice from my boyfriend on how to take care of my skin.

"So how is everything going?" I asked, trying to switch the conversation.

"Fine, Dr. Lettino introduced me to some other surgeons that were visiting our hospital yesterday." He let out a yawn and sat up in bed. "I didn't come home until ten last night, so it's a good thing you're there."

I felt a little better knowing he could have this time to concentrate on himself instead of worrying about me. Maybe it's better that I am here.

We chatted a bit more. He told me what he had planned for the rest of the week, while I tried not to talk about what I was doing so he wouldn't think I was still miserable.

"I love you, babe." He said, his lips turning up into the cute smile I missed.

"I love you too."

We hung up and I walked to the mirror and stared at what looked back at me.

6

Sei

riflettere - to reflect

Josh was right. My eyes were baggy, my mouth was frozen into a frown creating a new line of wrinkles that I'd never seen. My hair looked matted and void of the vibrant brown highlights that usually framed my face. I needed to take care of myself and look somewhat alive. I pulled up a chair, took out my magnified mirror, and plucked and exfoliated until my face felt clean. I applied every cream I had, making sure to add more under my eyes where they needed it, and apply some makeup that freshened up my look.

That was a start. I was finally proud of what stared back at me in the mirror.

I needed to go outside, move my body, and show Alessandro that I'm not some rich girl that wouldn't work. I failed at my first job, then I failed working for Michael, but I wouldn't fail at this. I wanted to show everyone that I was capable. A fire started burning from inside my core and sparking something new. I clenched my jaw and found a pair of shorts and a t-shirt. I laced up my new sneakers, and headed out to the farm, ready to show everyone that I was not weak. I could do anything I wanted to.

My shoulders slumped as I saw the amount of mud that was surrounding the farm. I looked around for a place to step so I could get to the gate. The mud wasn't going to stop me though. I tiptoed around it, trying not to get my new sneakers dirty, and tried to open the gate like I remembered my nonna doing.

After five tries, I gave up and looked around to see if I could somehow climb over the fence. The wired fence was held together by wooden posts that reached my shoulders, and I looked around to formulate a plan to get over it. I saw some bricks piled against it and figured I could use those as a stepping stool to help me climb over and reach the roof of the chicken coop on the other side. I plotted out the course in my head and started stepping on the bricks. My feet wobbled slightly on some loose stones that were piled on top. I tried to regain my balance, holding on to the fence, and readied myself to climb over.

My knees started to give out as my fear of heights reawakened, a fear I had not truly tested in years. When I tried to straighten my legs, I couldn't because fear had now taken over my body.

Why did this seem easier in my head? I was stuck. I kept looking for a way down, my knees still bent, my hands holding the fence, and one leg reaching down, hoping to feel something, anything.

I will not let this break me. I can do this. I am strong. I repeated words of encouragement to myself, holding back the usual tears that started forming, almost as if reminding myself that I am a rich girl that can't do anything. I tried again, carefully reaching a foot down. My other foot was now giving out as the brick wobbled beneath me. My knee scraped against the bricks as I held on to the fence, trying not to fall the rest of the way down.

"Do you need help?"

I rolled my eyes as I heard the familiar voice. He was enjoying the scene of me struggling, laughing in his head knowing all along how right he was and how I couldn't do anything.

"No, Alessandro. I'm fine. I couldn't open the gate, so I tried to climb the fence." I swore I heard him let out a laugh as he walked over to the gate and fiddled with it, making it open right away.

I clenched my jaw, refusing to look over at him and give him the satisfaction of being the hero that saves the damsel in distress. I was not a damsel in distress. I was simply a city girl, trying her hardest to adjust to this lifestyle.

I looked down at the ground, longing to reach it. I can still climb down the bricks; I know I can. I was trying my best to block out Alessandro who was holding the gate and staring at me. I just needed to find my footing again. I looked up, trying to blink away the tears and push away the negative thoughts, but I knew deep down that I wasn't going to be able to get myself out of this situation alone. Just when I was about to turn and yell at him for watching me suffer, I saw his hand reaching out, ready to help.

"Just take my hand, Cristina. I can help you get down. You almost got it."

I nodded my head, pressed my lips, and took his hand as he helped me place my foot on the right bricks to come down.

As soon as I reached the ground, I looked at my knee and noticed the scrape.

"You got hurt?" He said, looking at the small beads of blood poking through the scratches.

"It's not bad. I can handle this." I wasn't in the mood to hear that I was weak or have him laugh at me again.

"I'm sorry. I don't want to make fun of you, I was only trying to help you." His eyes softened and I let out a breath, relaxing my shoulders.

"It's okay. I want to help my nonna out, but I'm starting to realize there is a learning curve to adjusting to farm life." My voice was gentler, I realized it was hard being hostile towards him.

"I'll teach you to open this gate. Watch—you need to push it towards the post while trying to unhook it. That's the only trick." He effortlessly pushed the old wooden gate open and then closed it again, motioning for me to try.

I went closer, pushed it towards the post like he showed me, and unhooked the latch, watching it swing open.

"Wow that was it?" I said in surprise. "That's not difficult at all. The fence just wasn't aligned right." Alessandro stepped back, amusement crossing his face. I calmed myself down, trying to shield my embarrassment.

"Don't worry." He said, his face gentler than before as he nodded his head towards me. He headed back to his tractor, got on, and pressed his lips in a small smile as he passed me.

Maybe he wasn't so grumpy after all. I watched him drive away on his tractor, remembering the fun times we used to have together.

I turned back to the farm, ready to help my nonna as much as I could. But what should I do? I walked over to the rabbit cages, being careful not to step in the poop, and saw the rake that my nonna used to clean up the poop from under the cages. I tried to handle the rake the best I could, moving everything from under the cages and made a pile in the middle. I looked around to see if there was a pile of hay placed somewhere. I noticed one in the corner of where the chicken coop was and moved it towards there.

I can do this. My confidence began to build up as I went to look at what I could do next. Water. The animals need water. I looked for a bucket, walked over to fill it with fresh water, and placed some in all of the animals' drinking spots. My body felt strong and confident. I looked around, searching for more things to do, as I noticed the turkeys off in the corner, walking towards me, gobbling as they moved.

They look harmless. No need to be nervous about them moving towards me. I looked around for the chicken feed, ready to sprinkle some on the ground, when one of the turkeys pecked at my leg, hard enough to make me flinch.

"Ow!" I screamed and jumped away as the other turkey was ready to peck. "What the—!" I was about to scream again when I noticed my nonna and Arianna shoo-ing the turkeys away.

"*Via, via!*" My nonna shouted at them, making them move to the other side of the fence. I looked down at my leg, and between the scrape from before and the trickle of blood that the turkey just made, I looked pretty beat up.

"Everything okay, Cristina?" She asked, a smile forming on her face as she saw the rabbits' area cleaned out. "You did this?"

I nodded my head and looked over at Arianna who had a huge grin on her face.

"*Grazie.*" My nonna said, her eyes becoming cloudy. She smiled again, said something to Arianna, who then turned to me.

"Cristina, you have to go out with me for pizza tonight—please?"

I looked over at my nonna, guilty for leaving her, but saw her nodding yes.

"*Non ti preoccupare di me*—don't worry about me, Cristina. I am fine, I can cook. You go out and have fun with Arianna.

I needed a night out, to talk to another girl, and get my mind away from all of this. I agreed and exchanged numbers with Arianna who told me she would call me before she came to pick me up.

She came by the house around eight. I was surprised it was late, but she told me that it was actually almost early for pizza and that most of her friends were meeting later to get together.

We sat down at a little pizzeria in the main town. The tables were all filled and bustling with people laughing and talking loudly.

I looked around and noticed everyone seemed happy, putting slices to their mouth and talking animatedly with their hands. The energy in the room was contagious, instantly putting me in a better mood as I looked at the menu.

"So, how do you say *gluten free?*" I asked, trying to search for the option on the menu.

"Oh no, are you allergic? I'm sorry, your nonna didn't say that. The pizzerias in small towns don't usually have that option—you would have to go to a bigger city. Do you want to leave?"

She looked flustered and I felt guilty making her feel bad. I definitely wasn't allergic to it, just avoided it after Laila told me to.

"No, it's okay, I'm not allergic. I'll just pick something." I said, flipping through three pages of pizza toppings, amazed at all of the different possibilities that existed. I finally settled on a vegetarian pie, hoping that the vegetables would counterbalance all of the carbs I was about to eat.

"*Per me una tonno-cipolla, per favore.*" I heard Arianna say to the waiter as he came. The waiter then looked at me and I tried to copy what Arianna said instead of asking her to order.

"*Per me una vegetariana.*" I said, much slower than Arianna had said and probably with a thick American accent as well.

Arianna nodded her head and smiled.

"I used to know more Italian, but I lost it through the years."

"Well, that was pretty good." She said, her smile still wide and her eyes twinkling. "You'll start to learn more as you hear it and speak it yourself."

We started chatting, Arianna telling me all about her friends that moved to different cities because they found it difficult to get a job in the town or anywhere nearby.

"A lot of them didn't want to work on their parents' farm, so they went looking for jobs up north where there are more factories and positions. It's a shame because if you drive around, some of the houses and properties are abandoned, with the trees and plants growing over them."

I did notice that when I drove with Arianna to the market, there were houses with windows bordered up and grass that was overgrown. It was such a beautiful town, and it was sad to see it become abandoned.

"So what do you do for fun?" I asked Arianna, curious to know how I would spend the next month here.

"You are so lucky. In a week the feasts will start in this town. Almost every day the town has some type of feast, honoring a saint. Basically, it's an excuse to throw a party almost every night. If this town isn't having a party, then one of the neighboring towns is and we usually drive there."

"Wow, that sounds amazing! But what do you do at the feasts?" I asked, picturing the ones we had back home with carnival rides and games.

"Well, there is some type of concert or band that plays songs, and people usually dance, so that's fun. Then they have food, some games with prizes, and candy. People typically meet up and walk up and down the piazza, listening to the music and dancing most of the night."

That can make the weeks go quickly. At least it would make me tired enough so I wouldn't have to go to sleep anxious or depressed.

"I'd love to go with you!" I said and saw Arianna's face light up.

"Yes! But only if you promise me something." She said, her eyebrows slightly rising and her hands were now clasped together on the table. "Can you teach me how you do your makeup?" Her voice was barely audible, and I could tell she was embarrassed to ask.

"You like my makeup?" I asked, almost incredulous since I didn't do anything special.

"Yes! I grew up with two older brothers and I didn't know how to put on eyeliner until I was almost twenty." She exclaimed, letting out a chuckle. "I'm really behind. This took me an hour to get right before I came here."

I smiled, picturing her trying to line her eyes correctly and told her I would definitely help. My phone started buzzing and I reached to answer it after I saw Josh was calling.

"Hey babe." He said smiling, dressed in scrubs.

"Hi. I love you in your scrubs."

"And I love when I see you happy." He answered back.

"I'm at a pizzeria with my friend, Arianna." I turned the phone to Arianna who waved timidly at Josh.

"Oh, I just wanted to check up on you. Love you." He said, before saying goodbye.

I put the phone away and saw Arianna's expression change to curiosity.

"Is that your boyfriend?"

"Yes. We have been together for two years."

"And he is a doctor?" She added.

"Yes, a cardiothoracic surgeon. I have no idea how to say that in Italian." I added.

"I think I have an idea of what type of doctor he is. That's amazing!"

"What about you? Are you and Alessandro together?" I asked, but instantly got confused when I saw her let out a huge laugh.

"Nooooo. He is like my brother. Actually, he was my fiancé's best friend." She added, her face now becoming sadder.

"Was? Did they have a fight or something?"

"No. My fiancé died almost two years ago. He had leukemia."

My brain stopped functioning for a moment as I tried to figure out how to react. She was around my age and already went through a loss that big. I couldn't even imagine what it would be like to be in her shoes, yet here I was complaining about staying in Italy for just a month.

"I am so sorry; I had no idea." I stammered out, looking down.

"Don't apologize! I am okay. I mean, I still miss him, and sometimes I catch myself crying for no reason, but I am fine. Alessandro took it hard too since they were like brothers, but he is slowly getting better."

I couldn't match any emotions I had gone through with what had happened to them. It made me feel like everything that I'd ever been sad about was now suddenly invalid. I reached out my hand and grabbed Arianna's, squeezing it gently, no words felt adequate enough to say how sorry I felt for them.

"Anyway, let's talk about something different!" She said, returning to her bubbly self as our pizzas were arriving.

The waiter placed them in front of us and I instantly got stuck by the amazing smell emanating from it.

"Is that tuna and onion on yours?" I asked, my nose scrunching up. I had never seen tuna on pizza before.

"Yes, and you must try it!" She exclaimed, pushing the slice she had just cut onto my plate. I held it in front of me, not sure whether I would like it, but proceeded to take a bite, not wanting to offend her.

"Oh my God this is heavenly!" I exclaimed, my mouth full of the pizza. The dough was the perfect amount of crunch and chewiness that made me want to eat all of it.

Arianna laughed at my reaction and proceeded to cut more slices of her pizza, using a fork to put it to her mouth. I made sure to do the same with mine, remembering that Italians eat pizza with a fork and knife, something that was usually a huge debate back in New York. My pizza was just as good as hers and it made me realize how much I missed gluten. I decided to just relax and enjoy it, eating most of the pie and finally feeling satisfied for the first time in the past few days since I've arrived. I took a picture of the last slice left on the plate and posted it to my Instagram account, wanting to show everyone that I was having fun and was not someone that they should feel sorry for. I didn't want to be pitied anymore and decided that I would try to make the best of my time here.

We chatted a bit more and Arianna drove us back home, making me promise I would teach her how to apply her makeup. I told her we would need to drive to a store and that the market wouldn't be good for that. She laughed and agreed, making a date for the next day to pick me up and go shopping. I turned my attention back to the car window, looking out and watching the rolling hills as we drove past with the twinkling lights of towns in the distance. I didn't realize that I had missed this view from when I was younger.

When Arianna dropped me off, I found my nonna sitting at the kitchen table and watching a show almost as if she was waiting for me to come home. Her face seemed relaxed tonight and she eagerly asked me how the night went.

"Arianna told me about her fiancé." I instantly saw my nonna's face sadden as soon as the words came out.

"Yes, she has had it tough. But she is a strong girl. You know, her family doesn't have much money from working on the farm, and she would always take any extra job she could to help."

I couldn't even keep one job and here Arianna was able to help out on the farm and do more than I had ever done, even though she had lost her fiancé. I closed my eyes tight, embarrassed by how I was depressed for being away from Josh for only a month, and then opened them up to see my nonna placing a hand on my shoulder.

"I think she is strong because she knows she is needed, that she needs to help others. She knows that her family can't help her with money, so she works extra hard to make sure she is independent, that she can do everything on her own. I remember when I was young, before we moved to New York, we had no money. Your nonno had to work in Switzerland for a year, and I worked really hard taking care of the garden and animals alone. I needed to sell as much as I could to save money for a house in New York. We wanted to give your mother a better life than this. It was hard, but sometimes you have to find that strength inside of you and keep going, because you are the only one who can push yourself to do it."

I nodded my head and listened, taking in everything she was saying.

"*Va bene*, it's late, *vado a letto*." She said, getting up and announcing she was going to bed. "*Buona notte*." She leaned over and gave me a kiss on my head before heading to her room.

I walked to my room, still thinking about what my nonna said, and laid down on my bed with my phone. So many emotions were going through me, and the confusion was leaving me more unsettled than before. How strong could Arianna be if she had gone through something like that and could still smile? I thought of my friends back home and how Laila got upset if they didn't have a certain makeup product in stock and suddenly, I felt ashamed.

Thinking of Laila, I looked through my texts and noticed that she hadn't texted me, so I wrote to her quickly, asking how she was doing, and while waiting for her response, I continued scrolling through my feed.

I checked my notifications and saw that Blake had commented under my picture of the pizza I had posted earlier. Something inside of me begged to hear from her again so I clicked on her name to FaceTime her.

"Cristina! How are you? I miss you so much!"

There was Blake, her hair in a high ponytail with a big dog on her lap while sitting on a couch.

"Hi Blake, I missed you too. Where are you?"

"I'm at Matt's house." She said, finally giving her mystery boyfriend a name. "Where are you? That pizza you posted doesn't look like it's from here." She said, petting the dog in her lap.

"I'm in Italy, at my nonna's house. It's a long story, but I'm only here for a month. How have you been?"

"Good. Happy, I guess. Really happy." From the look on her face and the way she seemed so content just petting the dog, I could see it. I was happy for her and I felt guilty that I hadn't kept in touch all of this time. I was amazed that she didn't make a comment about that and just seemed as if we never stopped talking and were always friends.

"So catch me up. What have you and Laila been up to?" She said, laying down on her back, positioning the phone above her.

I didn't want to go into details about how I ended up in Italy, so I just explained that I came here to help my nonna while Josh was working hard at the hospital, so the timing worked out. I talked about how Laila still hadn't settled down, jumping from one guy to the next without a care in the world and we laughed reminiscing at some of the silly things we had about when we were younger.

"It was good hearing from you, Cristina." I nodded my head and we promised to make sure that we kept in touch more often.

I checked my phone to see if Laila had texted back, but noticed she hadn't yet, so I decided to fall asleep, my stomach finally full and content.

The next morning, I decided to venture off to the farm earlier, happy that I could open the gate with ease.

I made sure to stay away from the turkeys and filled up the animals' drinking spots with fresh water, and scattered some more crushed corn around the floor for the chickens. I noticed them hesitating around me, but as soon as I moved away, they clucked and gathered at the spots that I dropped the corn and picked away at it.

I shielded my eyes from the sun and looked over to see my nonna in the garden, leaning over some plants and tying them to stakes. I headed over to see if she needed help.

"Buongiorno, Cristina." She said, as I approached her, noticing they were tomato plants that she was tying.

"Ciao, Nonna." I reached for some string and tried to copy her, tying each little stem to a stake that was already in the ground.

"Così—like this." My nonna said, mimicking how I needed to take the right stalk so the tomato plant would stay upright. It took a while to pick up what she had been doing, but I followed along, getting the hang of it.

"Arianna passed by. Are you going shopping later?" She asked, while I continued to the next row of tomato plants.

I had forgotten about my promise to her and instantly became excited about going on another adventure. The day went fast yesterday when I actually did something, so as long as I kept myself busy, this month would fly by.

I went back to the house and decided to start getting ready for lunch. I knew my nonna loved pasta, so I started boiling the water, figuring that when she came back in, she would show me which pasta to throw in. I picked up my phone and noticed a missed call from my dad and decided to FaceTime him.

"It's early, Dad. What are you doing up already?"

"I'm always up at this time with this job. I start welding early and then load the pieces in the truck to get shipped out. We've been pretty busy lately."

I was happy that he was still working at the same job for the past six years. That was another thing he and my mom fought about. He had gotten injured at the first job he was working and took time off to heal. My mom got aggravated because our bills started piling up, and she thought it was a sign of weakness that he wasn't going back. He pushed himself to return, reinjured himself, and then had to take off even more time. That was when the fighting got worse. It was the same summer I had gone to Italy with them, right before they separated. Italy was supposed to be a last ditch effort to save their marriage, but it did the exact opposite, creating a rift that was too wide to heal.

"That's good, Dad. So...how've you been?"

"I've been okay. I heard you are staying in Italy for a few months with Nonna. Are you having fun?"

"Yeah, Michael and Mom thought it was best for me." I was sure he knew since he kept in touch with Michael more than he did with my mom. They started talking again the past few years, but Michael always texted my dad, making sure they were both on the same page with raising me. My dad never could say anything bad about Michael, in fact he would always mention how he is happy that he was also in my life.

"I know sweetheart. I miss you, though. Maybe you can come to visit when you get back? Lisa wants to see you too."

My heart ached that I hadn't seen him. I'd been trying to avoid visiting, because their house was small and I felt embarrassed for him. He seemed genuinely happy with Lisa though, and they had been together for over seven years. She was nice to me when we saw each other, but she reminded me of someone from an 80's poster with teased blond hair and bright blue eyeshadow, and snapping her gum whenever she spoke.

"Okay, I have to go. I love you, Dad."

"Love you too."

My nonna and I ate lunch and I got ready to go out with Arianna. She picked me up and brought me to a mall that was about twenty minutes away. I was grateful for the 50 Euros my nonna had slipped me before I left.

"Shh, don't tell Michael—but take this. Buy something nice for yourself."

I smiled as I held on to my bag. I didn't plan on spending it because I knew it was probably her own money.

We pulled into the parking lot of the mall thirty minutes later and I hoped that my face wasn't showing exactly how I felt. The mall looked like a cement warehouse. It stood out against the other buildings that were so architecturally thought-out and detailed, full of pastel colors that made each one unique. We headed in, and the inside resembled a shrunken version of the ones I was used to back home. Arianna led the way to the cosmetics store.

"I know the malls back home are bigger, but this is the best one we have in this area." She said, with an apologetic look on her face. She had been going out of her way to take me to new places, and I didn't want her to feel bad.

"Well, on the bright side, we definitely won't get lost." I said, trying to think of something positive to say.

The store we had entered reminded me of Sephora back at home, full of makeup, brushes, creams and perfumes. I recognized some of the brands, but also remembered to make sure I wasn't making her buy anything that was out of her price range.

"So, do you want makeup to go out with? Or something more for every day?" I asked, trying to get a feeling of what she needed.

"Both?" She didn't look sure of her response, and I knew she probably needed everything.

"Let's first get something to go out with. The feasts are coming up, right? You will need more dramatic evening makeup first." I said, as I headed over to the bolder colors that would make her hazel eyes pop.

"What do you think of this?" I showed her a palette and tried to gauge her reaction on the price tag.

"I love it, but it's a little more than I wanted to spend."

I nodded my head and went over to another brand that was just as good, but was more affordable.

"What about this?"

"Yes! This is perfect!"

"Great! Now let's get the rest." I moved with her through the store and picked out a primer and a tinted moisturizer, trying to save a few steps in her routine, and made sure she felt comfortable with the price. She got more excited as we went through the store, her smile growing wider every time I put more stuff in the basket.

"Let me know if it's too much." I asked, noticing the basket was getting fuller.

"No, this is fine. Maybe I can get one more thing and that's it."

"How about lip gloss? We can pick a fun color."

"Yes!" She said, her face lighting up which made me smile. It felt good to be able to help her in this small way.

"Wow, I can't wait to try these out." Arianna said as we walked back towards the car, swinging her bag.

It felt odd to be the one to give advice on what to buy, when I was usually the one begging Laila to show me what to get. I was always afraid I wasn't in style, and she would tease me for it. I especially felt that way in high school when the fear would linger over me, and my classmates would one day decide I wasn't enough for them.

Somehow, I didn't feel like Laila though. I took on her role, helping Arianna buy what she needed, but it didn't feel like the shopping trips we would go on. Instead, I felt relaxed, there was no stress of buying the right brand. I looked over at Arianna's happy expression and realized that this was different, in a good way.

7

Sette

cominciare - to start/to begin

14 years old...

Drrrriiiinnnng. My heart started pounding after the warning bell rang. I felt my breath becoming shallow and reminded myself to calm down before I embarrassed myself on the first day at a new school by having a full-blown panic attack in the middle of the hallway.

Cristina, calm down. You can do this. You are nice, sweet, and your hair looks amazing with that little poof you worked hours on. You will make friends. You will have a great school year. I needed to keep repeating this to myself and praying that this new little mantra would stick.

Michael had insisted that my mom move in with him and that I attend this *prestigious* (as he liked to put it) private school that was near his apartment. I looked down, pressed my dark blue pleated plaid skirt flat, and adjusted my white button-down shirt, triple checking that there were no chocolate milk stains on the front. I looked around, my fingers closing together in the usual preemptive warning that a panic attack was about to strike, and quickly remembered the deep breathing techniques my therapist had taught me and put those into action.

"Are you new?" I turned to see a striking girl with hazel eyes ask, as she pushed her perfectly smooth dirty-blond hair back over her shoulder.

"Yes, I am." I stared at her hair and automatically went to touch mine, feeling my split-ends. I made a mental note to ask what hair products she used.

"My name is Blake. Let me see your schedule so I can help you out." If my heart could jump out and hug her, I would've let it. I couldn't believe that someone wanted to help me. I followed her down the hall, quietly continuing the breathing techniques through my nose so I wouldn't sound like a three-year-old trying to blow out their candles on a birthday cake.

"Where did you move from?" She asked, her mouth forming into a delicate smile.

Also, I needed to ask about the lip-gloss she uses. "Um, PS 127."

I saw her brows pull together before I continued. "It's in Brooklyn. I just moved in with my mom's boyfriend..." I worried that I'd said too much. I had never seen so much shiny hair and expensive cars in one school. I needed to act cool. The less I said, the better chance I had of them not figuring me out.

"Well, you'll love it here." She said, turning to me with a smile. I saw her gaze move over to someone down the hall. "Laila! I found a new friend here!" A girl down the hall with equally shiny pin-straight hair stopped walking and turned around. "Wait, what's your name?" She turned to me and whispered.

"Cristina. Without an *h*. My parents are Italian, and they don't spell it with an *h* in Italy." I closed my mouth as fast as I could—for some reason I couldn't stop talking. What next? Did you want to tell her your whole life story so you can chase away the only potential friend you made? I shook my head and went to say hi, hoping not to embarrass myself more.

***

"Okay, girls. Terrence's parents are away for the night. He is throwing a party and I heard that there will be lots of Juniors there!" Laila exclaimed while we were in her bedroom looking through some magazines.

The walls were covered in periwinkle with thick white molding around the ceiling. A sheer canopy covered her bed, draping off the sides, creating a refined vibe, exactly the type of bedroom I pictured her to have.

"Oh, that sounds like fun." Blake said, flatly. I looked at her incredulously, wondering how she could remain so calm while I was a bundle of nerves imagining what this party would be like.

"*Blakey!*" Laila squealed, smacking a magazine against her arm. "Come on, this will be fun! Do you know how many cute Juniors there are? Luis Guerra, Dante Johnson, John Interro—do you want me to continue?"

Blake let out a laugh and turned onto her back. "Alright, alright. Is George driving us?"

George was Laila's family's personal driver, but so far, I had only seen him drive Laila around. When Blake mentioned that Laila had a personal driver, at first I laughed, thinking she was playing with me—until I saw a nondescript black car pull up to pick her up from school one day, my mouth dropped when I realized it was the truth. Small things would still shock me every day in the new school, and it almost became a game to see what would happen next.

"So, what are these parties like?" I asked, not wanting to sound completely clueless, but at the same time needing to prepare myself to avoid any potential disasters.

"You know, everyone who's anyone will be there. There will be drinks, music, some hooking up..." Laila said, while flipping through a magazine now lying stomach down on her bed.

"Cris—don't worry about it! If you don't like it, we'll go back to my house." Blake said, still not showing a trace of enthusiasm as she turned on her back and held out a page of a magazine in front of her to read.

Laila turned to look at Blake and raised both of her brows. "Umm, not if Luis is there. Sorry, Cris, Luis has been looking pretty fine lately."

They both laughed and continued flipping through the magazines. I let out a nervous chuckle and prayed that my stomach would stop doing acrobatic stunts so I could relax my nerves and not appear like a complete mess.

LAILA: **Here is the address—it's right by your house. We'll meet you there.**

It was the day of the party and I looked down for probably the thirtieth time at Laila's text message and memorized the address and how to get there. I nervously checked the time on my phone, and looked back down at my outfit, praying it would be okay for the party.

"Hey!" Blake shouted, coming over to give me a hug. Laila was right behind her and gave me a double-cheeked air kiss explaining how she didn't want to smudge her fresh makeup.

We all walked into the party and I made sure to stay behind them to check out the scene. The apartment, if I could even call it an apartment since it reminded me just like Michael's duplex, had windows on all sides of an enormous open-concept space where people were mingling all over. Exposed brick covered one of the rooms that had two white leather couches in front of a fireplace. I noticed a couple making out on one of the couches, and another couple whispering into each other's ears next to them. Another group was dancing in the far corner of the room and a few upper-classmen were surrounding the kitchen island with red solo cups in their hands. A shudder ran through me as I thought about drinking for the first time.

Blake and Laila walked further in and started mingling with some of their friends. Even though they had introduced me to everyone they talked to, I still stayed quiet and tried to absorb as much as I could without accidentally revealing something embarrassing about myself.

"Who is this new girl here?" A higher pitched, somewhat nasally voice asked, making me turn my attention to her. She was a few inches taller than me, wearing some strappy sandals with heels that were too high for me to even imagine myself walking in. Her head was tilted so upright that I am sure the doctor would have no trouble using an otoscope to fully check her nasal passages.

"Hi. I'm Cristina. I'm new here. It's my first year, and, um..." I tried to stop my mouth from talking but it's almost as if I couldn't help give her my life story.

She looked me up and down, with an exaggerated gaze that started at the top of my head and then took what seemed like 10 minutes to finally reach my shoes.

"Oh no, honey. Are those shoes from *Walmart*?" She let out a horrible laugh, one that I knew would give me shudders for years to come. She proceeded to tilt her head back and continue laughing while I looked around to find the quickest exit out of there. She then placed a hand on her heart, looked at me with what seemed like the most pitiful look anyone had ever given me, and shook her head. "Laila, someone needs to teach this girl to shop."

"Irene, that's uncalled for." Blake said, her face becoming redder as her fists clenched to her side.

"Don't worry, Blake." I said, placing a hand on her arm. "It's okay. You know what, I'm not feeling that great anyway, I'm probably going to head home." I looked back at her and noticed a pained expression on her face. She nodded her head and whispered something to Laila, and they both walked with me outside. As soon as I stepped out of the building, a few tears had managed to escape.

"No, don't cry, Cristina." Laila said, wrapping an arm around me. "Listen, I can take you shopping tomorrow. I'll get George to drive the three of us and we'll make a day out of it." I nodded my head, wiping the tears that had already reached the middle of my cheek, and walked back to Michael's apartment with them. I vowed that I would never let Irene, or anyone ever laugh or judge me like that from that moment on. I would make sure I fit in as much as Laila and Blake did and never give Irene a chance to laugh at me like that again. I let out a huff, marched into the apartment, and shut my jaw tight, trying to make sure that this night would be a memory I would quickly forget.

8

Otto

lavorare - to work

Now

I needed to clear up the field. There is no way Nonna could walk through the garden and reach the pepper plants through this mess. I decided the next few days that I would focus on clearing as many weeds as I could that had grown in between the plants. They seemed to have almost taken over the garden. I spied my nonna one day, trying to clear a little path, but I saw her give up after she had wiped her brow and held her broken arm, almost as if she had known she had pushed her limit as well.

After four days of hard work, the garden was practically weed-free. The plants looked more vibrant, and I walked around with a basket, collecting some of the string beans that were ready for harvest.

"*Che brava che sei, Cristina!*" My nonna exclaimed, after admiring all of the work I had done. She pulled my cheek towards her, kissing me, and repeated how proud she was of me before heading inside to get lunch ready. I continued to collect string beans as I saw Alessandro jump off his tractor and walk towards me.

"Wow, Cristina. I am impressed. You have been working hard these days."

I looked at him and saw a grin appear on his face. It was the first time that he had a smile towards me instead of his usual smugness.

"*Grazie,*" I said, looking back at the garden and admiring the work. I was sure that this type of work was nothing for him, but his words sounded sincere.

He headed back to his tractor, and I continued collecting more string beans before deciding to head back to the house. I wiped the sweat from my forehead and grabbed my phone to check the time. I was about to put it away when I heard Josh's voice.

"Josh?" I said, surprised to see him on my screen.

"Hey, you just FaceTimed me. Is everything okay?"

I must have called him by accident. "Yeah, sorry, I guess I accidentally hit the call button as I was putting my phone back in my pocket."

"Cristina, were you playing in the dirt?" He said, laughing. I quickly looked at my small insert on the screen and my eyes widened when I saw dirt smeared across my forehead and my hair sticking out around my crown.

"I was just helping my nonna with the garden." I hastily tried to rub my forehead clean. "Anyway, how are you?" I tilted the camera so my forehead and hair were cut out of the screen.

"Everything is good. I have to go though. I'll call you later. Bye, babe."

"Bye." I hung up, embarrassed that he saw me like this. I made it back to the house and was surprised to hear music and my nonna singing along.

"Nonna?" I could faintly hear the words to the song, but I was able to make out that she was singing along to the classic *Ti Amo* song I heard at our relative's Italian weddings.

I followed her voice to the garage in the back of the house. The garage was more of a huge walk-in pantry with dried meat and cheese hanging all around, than anything else. As I walked in, I watched her swaying her hips as she rolled out dough with her one good hand on top of a table. I shook my head and laughed because she still hadn't noticed me, but instead started singing the chorus of the song even louder.

"Nonna?" I said, slowly making my way behind her.

She spun around and a flush crept across her cheeks before she moved to lower the volume. She waved her hand as if to stop any conversation before it happened and grabbed the rolling pin again.

"It can get a little lonely by myself sometimes, so the music helps me feel better." She said, while positioning the rolling pin on top of the dough again.

All of this time I never thought about how my nonna felt all by herself in this house. She had Alessandro's family next door and Arianna came to visit, but most of the day she spent outside in her garden or on the farm, taking care of the animals. I knew I couldn't go a day back home without a lunch date with a friend or seeing Josh. I couldn't even imagine how lonely she felt. I walked over and put my arm around her shoulder.

"Nonna, can I help you? I want to learn about whatever you are making. The chicken I tried to make, well, that was bad."

She let out a laugh, looked up at me with raised eyebrows, and handed me the rolling pin.

"*Va bene*, okay. Cristina, we are making pasta for lunch today. So roll out the dough now." She gestured her hand towards the dough.

I rolled it flatter, but she positioned my body over the dough so I would be able to put more strength into it. She told me when to flip it and turn it, explaining how I needed to create a uniform square that would be easy to shape. I was surprised about how much strength I needed to put into making this mixture of just water and flour flat. All of the times I had seen my nonna do it, she made it look effortless.

As I cut the dough in strips, I looked over and noticed a gleam in her eyes while she continued to direct me on what to do. She handed over what looked like a long knitting needle and explained how this was now the hard part.

"This will take a lot of practice, Cristina. *Guarda.*" She said, telling me to look at her. I studied her hands and movements as she placed two pieces of dough under the needle and positioned her palms above the pieces, then rolled them forward, creating two perfect spiral-shaped pieces of dough.

"Now you try, but with one. It is easier with one."

I mimicked all of the movements she had done but let out a sigh when my piece looked like a Pinterest fail compared to hers.

"You have no confidence, Cristina." She whacked me lightly with the towel she was holding. "You start things like you expect to fail. You are smart, brave, and strong. Look at how beautiful my garden is. Find that part of you, Cristina, and try again."

I was taken aback by her abruptness but had a feeling this was more than a lesson of just making pasta. I couldn't help but see where she came from. There was always a feeling of anxiety in the pit of my stomach before I tried anything new, doubt always crept up and took over my thoughts, making me feel like I couldn't master anything. It made me feel like I always had to rely on someone else to do it for me. I took another piece of dough, let out a breath before I attempted it again. I shut my eyes, trying to push the doubt down and out of me. I rolled the needle, my palm firm, and at the same time applied a gentle pressure to shape the dough. I opened my eyes and let out a small gasp when I noticed the shape was almost identical to the ones my nonna had made.

"*E brava*, Cristina. You see? You are strong, you always were. Come on, let's finish."

I finished cutting and rolling out the dough, my nonna letting me know she was going back to the kitchen to check on the sauce and start boiling the water. I wiped my hands against my shirt, the flour from my hands leaving a small dusting against it, and took the finished pasta to the kitchen.

"*Allora, mangi la pasta?*" My nonna asked if I was eating the pasta, as I helped her scoop the now cooked pasta into a bowl and then added some fresh sauce on top.

I debated if I should eat it, but argued that if I worked harder outside, I would burn it off. I nodded my head, grabbed another bowl, and filled it only a quarter of the way so I wouldn't feel guilty.

We sat down, our bowls in front of us, and I grabbed a few of the pasta pieces I had made on my fork.

"These are called *fusilli*." My nonna said, before taking a bite of hers.

I bit into them, and I felt my body reacting in joy to the taste. The fresh flavor of the pasta with my nonna's homemade sauce was a taste that I hadn't realized my body needed all of this time. It was as if my stomach was thanking me for finally returning to my Italian roots after eating it.

I finished the plate quickly and saw my nonna's widening eyes as I went to fill my plate with more.

She was silent as I kept eating, stealing glances over at me as I continued to enjoy the pasta, not wanting to say a word either.

"*Mangia un po' di formaggio.*" She said, handing me a piece of fresh provolone. I figured the harm was done already, so I took the piece from her and bit into it.

"Nonna! This is the best thing I have ever eaten. Where did you get this?!" I had never tasted anything so good, and I couldn't even find the right words to describe the taste. My brain was trying to compare it with other foods I had eaten, but I ultimately had to give up as my stomach commanded more.

"I made this, Cristina. *L'ho fatto io.*" She said, after handing me another slice. "You need to eat bread with this, *aspetta.*" She handed me a piece of fresh bread, the one I noticed my nonna getting from a van that passed by the house every day.

I put the provolone on top of the bread and bit into it, shaking my head in disbelief that I had denied my body of this for years. Was it always this good? I tried to remember eating with my nonna when she would visit us, or when I visited her those few times.

"I want to learn how to make this. Can you show me?"

My nonna dropped her fork as she stared at me, and then placed a hand across her chest. "*Certo.* Sure." She said, a smile slowly forming on her face as she picked up her fork again and finished eating.

I went out after lunch, wanting to take a walk to help digest all of the new food I had eaten, and decided to go towards the farm to check on the animals. Even though my stomach was fuller than it had been in a while, I somehow felt happier and satisfied. For some reason it made me want to go outside and enjoy the air. I checked my phone and saw that it was still early to call Josh and I was about to put it away when I noticed Laila hadn't texted me back.

That's strange. She was pretty good with texting me back, so I sent her another quick text to see if everything was okay. I put my phone away, and pushed the gate towards the post, before I unlatched the hook.

I eyed the turkeys, making sure they stood on the other side of the gated area, and walked towards the rabbits, checking to see if they had food.

One of the cages had four smaller bunnies inside that were

scampering around, so I went to lift the lid, scooped one of them in my hands, and walked towards a tree stump, relaxing with the bunny in my hand and admiring the view around me.

I could feel the bunny's whiskers tickling me, probably nervous to be in a stranger's hold, and ran a finger between its ears, trying to calm it down. It settled in after a few more caresses, and I held it against my belly, cradling it, and watched the chickens cluck and peck at the corn pieces on the ground.

"Are you stealing rabbits now?"

I jumped and turned around to see Alessandro behind me, on the other side of the fence, his mouth twitching into a smile.

"Oh, hey. You scared me. I was just relaxing here." I said, sitting back down on the stump. I turned and saw that he was gone, and I looked around to see where he went, until I heard the gate open and he was walking towards me.

"Is it okay if I sit next to you?" He asked, his hand gesturing to a crate that was turned upside down.

I nodded my head, and he pulled the crate closer and sat down next to me. He was quiet, staring straight ahead, and I wondered what he was doing.

"So, your nonna is really proud of you. She keeps telling my mom about all of the work you are doing for her." He said, his body leaned forward, his arms resting on his legs as his face turned to mine.

"Really? I'm not doing much. I mean, she has a broken arm and is still doing more than I could ever do." Alessandro let out a laugh.

"Well, Italian women are strong. When they have work they need to get done, they do it. No matter how hard it may be." He added, letting out another laugh.

"How are your parents?" I asked, curious since I hadn't seen them since I had arrived.

His face saddened a bit as he went to tell me that his mother moved in with his sister down the road when his father had passed away five years ago.

"I'm so sorry." I said, placing my hand gently on his arm. I noticed him flinch, so I pulled it back, embarrassed.

"It's okay." His expression changed slightly, becoming more serious as he sat up straighter.

"How's your sister doing?" I asked, changing the subject. "I remember she has a son, right? I saw a boy playing down by your vineyards the other day."

"Yeah, he's 10 and full of energy." His face now relaxed. "What about your family? I remember your parents are divorced. That must be hard."

An image of my dad walking out of our apartment, one small suitcase in his hand, pinched my heart. "It was hard, but so many years have passed since then and I'm fine now. Plus, I like Michael, my mom's new husband. I have two sisters that are around your nephew's age, and instead of being full of energy, they are full of sass."

"*Sass?*" He asked, his eyebrows knitted together and his head pulled back.

"Oh, it means that they are full of energy, but in a feisty way." I saw him nod his head and his lips formed a small smile, as he leaned forward, his arms resting on his legs again.

"I'm sure you can't wait to go back home." He turned towards me again and I could see amusement dancing in his eyes.

I smiled and nodded my head. "I like it here, but my whole *life* is back home. That doesn't mean that I'm not happy I came, though. Well, I get happier about it each day I'm here. I think I was a little bit in shock." I looked over and saw that he was laughing and shaking his head.

"Okay, I wasn't that bad, Alessandro." I looked at him and he raised his eyebrows. "Okay fine, I was bad, but you have to realize that I hadn't been here in years, and I left everything back home."

He nodded and got up, his eyes gentler than they had ever been since I had arrived.

"You are right, Cristina. This is definitely different for you than from back home. I need to check on the vineyards and finish up before dinner. *Ciao.*" He said, and he walked out of the gate before turning around to wave.

Maybe he didn't hate me after all. I hoped that the way I acted when I was fifteen didn't completely ruin the friendship we first had. I walked over to the rabbit cage, ready to put the bunny back, and my heart melted when I realized that it had been sleeping soundly against my stomach the whole time. I carefully lowered it in, but it woke up and hopped off my hand, joining its other brothers and sisters that were already in the cage.

The next few days I kept up the chores around the farm. Arianna had stopped by a few times to collect the eggs and chat with me, but I made sure to add cheese-making lessons to my routine after falling in love with the provolone my nonna had made.

"Andiamo da Alessandro." My nonna said one day, telling me we had to go to Alessandro's house. "We can get the milk from him if we want to start right away."

I gave my nonna a hug, excited to be able to learn how to make the best cheese I had ever tasted, and quickly headed outside with her towards his house.

We walked across the cut wheat fields that were now yellow and dried, crunching below our feet as we reached his house, about 500 yards from ours. I wasn't used to walking on anything but concrete or asphalt and I was starting to love the feeling of the different textures under my shoes. The softness felt comforting under me from the tilled dirt to the soft grass we fed to the animals. Alessandro's house was a white-stuccoed one floor building with dark-red shutters next to the windows. I could see it between the cherry trees from my nonna's kitchen window, but I hadn't visited it since I was 15 years old.

"*Buongiorno!*" Alessandro called out to us as he opened his door and walked down the steps. I recognized his mother and sister following him close behind, walking quickly my way with big smiles on their faces. His mother approached me first, her flowy black dress moving with the slight breeze and her once dark hair was now peppered with white and cut short away from her face. Her eyes reminded me of Alessandro's, but there was a hint of sadness behind them.

"Cristina, *ma quanto sei diventata bella!*" His mother said, exclaiming how pretty I had become. She squeezed my cheeks with one hand, and I bent down slightly when she gave me two kisses. She turned to chat with my nonna while his sister greeted me as well. While Alessandro's expression seemed more serious and dark, his sister Rosina's was bright and playful, with both her hair and eyes lighter than his. Her thick, curly hair was pulled back in a loose braid and her long, tan legs stood out against the sunny yellow shorts she wore. Even her outfit was a bright contrast to her mother's, the vibrant colors matched the smile that reached her eyes. I looked over to see Alessandro closely watching our interaction. Even though it had been a while since I had seen them, it felt as if little time had passed. His sister and mother then said goodbye, mentioning the farm needed work to be done, and we waved to them and followed Alessandro down a gravel path toward a barn.

The barn had the same white stucco and dark red accents as his house, but it was more simple and boxy with a gabled roof. I could hear the cows mooing from the outside and when Alessandro slid the barn door open, I could smell them too.

"*Allora*, what are we making? Provolone today?" Alessandro said, smiling. I tried to suffer through the smell, but ultimately pinched my nose when it was more than I could take.

My nonna nodded her head and Alessandro took a contraption consisting of hoses at the end and put them directly on the cow's teats before turning on the machine. I must have had a horrified look on my face because Alessandro looked at me and let out a deep laugh, and then promised me that the cows were fine and were used to the feeling. After the bucket was filled, he handed it to my nonna and refused the money she was trying to stuff in his pocket.

"*No, no. Non posso.*" He said, explaining how he couldn't take it. "Maybe I will just take a slice of cheese next time I come over." His smile grew wide when my nonna hugged him. We headed back to our house and straight to the garage.

"*Va bene, cominciano,* let's start!" She took the time to explain, half in Italian and half in English, the steps to make the cheese. First we heated the milk, then added the culture and rennet at the right moments, letting it sit and curd, and then tested the curds to see if they stretched the right amount. It took the whole day, and I took pictures, posting it to my feed as my nonna's hands started shaping the provolone.

"So now you make cheese?" Josh said, while we were FaceTiming each other later in the day.

I laughed and laid on the bed, happy to have a few moments with him before his next shift. It was difficult to find the right time to talk since we were both in different time zones.

"I'm becoming an expert." I joked back, watching him smile. "By the way, what is up with Laila? She's only been answering my texts with one-line responses. Is there an event she's been planning that she hadn't told me about?"

Josh paused for a half of a second before responding. "No, not that I know of. I know she has been hanging out with Irene lately though."

Irene. That was the one girl I still could not stand. We had never clicked, from the time at Terrence's party to now. The haughtiness about her made her unapproachable and rude. Blake didn't like her either, so Laila would hang out with her without us sometimes, making sure that our paths never crossed.

"Work is good?" I asked, switching subjects, not wanting to show my irritation in front of Josh.

"Yeah, everything is going well—I need to get going though, love you."

"Love you too." I hung up and walked over to the kitchen, looking for something to snack on.

"Nonna?" I said, walking over to her as she sat in a chair, her elbow against the table and her hand on her forehead. She looked pale and her face was pinched as if she was trying not to show she was in pain.

"Nonna, *stai bene?* Are you okay?" I put an arm around her shoulder, nervous to see her like this.

"Sì, sì. I'm fine. My stomach just hurts. I will make some *finocchio* tea and I will feel better."

Before she could get up, I rushed and grabbed the tea kettle, filled it up with water, and put it on the stove. It was a shock to see my nonna in pain, because even with her arm in a cast, she still was the strongest woman I knew, never complaining about anything. I grabbed the fennel tea, placed it in the cup, and drummed my fingers on the counter waiting for the water to boil. I looked over at her, saw her adjusting her position on the chair as if she was trying to find a way to relieve the pain.

"Nonna, I can call the doctor if it's bad." Worry started to take over and I wanted to help her in any way I could.

"No, Cristina. It's just a stomachache. *Basta*, enough. I will drink the tea and be fine." I let out a breath and walked over to the kettle, pouring the boiling water in the cup. My nonna took her time drinking it and I decided to walk outside.

The air was dry and hot, but not the stifling heat of New York City air. I let the sun hit my shoulders and arms, admiring the tan that I was getting. When I worked outside, I made sure that the sunscreen I was using protected my face, but I liked the deeper tones to my skin. I took in a deep breath as I headed towards the farm, the gravel road crunching beneath my shoes.

"Look who it is." I heard a deep voice behind me. I turned around to see Alessandro, walking up from his property towards the gate.

"*Ciao!*" I said, happy to see him. "Thanks again for the milk. My nonna made the provolone. How do you guys have the patience to wait a month before eating it?"

"Trust me, it's worth it. Your nonna is famous around here for her provolone. Where are you going?" His hands dug into his jeans pocket as he looked at me with his intense, dark eyes.

"Nowhere, really. I just wanted to go for a walk."

"Can I join you?"

"Sure."

We walked quietly along the gravel road, away from the farm, and headed towards the river that flowed down at the bottom of the valley. There were a few apple trees along the path with some already fruiting along the branches. There was something about having fruit trees all around that created a sense of security. Almost as if wherever you went, there was always something to eat.

"So, what are summers back in New York like?" He asked, turning his head to me.

I went on to explain how we would usually stay at a friend's house in the Hamptons, and when he looked at me confused, I pulled out my phone to show him on Google Maps what part of Long Island it was. He nodded his head as I continued to talk, but I felt silly about what I was saying. Summers for me just involved laying at the beach and going to parties at night. He probably sensed my embarrassment when my voice became quieter because he added that it sounded a lot like the summers around here, friends getting together, going to the beach during the day and then feasts at night.

We reached the river, sat down by the bank on soft grass, and Alessandro picked up little pebbles near him and threw them in the water, making them skip across the top.

"Wait—how do you do that?" I asked, watching the rock skip five times across the top before it finally sunk under water. I grabbed one, tried to flick my wrist the way he had done, but let out a sigh after it sunk on the first hit.

"Like this." He said, showing me the motion of how far to pull it back before letting it go. I tried and laughed after it had made it to two skips before it sank.

He took another pebble, made it somehow skip six times, and turned to me, his face beaming.

"Show off!" I hit him playfully on his shoulder and laughed as I looked at him.

He stopped smiling and stared at me, his lips pressed straight as his eyes jumped to mine.

"I missed that smile. You are as beautiful as I always remembered you, Cristina."

I held my breath and my heart fluttered. I didn't know how to respond. He got up, gave me his hand to pull me up, and we headed back, silent for a few minutes more.

"I'm going to walk over and take care of the animals." I said, my voice slightly betraying the fact that I was still flustered after what he had told me. He nodded his head, smiled, and headed back across the fields.

I couldn't stop repeating what he said in my mind, replaying his face and expression, my cheeks warming and my heart beating a little faster as the memory burned into my brain. My phone vibrated with a message from Josh, breaking me out of the daze I was in.

JOSH: **Thinking of you babe.**

Guilt crashed over me, as I started hating myself for having a reaction to just one sentence. I wrote Josh back, expressing how I missed and loved him more than I normally would, and then put my phone away, trying to convince myself I shouldn't feel guilty for responding like that to a compliment.

It's fine to blush after someone gives you a compliment. It's just a natural reaction. I kept repeating this in my head and the guilt slowly retreated after I had convinced myself enough. Besides, Alessandro was just trying to be nice. He probably saw that I had been miserable the first few days and wanted to cheer me up. I seemed more satisfied with that logic and started to take out my phone to see if there was any response from Laila, but I froze midway. A memory from when I was 15 tore through me again, ripping through my heart, and reminding me of what I had done to Alessandro.

9

Nove

diverso - different

15 years old...

"Why are we here, Mom? I wanted to stay with Dad!" I said, slamming the car door as loudly as I could.

"How can you stay with him when he is living in a one-bedroom apartment?" My mom said through gritted teeth as she exited the passenger side.

"Ladies, it will be fun, you'll see. Remember, you are the ones who have to show me around here, I've never been to this part of Italy." Michael said as he got our bags out from the back of the taxi.

My mom had just married Michael, and this was a part of their honeymoon. They planned on traveling to Italy for a week before dropping me off with my nonna while they continued on to Greece and France by themselves. I looked over to see my mom grabbing Michael's hand and planting a kiss on his cheek.

I wanted to hate him when they started seeing each other, but I couldn't. He had been nice to me from the very first day—never pushy or forcing the whole "I am your stepfather, so now you will treat me with respect" act. Instead, he praised my dad in front of me, telling me he completely understood how I felt, and never made me feel like he was replacing my dad. I did give him the silent treatment for the first month we moved in, but he was *still* nice to me, telling me he would be patient until I was ready to talk to him.

My mom went from being miserable with my dad, to a teenager in love again with Michael. It brought out a side of her that I hadn't seen in the last few years my parents were together, and for that I was grateful. But, as any child of divorced parents knows, I still prayed that my parents would miraculously get back together but knew deep in my heart that it would never happen. I took a breath in and smiled when I saw my nonna running out of the house towards me and scooping me up into a hug.

"*Ma, sei grande*, Cristina!" She said, exclaiming how big I got. I laughed; it had been three years since the last time I saw her. She hadn't come to visit us after the divorce or even attended my mom's wedding to Michael. I had missed her all of this time. She always balanced out my mom and had a soft spot for me.

"*Piacere*, Michael." Michael said, reaching his hand out to my nonna. My nonna looked at him with a confused face but shook his hand and nodded her head.

"Michael, you can hug her. They hug and kiss a lot here." I whispered to him, noticing my nonna was not sure of what to do.

"Oh, okay." He said, and then went in for an awkward hug. My nonna just shook her head and gave my mom a brief hug and a pat on the back.

"*Il tuo papà sta bene?*" She asked, wondering how my dad was doing.

"*Sì, Nonna. Ti saluta.*" I said, telling her he said hi.

I could see my mom's eyes narrowing, she was definitely upset that my nonna was still asking about my dad even after the divorce. I smiled back knowing full well what she was doing, and I secretly loved her for it.

As soon as I settled inside, I jumped on the bed and pulled out my phone, ready to text my friends.

CRISTINA: **Hey girls. I'm at my grandma's house. This is sooo boring.**

BLAKE: **Going to Laila's house in the Hamptons now! We miss you!**

LAILA: **Hurry up back home, girl! The Hamptons are not the same without you...oh, and there is this cute boy who moved into the house next door.**

My heart ached knowing that my friends were having fun without me. I looked down at my outfit, knowing that Laila would have approved of my Gucci sneakers and Seven jeans, but started worrying that everything would get dirty here, especially if I helped my nonna on the farm. I wasn't used to spending so much money on clothes, but Laila warned me I needed to buy certain brands if I wanted to fit in. Blake would usually roll her eyes at whatever Laila said, but I was afraid to be an outcast, so I would always ask Laila to shop with me, using Michael's credit card that he graciously lent.

"Cristina, *andiamo*. Let's go feed the animals." I hesitated when my nonna called, looking down again at my sneakers, I was so annoyed that I hadn't bought another pair.

"Nonna, I'm tired so I'm going to stay here." I said, instead laying on the bed, scrolling through my phone.

I checked Instagram, a new social media app that my friends started using, and went through their pictures that they posted, which made my heart hurt even more. They were having fun without me, while I was stuck here, surrounded by dirt and dirty animals.

Michael and my mom left a few days later, leaving me with my nonna. I ventured out one day to the farm, using my least expensive pair of sandals, but I turned right back around and went straight to the house when I stepped in a bunch of chicken poop.

"*Scusa!*" I said, bumping into someone, not looking ahead where I was walking.

"Cristina?"

I looked up and saw him. It'd been three years since I last saw him. The kiss we shared was forever an image burned in my memory.

"*Ciao, Alessandro.*" I said, noticing he was much taller than I had remembered and a bit more muscular. He was in a t-shirt with his hair still wavy, but swept away from his deep, serious eyes that always seemed as if they were reading into mine.

"How are you? It has been three years, right?" He asked, now holding my elbow, which made my breath stutter for a beat.

"Yes, three years. Your English is amazing though! Have you been studying?"

"Thank you, and yes, I have. It is still not perfect, but I am try-ing." I smiled, noticing how he was making sure to pronounce every word perfectly. I pictured him studying in his room, his intense eyes reading books and his full, perfect lips, pronouncing every word.

I shook my head, trying to get myself to not think of him or his lips in any other way, and went back to asking about his family.

"Everyone is fine. My sister had a baby boy. So, I am an *uncle*, right?" He said, his face now beaming.

I congratulated him and he said he would stop by later after he finished feeding the animals. I skipped a little, remembering all of the adventures we had last time I visited, and thought that maybe it wouldn't be so bad staying here after all.

"Cristina, do not do it! *Non ci pensare!*" Alessandro warned me not to even think about what I was about to do, hose in my hand, ready to turn it on him. The gleam in his eyes said otherwise, almost begging me to splash him with water. It would be the perfect coolant against this heat.

"Oh, I'm going to do it. You have three seconds to run." He started to flee from me, but didn't make it far as I said, "one...two..." and didn't finish counting before spraying the hose directly on him. He let out a laugh, looked down at his clothes, and then shook his head, now looking at me.

"You better run, Cristina." He said with a mischievous smile. I dropped the hose and started running away from him through the vineyards, laughing as he quickly caught up.

He ran up behind me, took me in a bear hug, and I tried to wriggle free. I felt his wet clothes against me. When he put me back down, I turned to him, and we both stood there, smiling, but our eyes were reading each other's in a different way—one that sent shivers down my body despite the sun's heat that was beating down on us.

"Come here." He just said, taking my hand in his, and leading me towards the edge of the vineyards, on the side further from my house. "This is one of my favorite views." We sat next to each other, my hands slightly behind my back, supporting me as I took in the rolling hills around us. Patches of grass and wheat fields scattered all around us. It created a simple beauty, one that I wasn't used to seeing anymore. I knew I had to take this chance to appreciate it. It was a view I would never get back home.

We spent the next few days glued at the hip, sometimes at my farm and helping my nonna or going to his. He knew how much I loved tractor rides and would always call me whenever he was going to use it. There were times when I swore that he really didn't need the tractor, but just wanted the excuse to be with me.

***

"These are my favorites." Alessandro said one day, pulling a ripe fig off the tree. We had just finished watering my nonna's garden and decided to take a break together.

"Mine too!"

"Here, take it and we can sit."

We walked to a log laid down on the grass and ate the figs sitting right next to each other. He looked over at me, one side of his mouth tugging up into a smile, as he gently used his thumb to wipe something off my lips.

"*Sei un disastro*, Cristina," he said, teasing me, saying that I was a disaster.

I didn't smile back though. His gentle touch across my lips triggered a memory from the time when we shared that first kiss. I noticed a look in his eyes changed too. My heart started beating faster, sending the blood through my body. I wanted to touch his lips with mine. I leaned towards him and saw his eyes widen for a brief second, then close, as the gap between us lessened, until there was none. I parted my lips as we connected, his tongue gently touching mine, making everything around me feel like it was spinning, even though my eyes were still closed. I felt like I was floating. We both pulled away, and then heard someone calling his name.

"That is my mom." Alessandro said, his face was still close to mine and his eyes turned serious, probably not sure what had happened either. "*Dobbiamo andare da mia zia. Scusa.*" He spoke in Italian, flustered from the moment we shared, and explained how he had to go to his aunt's house.

He grabbed my hand, walked me back towards the other side of the yard, closer to my property, our fingers gripping each other's. I let go as soon as his mom came to view and then waved bye as I ran back to my house. I couldn't wait to share what happened with Laila and Blake and needed to text them immediately.

CRISTINA: **You guys are never going to believe this! My cute neighbor next door and I kissed three years ago and now we have been hanging out again!**

LAILA: **Cristina, are you serious? He works on a farm in Italy. Aiden has been asking about you. The same one whose dad has his own financial firm. Don't go messing around with dirty farm boys, that's so beneath you.**

BLAKE: **Laila, lighten up on Cristina. I say go for it!**

My heart dipped. *Dirty farm boy*? What was that supposed to mean? They knew that I didn't grow up with money like they had, but sometimes I felt like I would never be cool enough for them. I worked hard to dress the right way with the right brands but wondered if my past was going to follow me eternally. I was afraid I could be all alone, with everyone figuring out that I was a fake.

CRISTINA: **I won't go for him, just wanted to share!**

I wasn't sure exactly what to say so I wrote back hesitantly, feeling my heart sink further in my chest. That kiss felt right, but something in me snapped, and I knew that I couldn't be with him. I needed to be with someone from New York, who would fit the profile that I was trying to obtain.

I stood in my room the rest of the day, not wanting to go out, until I heard the doorbell ring. Alessandro was at the door, with a big smile on his face. He just got back home and wanted to know if I wanted to ride on his tractor to the vineyards.

"No, I'm going to stay in. I'm busy today talking to my friends on my phone. I haven't heard from them in a little while and need to stay updated on everything that's happening back home." I said as I bit down on my lip, almost to the point of hurting myself because I knew I was hurting him. He took a step back, and I closed the door.

The next few days, I tried to avoid him, turning my head when he waved hello, or walking away when I saw him come up to me. By the end of the week, he stopped waving at me, and I felt like the worst person on Earth. I had truly made him hate me.

My nonna asked if everything was alright between us, but I just made excuses that he wasn't who I remembered him to be, but I knew she could see through my lies.

I left that summer feeling like I'd changed and didn't know if that was for the better.

10

Dieci

Sentirsi male- to feel bad

Now

"Nonna, I should call the doctor. It's been two days since your stomach started hurting." I put my hand on her shoulder, she was laying in bed, too weak to get up.

"Don't worry, Cristina. This has happened before. It stays for a day or two but then I feel better. There's no need to worry. I'm fine."

I went back outside, started taking care of all of the chores, and saw Arianna get out of her car. Her expression changed to worry after I told her my nonna was still in bed.

"She is stubborn. She doesn't want to see the doctor?" She asked.

"No. She said it's happened before, and she usually gets better. Are *all* Italian women this tough?" I asked, trying to lighten up the mood. After what Arianna told me about her fiancé's death, it bothered me to see her anything but her bubbly self.

Her mouth curved upwards slightly and she nodded her head. We laughed and walked towards the farm, collecting the eggs.

"So... have you tried the makeup yet?"

"Not yet. I'm nervous that I will end up looking like a clown. It would be great if I could watch you one time before I attempt it."

"Okay!" I said. "We can get together again and I will show you." I had been meaning to make plans to hang out with Arianna again anyway after the shopping trip.

"I would love that!" Her face brightened up. We collected the eggs, she brought them into her car, and I waved 'bye before she left. I walked back to the farm to fill up the drinking spots for the animals, when I heard a baby lamb crying out.

I looked over, frantically trying to find it and spotted it tangled up, its leg caught in the wire as it tried to pull itself out. I carefully walked over, trying not to scare the baby lamb, and went to delicately remove its leg out of the fence. It kept kicking at me, and I started panicking more and worrying that it was hurting itself, and I couldn't help. I looked up and saw Alessandro working on his garden, close to ours, and called him over to help.

"What happened, Cristina?" He said, his breathing heavy after jogging across the field.

"The baby lamb is stuck." I said, pointing over to her struggling. He knelt down next to it, trying to calm it down, before carefully pulling apart the fence that was wrapped around its leg, giving the lamb space to get free. She hopped a little, avoiding placing the hurt leg down, towards her parents up the hill.

"Thank you, Alessandro. I panicked. My nonna hasn't been feeling well, and I'm trying to take over, but I'm not sure if I'm doing everything right." My words sputtered out, realizing how overwhelmed I'd been feeling about having to take care of everything.

"Did you call the doctor?"

"No, she doesn't want me to."

"Ah, so like her. I'll try to convince her," he said, shaking his head. "Listen, you need to take a break too. There is a feast tonight, why don't you ask Arianna to go? She really needs to get out too, so you would do both of yourselves a favor."

"I don't know if I can finish everything before then." I looked around and noticed the animals still needed to be fed and cleaned.

"Well, since you are also doing me a favor by taking Arianna out for some fun, let me do you a favor and help out." I started to open my mouth to protest because I didn't want to owe him any favors or think I couldn't handle this on my own. "No Cristina," he said before I could get anything out. "I insist. My sister and her husband are working on the garden now, so I have time."

I wanted Arianna to have fun, so I nodded my head and finished up the chores. He picked up right where I left off, already knowing what to do. He put the right feed in the animals' pens and together we cleaned them out. He worked with an effortless swiftness, moving twice as fast as me with no hesitation or worry that he may not be doing something right. We finished within the hour, and I looked around in relief, happy that everything got done, and more importantly, got done right.

"Give me your phone." He said, wiping his hands on his pants. I pulled it out and handed it to him. "I put my number in there—if you ever need help, just call me, and I will come over. It's not easy taking over all of this, especially if it's something new. I remember the stories my parents would tell me from when your nonna first came back and needed time to readjust to the farm again. They helped her without a second thought. I want to be there for you too."

I felt grateful to have him as a neighbor and a friend. I headed back to the house to check on my nonna and was surprised when I saw her in the kitchen, over a pot of boiling water.

"Yes, Cristina- you see? I am fine." She had a wooden spoon in her hand and pointed it in my direction as I walked in. "Lunch is almost ready."

I helped her boil the pasta, put sauce on it and sliced some cucumbers and tomatoes to make a salad. We sat down and ate, and I kept a close eye on her to ensure she was actually feeling better.

"Cristina, are you going to the feast tonight?"

"Alessandro told me I should go with Arianna, but I don't want to leave you if you aren't feeling well."

"I'm fine, *basta!* Enough! Go spend time with Arianna and have fun. You are only young once."

I smiled, happy to see she had some of her energy back and took out my phone to text Arianna after we finished our lunch. Her text back was hesitant, saying she wasn't sure if she wanted to go out. I needed to come up with a plan to convince her.

CRISTINA: **Can you pick me up and I can help you put on your makeup for tonight?**

I thought it might have been the push she needed.

ARIANNA: **Are you sure? I don't want to bother you.**

CRISTINA: **I'm absolutely sure! It will be fun!**

She responded back with a smiley face and I put the phone down, satisfied that I was able to convince her to go.

"Wait, so what is primer?" She asked, while I put some on her face.

"It's just something you use before you put your makeup on. It helps everything stay on and look better."

"Oh, interesting," she said, pulling away to look in the mirror. "Thanks again, Cristina. There was no way I could have done this."

I smiled and started to add bronzer, showing her in front of the mirror where to add it on her face and where to add highlighter. She nodded her head, her eyes focused on all of the steps I showed her. When I moved to the eyes, I paused before each step, having her open her eyes to see what I'd done and see if she liked it.

"Wow, that really makes a difference, huh. I like how it enhances my eyes." She said, getting close to her reflection. "This is what I always wanted my makeup to look like but was never able to figure out how to do it myself." She continued admiring what I did, turning her face side to side.

"You are naturally beautiful, Arianna. The makeup only just brings it out more." I said, taking a step back and really seeing how striking she was. She kept staring at herself in the mirror, her lips slightly turned upwards, before she turned to me, her expression now serious.

"What am I going to wear? Now I want to look really good." She hopped up from her seat and went towards her closet.

"Let's see what you have." I rifled through her clothes and picked out a short skirt, some strappy sandals, and a blouse that matched, and paired it with a cardigan for when it got chillier at night. I remembered when I was younger that the main part of the town was always chillier at night since it was high up on the hill.

I took out my own clothes, freshened up my makeup, and tried on several outfits I had bought, seeing which Arianna liked better.

"Wow, these jeans don't button." I said, trying to lay on the bed and pull the button closed. I gave up, took them off, and opted for a pair of black dressy shorts and white tank top, with a small jacket on top. I decided to FaceTime Josh, wanting him to see me all dressed up instead of in my usual farm clothes.

"Hey babe." He said, his smile almost looking forced as he moved the phone around his apartment.

"Hey, is this a bad time?"

He finally stopped moving the camera and settled in the living room. "Um, well, kind of, but I have a few minutes." His face relaxed as he leaned against the couch.

"Oh, okay. I'll let you go. I just wanted to say hi and show you my outfit that I picked out for tonight. We're going into town." I paused when I noticed Laila's orange Birkin bag across the room. "Is Laila over?"

He jerked his head back, confusion spreading over his face, and shook his head. "What? No."

"Oh, I thought I saw her orange bag by the window."

He turned back and laughed.

"Oh that, that's my sister's. You know she copies everything Laila buys. She's over because we're planning my dad's surprise 60th." His sister sometimes tagged along on shopping trips with us. She was three years younger than us, but we sometimes included her when we got together, especially seeing how it made Josh happy.

"You do look nice by the way."

I smiled. "We're going to a feast, it's quite the adventure everyone says. I'll FaceTime you later to show you when I get there."

The town took on a different atmosphere at night, lights strung across the rooftops above the roads created a festive feeling, while the smell of the food trucks that lined the streets made me want to forget the music and just spend time trying everything they had. One food truck was selling *porchetta* sandwiches and I pulled Arianna towards it, needing to see if the taste matched the heavenly smell that was coming from it.

"You've never had *porchetta* before?" Arianna said, taking a bite of her sandwich as we walked up and down the piazza.

"No, and if I keep eating all of the amazing stuff here, I don't think I'll ever be able to fit into those jeans again. How do you do it? How do you live with all of this amazing food and stay thin?"

"Not sure, honestly. I like to eat what I want and try not to worry about that. My mother always tells me that life is too short to deny yourself of good food."

After finishing up the most savory and delicious sandwich I'd ever had, I started to agree with her. Arianna laughed and we continued walking up the piazza. We stopped in front of the stage and listened to a local cover band, my hips began swaying to the beat.

"So, tell me more about the infamous Angela who makes amazing gelato." I said loudly to Arianna, as I noticed two guys come up to us.

"*Ciao, belle.*" One of them said, alcohol coming off his mouth and his eyes were glazed.

"*Ciao.*" I said, moving slightly away, but still trying to be polite.

"*Non volete ballare con noi?*" He asked why we didn't want to dance with them.

"*No, no grazie.*" Arianna said more firmly, grabbing my elbow to move me away.

The boys followed, still calling out for us to dance as we reached a group of people and tried to push our way through. One of them reached my arm, pulling me towards him, and I tried to nudge him off, telling him *basta.*

"*Lasciale stare.*" I heard a strong voice telling them to leave us alone. The one guy let go of my arm, raised both of his hands against his chest, and moved away. I turned to see Alessandro's nostrils flaring as he glared at them as they moved across the piazza.

"You need to stop saving me, Alessandro. I promise I'm not always the damsel in distress." I said, smiling at him, but still shaking from how brazen those men had been.

He turned towards me, his intense stare softening, and then he moved his gaze to both of us, a small smile forming on his mouth when Arianna thanked him too.

"Andiamo al bar qui vicino." He said to Arianna, motioning for us to follow him to the bar that was nearby. Relieved to get away from the crowd, I followed.

The bar was in one of the buildings that lined the perimeter of the piazza and had a dark-brown awning that covered a few tables and chairs on the outside. I walked inside and took in the pale yellow stucco that covered the walls with rocks that jutted out every so often, giving the inside a rustic feel. I felt like I could breathe with the vaulted ceilings and exposed beams and trusses that had old-fashioned lanterns hanging on them. We both sat down at the bar next to a group of guys who Alessandro introduced me to as his friends. Arianna went straight to talking to them. I took a seat next to her on an empty stool and tried to follow along.

"You don't understand a lot of what they're saying, right." Alessandro said, sitting in the stool next to me. He was dressed in dark-gray pants and a black short-sleeved fitted polo shirt, definitely different from what I was used to seeing him in when he worked on the farm. "Here, try this and tell me what you think." He handed me a glass of red wine and offered one to Arianna who refused, reminding him she was driving. I lifted my glass to the others, took a sip, and put it down quickly before turning to Alessandro.

"Write down the name of that wine because I need my nonna to buy this. I never drink red because it's either too strong or has an unpleasant aftertaste. But this—this is amazing!"

Alessandro's full lips parted to show his straight teeth, something I hadn't really paid attention to.

"You know he makes this wine, Cristina, right?" Arianna said over her shoulder, her lips closed together trying to stop the smile that was spreading across her face too. "But don't let it get to his head that he makes the best wine. Just tell him it's okay." She added, looking at Alessandro with a mischievous grin.

"I didn't know you sell the wine you make! That's incredible,

Alessandro! You should market this for New York too—people would go crazy for it!"

I saw him glance down and I swore his cheeks flushed, before he looked back up at me, staring into my eyes. I had never really noticed him, but dressed up tonight, with his hair gelled back in soft waves, he looked handsome. I became mad at myself that I could even think of that, but then reminded myself that I was human, and it was normal to still think other guys were good-looking.

"*Grazie*, Cristina. But I don't sell it. My friend who owns the bar has a couple of bottles behind the shelf for when we come, but I don't think it's good enough to sell."

I was about to protest when I felt my phone vibrating and went to pick it up.

"Hey, babe. Sorry about before, it was crazy with my sister over and planning. I have more time now." Josh said, before his expression changed quickly to confusion. "Are you at a bar?"

"Hey, yeah. I came with Arianna." I moved the camera towards her, and she gave a quick wave before I moved it back to me.

"Oh, there's a lot of guys there too."

"Yeah, it's my neighbor, Alessandro, and his friends." I said, all of a sudden feeling uncomfortable I was out with them.

I glanced quickly over at Alessandro, who was looking down, his body now positioned away from me.

"I'll let you go babe. Have fun. I'll talk to you tomorrow. Love you."

"Love you too."

I hung up, turned back to Alessandro who was still staring down, his foot kicking gently against the edge of the bar. I was about to say something to him about the wine, but he looked up at me, his expression now unreadable, and said that he was going to go home. I said goodbye, secretly hoping he would change his mind and stay, but watched him nod his head to his friends and head out of the bar.

I chatted the rest of the night with Arianna, not knowing what to say to the other guys, before we decided to head out and try one of Angela's famous gelatos. I felt great after the wine, not even slightly buzzed, as we picked out gelatos and walked the rest of night, listening to the songs.

"Seriously, this gelato is absolutely delicious! Arianna, why didn't I get it last time? Why did I waste two weeks not eating this every day?" I said, while enjoying the creamier version of America's cousin of ice cream.

On the drive home, I stared out the window into the darkened fields and thought about how everything that changed in the short weeks since I arrived. I felt good— free, and comfortable, in a way I'd never experienced before. I didn't know how to explain it, but my body felt different, and I wanted to know why.

11

Undici

aiutare - to help

"No, come back here! Oh no, don't run that way!" I tried cornering the baby lamb, the one that had its leg stuck in the fence had now somehow escaped and was trying to run across the field. I had managed to corner it against the fence but didn't know how I was going to push it towards the gate which was on the other side.

I need to call Alessandro. I thought, taking out my phone and dialing his number. A few minutes later, he was running across the fields, a big smile on his face when he saw the situation I was in.

"Okay, you go behind it and I'll move to the side of it so we can push him towards the gate." He said, coming up with a plan faster than I would've been able to. We finally reached the gate, let the lamb back inside, before we each let out a breath of relief.

"That baby lamb is going to kill me. Thanks." I said, smiling at Alessandro. I saw his smile fading as sadness took over his eyes and wondered what he was feeling.

"Alessandro, you need to sell that wine. You know I'm going to ask you for some bottles now that I know you have a stock back in your cellar."

I saw some life come back to his eyes as they crinkled, a smile forming also on his face.

"Thank you. But I don't think they would sell like you think they would."

"Are you kidding! It's better than the $200 bottles I've tasted back home!" I said, grabbing on to his arm to yell at him. My breath hitched when I felt the muscles on his arm and a feeling of warmth centered me. I took my arm away, embarrassed by the touch. "So," I continued, smiling in a playful way, "what do you need to do to sell wine? Learn marketing?"

He inclined his head towards me. "Cristina, I never even finished my last year of high school. School is not easy here and many of the kids that *do* graduate can't even find jobs. I'm meant to spend my time on the farm and maybe finish up that last year, but I would never be able to attend university. Plus, university is so difficult, it takes some people 8 years to graduate."

I never realized that the schooling was different here than in the States. I was used to every kid following the same path from high school graduation to college. I had finished my bachelor's in four years, getting a degree in business that I didn't even know what to do with. I didn't even really want to go to college, but Michael insisted I needed a degree.

"I never realized that. But we need more people to taste that wine. A lot of entrepreneurs never went to college." I looked back at him and saw a small smile form. I loved watching him smile, and I wanted to make sure he did often, just like I wanted for Arianna. They were both hard-working, caring people that didn't deserve to feel loss at such a young age, and I almost felt as if it were my job to make sure that they were happy. When I saw them smile, it made my heart full, as if there was a piece missing to it that I couldn't quite understand.

We kept walking and I stopped Alessandro, holding his arm gently again, but taking it away quickly when I still felt a subtle electric current.

"Can you do something for me?" I asked, after an idea popped into my head.

"*Certo*, sure." He said, his eyes locking on mine.

"I want to surprise my nonna and make a good meal for her, but I have no idea how to do anything besides boiling water and putting the pasta in."

"I will help you. Come over to my house in an hour, and we will put something together for her that she will love."

I thanked him and headed back to the garden. I continued pulling out the weeds and realized that I was still smiling. I picked some of the vegetables to bring over to Alessandro in case he wanted to cook with them, and then FaceTimed my mom, showing her the garden instead of always talking to her from my bed.

"Honey, you are incredible. Nonna keeps saying how she wants to keep you there."

"It's not that bad. I hate to admit it, but you were right, I needed this time to get away from Manhattan for a bit."

"A few more weeks and you can come home, are you excited?"

"Yeah, I miss everyone a lot, I can't wait to see them. Give a kiss to Stella and Samantha."

"Soon, alright, I love you," she said.

"Love you too." When I hung up I started thinking about everyone back home. I was taken aback when I realized that I still hadn't heard much from Laila. It was unlike her to not talk to me everyday and keep me updated. I put it out of my mind thinking about how she was the type that got caught up in the moment and became oblivious to whatever was happening around her. I imagined her laying down on a lounge chair at her beach house, enjoying the view, and not wanting to be bothered by anything else.

I ran back to the house telling my nonna not to cook anything tonight, and that she would be surprised and then skipped over to Alessandro's house with the bag of vegetables I had picked.

"What do you think about *lasagne*?"

"I love lasagna!" I said, remembering the last time I had it was when my nonna had made it for us when she visited, probably more than six years ago.

"No, Cristina. It's *lasagne. E,*" he said, jokingly scolding me for my mispronunciation.

"Sorry. *Lasagne.*"

"Please, that and bruschetta. Make sure you tell your American friends that it's not *broo-shetta*. It's *bruschetta.*"

"*Broo-skeh-tah.*" I said, phonetically sounding out the syllables.

He looked pleased after I said it and patted my back, which made me laugh.

We started on the *lasagne,* and he went over to grab a pot with tiny meatballs and sauce already cooked and placed it near me.

"Wait, so I just skipped five steps, Alessandro! This is cheating! You already have the sauce, meat, and meatballs ready?"

"We need hours to cook the meat sauce, Cristina, and you were lucky because I had started it earlier already for tonight. Besides, that's a lesson for another day, when we have more time." His eyes playful as he turned his attention back to the pan.

"Put a little oil on the bottom, add some sauce, and then put the layers of the *lasagne* on top."

I did exactly as he said, carefully aligning each of the noodles in the pan.

"Now put more sauce on top, add some *scamorza,* and then the meat."

"*Scamorza?*" I asked, looking at the cheese he handed over to me. "I don't think I've ever had this before."

"Try it."

I took it from him, still not knowing what type of taste to expect.

"Why does everything have to taste so good here!" I exclaimed, savoring the taste of the cheese.

"It's like mozzarella, but dried." He added, delightment crossing his face as he watched me eat it. "Once you are done, there is a big question to ask."

"What?"

"Do we add hard-boiled eggs or not?"

"Hard-boiled eggs? I had never heard of that in *lasagne.*"

"So, some people swear that it's the original way, but some people tend to skip it—up to you. My family and your nonna normally don't use it, but we can try it if you want."

"Nah, let's skip it. What's next?"

"Put some of the ricotta on it—I already mixed it with grated cheese and fresh parsley."

"Alessandro, you keep cheating!" I said, jokingly hitting him on the arm, and he took a step back to avoid me hitting him anymore. I loved watching his face light up as he explained the steps.

"Alright, now we repeat the layers, I add some more grated cheese on top, until we reach the top of the pan."

I kept going, remembering the steps to each layer, and was surprised that I became more confident in what I was doing, especially with Alessandro next to me, not judging, but explaining exactly what I needed to do. By the time the last layer was done, Alessandro had me turn on the oven and put the *lasagne* in, and then high-fived me.

I was grateful that he didn't make me feel embarrassed about not knowing how to make anything, but for some reason, I knew he wouldn't—which was why I had asked him. He pulled a chair out from the kitchen table and motioned me to sit down as he walked over to the cupboard and opened it. The kitchen reminded me of one that I had seen in a rustic magazine, with dark wood cabinets and open shelves decorated with copper accents. I was surprised how clean everything was and noticed nothing was out on the countertops. He came back with two glasses and poured some *acqua frizzante*, sparkling water, for both of us.

"Wait, are those Harry Potter books?" I asked, noticing a few books on a higher shelf across the room.

He looked over and let out a chuckle while looking down. "Yes. Someone made me want to read them." He said, his eyes meeting mine quickly and his lips pulling more to the sides.

I walked over and reached for one of the books and flipped through the pages. "Alessandro—this is in English!"

"Well, after *someone* read it to me the whole summer, I had to go and buy them and tried to read them myself."

My heart hugged itself, happy that a small moment we shared so many years ago made an impact on him later on. We sat silently for a few minutes, taking small sips of water, and breathing in the delicious smell of *lasagne* that was now coming from the oven.

"Should I call Arianna too and see if she wants to have dinner with us?" I asked, wanting to include her in this special culinary victory.

"That's a great idea. You know—I have to thank you for spending time with her. Ever since her fiancé passed away, she hasn't gone out or had fun. So, it means a lot that you are spending time with her and becoming her friend—thank you."

I could see an inner glow in his eyes as he thanked me, which made my body tingle with warmth, grateful that I was able to be there for someone when they needed it.

"Well, she's fun, and we have a good time together. She is honestly helping *me* more than I am helping her." He stared back at me when

I said that, his deep gaze holding on to mine, before it became too much for me. My heart quickened for a beat. I turned away to check on the *lasagne*. Guilt started creeping up again and I busied myself to move over to the bag of vegetables I brought from my garden.

"So, what can we do with string beans, cherry tomatoes, and zucchini?" I said, taking them out and placing them on the table.

I saw him study them for a bit, shrug his shoulders, and then pick up the tomatoes.

"Let's boil the string beans, then just put some olive oil and salt on them. Then, we can make *bruschetta* with the tomatoes, and well, for the *zucchine*, I will teach you my favorite recipe."

I became excited that we had more time together as he started explaining what I needed to do for the bruschetta. He made me repeat the name twice so I would pronounce it right, and then seemed satisfied enough to then have me start cutting the tomatoes. We chatted while preparing the food, talking about Arianna and what her fiancé was like. I asked if it was hard for him too, and he nodded, explaining that he was like a brother, often spending most of their time together.

"What do you do for fun besides working on the farm?"

"Why, it's not fun working on the farm?" He rebutted, matching my smile.

"No, seriously. Alessandro, all I do is see you work on the farm, in your garden, then somehow you have time to make wine and then sauce. You need to do something more fun than this!"

He thought for a moment, probably trying to come up with a response before adding, "Well, we go to the beach a lot in the summer with my friends, and then there are the feasts at night."

"Alright, alright. That sounds like fun. As long as you promise me that I will see you laugh and smile more." I noticed his eyes became more serious, his gaze strong again, and felt the heat from the oven, making the room hot and flushing my whole body with warmth.

I turned my attention back to the *bruschetta*, chopping up the parsley, basil, and garlic he had given to me, and then added some dried oregano on top. I drizzled the vinegar and olive oil over it, until he told me to stop.

"Always put a little salt at a time. You can always add salt, but it's very hard to take it away if it's too much." He said, as I sprinkled the salt over it. I tasted a spoonful, told him it felt like something was missing, and he added a little more salt until it was perfect.

"I feel like I can at least prepare a simple meal now. I'm definitely not Giada De Laurentiis, but it's a start." We drained the string beans and seasoned them, and then he taught me how to prepare his favorite *zucchine* dish, cooking it slowly with olive oil, onions, garlic, and parsley.

When we were almost done, I texted Arianna to meet us at my house and we wrapped everything up to bring it over.

"Che brava che sei, Cristina!" My nonna said, taking a bite of the *lasagne* from her dish. I started to blush, and I looked over to Alessandro, silently thanking him for all of his help.

"Nonna, Alessandro was the one who taught me what to do. He helped a lot but thank you."

"No, Cristina, it was your hands that created this, my words just guided you." He said, his face brightening.

Arianna had her fork close to her mouth, but just stared back and forth between me and Alessandro before shaking her head and taking a bite.

We sat there, talking about what it was like for my nonna when she first came back to Italy after living in New York, and we laughed at her stories of not being able to grow the vegetables like she used to. It took the help of Alessandro's family for her to get her gardening skills back. I looked around at all of their smiling faces as I took a helping of the *zucchine*. It felt good to have dinner with friends and family. I hadn't had this in years. Michael always worked late, and our housekeeper Maria would prepare the meals for everyone. Once I lived by myself, I would usually pick up something on my way home or go out with my friends or Josh, but it never felt like this. It felt good to sit at a table, with a homemade meal, and laugh. It didn't bother me that my clothes were snug or didn't fit, I knew I could always get new outfits, or wear something different—but I would never be able to get these memories back.

12

Dodici

nuovo - new

The sunlight hit my face the next morning through the open slats in the shutters as I reached over to grab my phone and check the time.

Two missed calls? I scrolled to see Josh had called me last night around eleven, and then at midnight, and felt bad that I hadn't answered. I made a mental note to call him later, when I was sure he would be up, and headed out to the kitchen to make espresso.

I dipped the cookies in the espresso cup, taking small bites, and scrolled through my feed before I noticed a message from Arianna.

ARIANNA: **So, I need a haircut and this place has an opening today. Do you want to come with me? You can help me pick a new style!**

I replied quickly that it was a date and asked if she could add me to her appointment. I wouldn't do anything drastic with my hair, but a simple trim would keep my hair healthy.

I worked in the garden with my nonna next to me before lunch. We talked about some new recipes we had planned to try with the peppers that were starting to grow fast.

"Nonna, *stai bene?*" I asked if she was well, after seeing her grab the side of her stomach. Her pinched expression on her face had me worried.

"*Sto bene, sto bene.* Sometimes if I have too much coffee, my stomach hurts. *Basta caffè.*" She said, saying she would stop having coffee.

I nodded my head but continued to check on her as we finished up weeding the garden and picking some of the vegetables.

"Nonna, you're sure you're okay?" I asked, after we had finished lunch. "I'm going with Arianna to get our haircut, but I can stay back if you need more help." She responded firmly that she was fine and then shoved a 100 Euro bill in my pocket after I protested taking it from her. I gave her a hug and waited outside for Arianna to pick me up.

"So, should I keep the length? Or should I go shorter?" She asked, one hand on the steering wheel while the other shifted the gears seamlessly.

I looked down and wondered how difficult it would be to drive a manual car. My nonna had one sitting in the garage that she hardly used. Maybe I could also learn how to drive one.

"You have a really pretty face, maybe go shorter so you can show it off?" I offered, not sure if she was ready to do something so daring.

"You always are so nice to me, Cristina. Okay, short it is."

I didn't think Arianna was the type that realized how pretty she really was. She was always hiding behind her hair or an outfit that was a size too big for her. I wanted to bring her in front of a mirror and make her see how beautiful she was, but I didn't want to force her to change either.

"Hey, have you ever noticed my nonna sick a lot when you stopped by to get eggs before I came here?"

"What do you mean?"

"I don't know. About a week ago she was sick in bed with a stomachache, refusing to see the doctor—and today, I saw her holding her stomach, obviously in pain, but then she brushed it off, saying that 'I worry too much.'"

"Hmm. And she won't see the doctor?"

"No. But maybe I should call anyway?"

"There's only one doctor in the town. I can call him if you want."

I thought about it more but didn't want to go behind her back.

"I'll wait a little longer, but if she is sick again, we will."

We reached the salon thirty minutes later. The salon was at the bottom of a three-story building, covered in dark cream stucco, with potted flowers next to the entrance.

"*Buongiorno.*" Arianna said as she moved the beaded curtains to the side before she entered. I greeted everyone too and sat in the waiting area before we were called in. There were four ladies cutting and styling hair, chatting away with their clients. The salon had a cozy feel, like you wanted to grab a cup of coffee and chat with the ladies, telling them everything that was going on in your life.

Arianna was called over first and I saw panic in her eyes as she hesitated before saying she was going to cut it short. The hairdresser started washing her hair after showing her some pictures of styles before Arianna had agreed on one.

"Cristina? *Puoi venire!*" Another hairdresser called out my name, telling me to come to her chair.

"*Allora, cosa vuoi fare?*" She asked, wanting to know what I wanted to do. I was hesitant to respond in Italian, and almost wanted to call Arianna over to help, but she had her head in the sink, hair all full of shampoo.

"Um. *Tagliare? Poco?*" I asked her in the best Italian I could for what I thought was the word for *cut* and *just a little*. I could see her squinting at my response, trying to put together what I meant, before nodding her head and repeating in proper Italian that I just wanted a trim.

"*Sì!*" I said, happy she had understood.

"*Va bene*, good. You want highlights? I can put little highlights in front. It is pretty for you." She said, effortlessly transitioning to English.

I was afraid to say yes and mess up what my stylist, Carlos, back home had done for me but I didn't want it to seem like I didn't trust her, especially since Arianna was getting something drastic done. What's the worst that can happen? I can always correct it when I go back.

"*Va bene!*" I said, a smile growing on my face as I saw my hairdresser's eyes lighting up. She quickly started mixing up some colors and prepared the aluminum foil strips for my hair.

About two hours later, we walked out together jumping up and down at the new us.

"Arianna, *sei bellissima!*" I shouted, admiring her asymmetrical bob cut with side bangs that showed off her gorgeous eyes. She touched her shorter hair, and her smile was so wide that I just wanted to hug her.

"And you are beautiful too, Cristina! Wow! You look really good with blonde highlights!"

I smiled and batted my eyes, which made Arianna laugh and smile more. I was pleasantly surprised when the hairdresser turned me around at the end to admire my hair. She added highlights around the frame of my face and a few scattered around that complimented my brown hair perfectly, making my tanned face somehow seem brighter than before.

"Cristina, we need to go somewhere tonight with our hair so nice! Let's go to the feast—I'll pick you up!"

"Yes!" I said, excited for a night out. I quickly felt guilty about my nonna, not wanting to leave her alone for too long if she wasn't feeling well. "Let me make sure my nonna is okay, though."

"Sounds good! Text me later if you can go."

She drove me home, chatting the whole way about how much she loved her hair, and thanking me for keeping her company. I waved goodbye when she dropped me off and skipped into the house, excited to show my nonna.

"Nonna, *guarda i capelli!*" I shouted as soon as I entered the house. I saw her sitting at the kitchen table, her hand on her stomach and a hot cup of tea in front of her.

"Nonna, are you feeling better? Is it still your stomach?" I said, putting a hand on her shoulder.

"*Sì.* But it is getting better. I just wanted to relax a little before I went outside."

She then got up, took another sip of her tea, and then placed the cup in the sink. I texted Arianna that it was probably better I stayed home.

I was working with my nonna in the garden when my phone started ringing, Josh wanting to FaceTime.

I forgot to call him. I moved over to the side of the garden and answered his call.

"Cristina? Is everything okay? I haven't heard from you." I saw his expression shift and his eyebrows pull together. "What did you do to your hair?"

"I'm so sorry. It has been crazy lately. I was supposed to call you, but then Arianna took me to get my hair done with her…"

"Wow, you trusted them to do your hair?" He let out a laugh.

I became slightly miffed at his response. "I actually think they did a great job."

"Well, you look happy—whatever you are doing, it's working." A small smile formed on my face, and I relaxed my shoulders to his response. "You know I miss you and I can't wait to see you."

"I know, I miss you too." I answered back and then spotted Alessandro walking across the fields towards us. "I have to go. I'll call you later."

"Oh, okay. Love you, babe."

"Love you too." I hung up right as Alessandro was about to reach us. I noticed his eyebrows were furrowed and he was rubbing his chin.

"*Signora Filomena, come si sente?*" He said to my nonna, asking how she was. It was sweet to hear him call her Mrs. Filomena.

"*Mamma mia, sto bene. Cosa sta dicendo Cristina?*" My nonna jokingly threw her garden tools on the ground, pretending she was mad and asked him what I had been saying. He smiled at her and then turned towards me, his intense eyes always drawing me in.

"So, you can't come to the feast tonight?" From the corner of my eye I could see my nonna staring at me, her hand on her hip, listening in.

"Well, I wanted to make sure my nonna was better and I didn't want to leave her."

"*Basta*, Cristina. You are going to the feast. I have lived alone for a long time, I am fine. Alessandro, please make sure she goes tonight!" My nonna said, her hands waving around and her voice sounding exasperated.

Alessandro shrugged his shoulders and smiled at me, one of his eyebrows raising. "I can't argue with your nonna, Cristina."

I shook my head, rolled my eyes comically, and looked back at my nonna who was motioning for me to go.

"Okay, I'll go." I said, still shaking my head as a tight smile formed on my face. Alessandro nodded his head, and then said he'd see me later.

My nonna stared at me a while longer after Alessandro left and then shook her head before picking up her garden tools to start working again. We worked for another twenty minutes before we decided it was enough and I ran back in the house to take a shower to get ready.

I took time with my makeup and FaceTimed Arianna to help her with hers. We giggled half the time as she kept picking up the wrong product to use as I was explaining to her the steps. We leaned our phones upright as we took turns modeling outfits before deciding on one. I opted for a navy blue maxi dress, the only thing that seemed to fit me lately, and a cardigan to put on top, while Arianna picked out jeans and a blouse that brought out her new hairstyle.

"*Ciao*, Nonna." I gave her a hug goodbye on my way outside to meet Arianna. I stepped out, taking in the cooler night air, and looked up at the ebony sky filled with glistening stars right as I heard Arianna's car approach.

"Arianna, I need to learn how to drive a manual car. Can you teach me?" I asked, ducking to get into her car. I felt bad that she had to drive me everywhere. I knew my driver's license was valid in Italy, but what good would it do if I couldn't drive their cars.

"You don't want me to teach you, Cristina." She said, letting out a laugh. "I wouldn't even know how to explain the steps. I would just tell you to look at me and then figure it out. I'd ask Alessandro to teach you. He has way more patience than I do when explaining."

My heart quickened. I couldn't ask Alessandro—he already did so much. I shook my head, certain that I could teach myself after watching a Youtube tutorial instead.

"No, don't worry. I don't want to bother him. Plus, I'm not here for much longer, so it probably doesn't matter much anyway." My heart dipped a little. I hadn't even thought about how much time I had left and I hadn't even asked my mom or Michael when they called. I missed home, but I didn't feel ready to go back. I needed a few more weeks to make sure my nonna was okay.

"I'm sure he wouldn't mind. Besides, have you seen what a good mood he has been in lately? He used to always keep to himself, just working on his farm, always with a serious expression. But lately I've seen him smiling and laughing so much more!"

I pictured his face, laughing after something I said, and remembering all the time we've spent together. That familiar warmth crept through my body remembering when I touched his arms, feeling the strength in them, and I quickly pushed those thoughts aside, guilty that I had them, especially since he was a good friend.

"Oh, no I can smell the *porchetta* stand from here." The delicious smell of the sandwiches filled the air as soon as I stepped out of the car. "You are going to have to pull me away from that tonight. Nothing is fitting me anymore! We need to do some serious shopping again."

Arianna laughed as we walked closer to the piazza, taking in all of the noise from the people that were chatting together on the streets, drinks in hands, laughing together. This was something that was missing back home—not just a place where people could eat and drink while listening to music, but a sense of community while doing it. Everyone knew each other here and you felt safe— like you belonged walking through the town and saying hi to your friends and neighbors with either a drink or gelato in your hand, or a *porchetta* sandwich which was my go-to choice.

"Che belle ragazze." I turned to the side to see Alessandro looking at both of us and letting out a whistle. Alessandro surprised me, giving us both a hug.

Arianna hugged him back and turned to him. "I was just saying to Cristina how happy you've been lately. See Cristina," she turned towards me, "we even got a hug tonight." He dug his hands in his pocket, looking away embarrassed.

"I'm not so bad, Arianna. What, I can't hug two beautiful girls hello?" He said, his eyes shifting towards mine and staying there. That warm feeling from before came over me slightly as my eyes drew to his arms. I saw the outline of his muscles under his dark-green t-shirt. I looked away, reminding myself that I needed to call Josh. Alessandro is a friend. It is normal to think another guy is good looking. I kept repeating that mantra in my head, trying to suppress those usual guilty feelings that seemed to take residence in my body lately. I was sure Josh thought other girls were pretty too, since it was a human thing to do.

He walked with us as we made our way closer to the *porchetta* stands, my will weakening and craving another one as we approached it.

"I am sorry, Alessandro, can you keep Cristina company? I just want to say hi to my friend from high school that I just saw."

"Sure." He said, his hands still in his pockets as we now walked together.

"Alessandro, I need to move away from this *porchetta* stand or you will see me climbing over it and making myself a sandwich."

He started laughing, pulled my arm closer to it, and bought two sandwiches, handing me over one.

"If your heart wants it, then you take it, Cristina." He said, before taking a bite of his sandwich.

His words made my heart flutter. *If your heart wants it, then you take it.* He was talking about a sandwich, but my heart created a story with my mind that I couldn't help. I took a bite of my sandwich, pushing any other thought away, and continued walking silently next to Alessandro towards the stage.

"So, who is playing today?" I asked, noticing a different band on the stage.

"Another local band. They play some good cover songs by Ligabue, one of my favorite singers."

"You listen to music? When? All I see you do is work." I said, taking the last bite of my sandwich, brushing the crumbs away from my hands.

"I listen to music. In the shower, in my car, and sometimes when I'm making wine. I put some Vasco Rossi or Ligabue on, and suddenly the hours feel only like minutes."

I scolded myself again, when the image of him in the shower listening to music popped up in my head. Enough! I tried to hold on to my emotions. I wondered if it was the haircut, the bright, dry sun, or just the fact that my belly was finally full that kept creating more of these images of him in my head.

We listened for a few beats, until I noticed him looking at me, his eyes intense like they normally were.

"Can I ask you something?" He said, his voice revealing a slight uncertainty.

"Sure."

"Why did you hate me that summer when you came back? You seemed happy those first weeks, but then you ignored me after."

My heart slumped, my face must have dropped, and I wanted to hug him and tell him I was sorry. Sorry that I could have been that mean when he was always nice to me. I didn't want to hurt him, to tell him what Laila had said about him and how I'd been so weak and listened to her. I tried to come up with something else, anything that wouldn't hurt him or make him lose that smile that I loved to see.

"I'm sorry. I wasn't myself that year. My mom had just remarried, they wanted me to go with them to Italy, but I wanted more time to adjust to my new life at home. I had started a new school with new friends, and I took it out on you. It was a hard adjustment for me." I stared into his eyes, hoping he would forgive me. "You were always so nice to me—I'm really sorry."

I saw his eyes jump up to mine and his expression change slightly. His face became unreadable as he continued to look at me and I didn't want to break his gaze.

"It was a shock. I mean, we had so much fun before that." He said, and my breathing stopped as I remembered the kisses we shared and the memories we made. He stopped too, and we both stared at each other silently, before I looked down, needing to break away.

He let out a small laugh and then said, "You just used me to ride on the tractor that summer, didn't you?"

I laughed, remembering the feeling of being free on top of his tractor. "Okay, so maybe the rides were a lot of fun. But it wasn't just that—I loved when we were on our own and going on adventures." I looked back at him and all of a sudden the band started playing again and everyone crowded near the stage. Someone bumped against me, pushing me right into Alessandro, who gripped my waist to steady me.

I was pressed against his chest, his hands still holding my waist, and I looked up at him. His lips were slightly parted, his eyes even more intense than I had ever seen. My body was not moving away from him; instead it was as if it was begging me to stay there, feeling as much of him as I could.

Reality finally hit me, my brain taking command, and I moved quickly back, saying sorry. He stood still with his lips pressed together, and one of his hands moved to the back of his neck.

"I need to go home, Alessandro. It's getting late." I said, my voice low.

He continued to look at me, his eyes stronger than they had ever been. I wished I knew what he was thinking. "I'll find Arianna." He said and left me alone with an empty feeling taking over my heart.

13

Tredici

guidare - to drive

It can't be too hard. I finished another YouTube tutorial on how to drive a manual car. I eyed my nonna's car that was sitting in the garage and mustered up the courage to try driving it.

"*Stai attenta,* Cristina." My nonna said, telling me to be careful as she stood next to me clutching her rosary beads.

I can do this. I left everything behind and came here and I'm doing fine. The car I drive back home is huge—how hard could it be to drive this little one? Nonna's car resembled a small blue semi-circle that could only fit two people. The trunk was flush with the back of the car and almost reminded me of a Volkswagon buggie.

I stepped inside and then looked down at my hands, trying to remember what to do with them.

Okay, left hand on the steering wheel, right hand on the shifting gear. Check. Now, left foot on the clutch, right on the break. Check. I felt a burst of confidence in remembering the most important steps from the tutorial. Ignition on. Okay, now slowly move my foot from the brake to the gas. Now lift the clutch.

"Uggghhhh...." I let out as the car sputtered to a stop and the ignition stalled.

Try again, Cristina. I repeated the steps and this time I moved it a few inches before the ignition stalled again.

One more time. I was determined to get it right. The car started moving. I maneuvered the steering wheel, turned out of the garage and onto the street, and started driving down the road when all of a sudden the pitch of the motor started going higher and higher.

"How do I shift gears?" I yelled out to myself in the car. The street was on a slight incline, which made the car slow down, but I still panicked trying to remember what the video had said. I pressed on the brake and decided that I would relax before I moved the car ahead again. Fear came over me as I started to feel the car rolling backward, right into a ditch.

"Really? It has to be this hard?" I said, slamming the door shut and looking at the car stuck in the ditch. It didn't take long for me to notice Alessandro standing in the distance, arms crossed in front of his chest, enjoying the scene.

"Are you happy with the entertainment, Alessandro?" I said, letting out an exasperated laugh, trying to calm myself down and not tear up.

He walked over, his smile fading into concern as he stood next to me. "Come on, let's get this car out of here." He pushed against the car, and I stared at his muscles twitching as he strained to get it out of the ditch. I silently scolded myself for staring too long and turned my focus back on the situation. Once it was back on the road, he ran inside and pulled the emergency brake so it wouldn't roll any further.

"So, you are like my knight in shining armor. Thank you."

"Knight in shining armor?" He asked, a quizzical expression crossing his face.

"You know, like in the movies. The princess always gets saved by the knight or the prince. It's called gallantry. Kind of an out-of-date notion now because women can do anything men can, and all Disney princess movies are about female empowerment now, but I still like to believe chivalry isn't dead." My face immediately turned bright red as I realized what I said.

"So what you're saying to me is that I'm your *hero?*" I could see a little glimmer in his eyes as he looked back at me, a smile slowly forming on his face.

"Ugh, I regret saying anything," I said as I looked back at the car. "I was trying to learn how to drive in manual by myself, but that obviously didn't work out the way I expected it to."

"You don't really need my help. You just need someone to guide you, that's it. You had it moving all by yourself. Give yourself some credit."

I knew it wasn't true what he was saying, but I appreciated it. The garden was thriving and I was getting the hang of cooking. "Thanks, Alessandro, but I haven't really done anything great by myself."

"Do you think people are just born knowing everything? No, Cristina. Someone shows them or they look at someone and copy them. Yes, there are those that are gifted and make their own creations, but we all had to start somewhere. You are starting, but you are going fast and creating. Your nonna's garden never looked this good before, Cristina, and that's thanks to you."

My heart stuttered and my breath hitched—no one ever said anything like that or made me feel better about myself. I was speechless. I wanted to thank him, but no words could come out. I stared back into his eyes, trying to come up with the words, but he interrupted me before I could even try to say anything.

"Let me help you. You know the basics—let me help you learn how to drive."

I nodded my head and headed into the driver's seat as he ducked into the passenger side.

"Fiat 500." He said, patting the dashboard as he settled in. "Show me what you know." He looked over at me, his full lips slowly curving up. Stop focusing on his lips! I yelled to myself. He is nice enough to teach you how to drive so Arianna doesn't have to keep driving you around. I placed my left hand on my steering wheel and my right on the shifting gear. He placed his left hand over mine on the gear and I froze. I couldn't look over at him and I completely forgot what I was supposed to do next. He probably sensed something because he took his hand off of mine, just hovering now slightly above it.

"*Posso?*" He asked for permission to touch my hand. My heart moved slightly towards him for asking me for permission. I nodded my head, still silent, and he placed his hand on mine again, electric sparks now shooting up my arm, forcing myself to remember to breathe.

"Okay, I will help you remember when to shift gears. I could hear that you weren't shifting gears when you were driving before. The pitch of the motor kept going higher and I was afraid you were going to break the car." He let out a laugh, which made me relax and be able to concentrate on what he was saying.

"The trick is, you have to play with your feet. Watch my feet and how I move them." I leaned over to see them and instantly got distracted again by the smell of bergamot and fabric softener coming off of his shirt. "The clutch is what controls the car the most. Push it down when you want to change gears and brake so the car won't stop."

My mind shifted, letting clarity sweep away the school-girl crush daze I had been in. "Okay, I think I got it."

"Show me."

I turned the car on, his hand moving away from mine as I lifted it from the gear to turn the key. I placed it right back and his hand hesitantly hovered over mine before placing it down once more. I took in a deep breath, moved my right foot slowly up off the brake as I lifted my left carefully off the clutch before it sputtered to a stop.

"Try to lift it off the clutch slower while your right foot steps on the gas."

I tried again, just like he said, and this time the car lurched forward and continued to move.

"Don't get too excited," he said, as I let out a screech. "My hand will help you shift gears as you keep going. Just remember to press down on the clutch."

As the motor revved up higher, I felt his palm against the back of my hand move, helping me realize that I should shift. I shifted seamlessly into second gear, and then again to third when he nudged my hand again. I was so afraid to look at him, but I could see from the corner of my eye that he was smiling and glancing over at me.

"*Brava.* Now, try to stop over here and we will turn around." It took a few tries to start again, but I felt that I had at least the hang of shifting gears. When we rolled up in front of my nonna's garage, I put on the emergency brake and looked over at him.

"That was good for today. Tomorrow we will go on lesson two, starting again on a hill." He started laughing to himself, maybe reliving the scene in his head of the car rolling into the ditch.

"I can't take time away from what you do throughout the day to help me drive. It's not fair."

"Well, I'm doing it for myself too. I don't want you on the road if you are driving like that." He said, letting out a chuckle.

"Okay. But then I have to do something to help you. It's only right."

He thought a moment before responding. *"Va bene,* tomorrow I'm going with my tractor to pick up some wood that I cut about a month ago to bring them up to the house. I could use help loading it." His hands were now in his pockets while his shoulders shrugged up.

"Absolutely, I'll definitely help." We said goodbye and I walked towards the farm, helping my nonna with the chores.

As I walked, I kept thinking about all of the feelings I had whenever he touched me or got close to me. I tried to tell myself it was only because I missed Josh. I knew I needed to talk to him more often.

"Hey, babe. What have you been up to?"

"I wanted to show you something," I said, walking towards the garden where my nonna was tending to the tomato plants. They were almost the size of her now, and she had mentioned they had never got this tall at this point in the season.

I turned the camera towards the garden, my nonna had her hand over her eyes to block the sun and gave a wave to Josh.

"So, this is what I have been up to." I turned the camera towards the garden and spanned it so he could see all of the plants.

"Really? What is that?" He asked, laying on the bed, one arm behind his head.

"Umm, the garden?" I responded, confused.

"Oh, yeah, I know the garden. I thought you were talking about something else. So, what, did you plant something?"

My eyebrows knitted together and my jaw slackened. Did I plant something? For some reason the question made me burn.

"Well, I helped my nonna take care of it, and the plants have grown a lot." I felt weird having to explain my hard work to him. "Never mind. How are things going?"

He talked about some surgeries he assisted in. Dr. Lettino let him take over for some of them. I asked him if he had heard from

Laila, but he shrugged his shoulders and said she was probably still hanging out with Irene and to not let it bother me.

"You're coming home soon, right? It's been almost a month."

"Yeah, but my nonna still needs help. I feel guilty leaving her so soon."

He got up on his elbow on the bed and adjusted himself to sit down.

"Why do you want to stay longer? You've practically been there a month, Michael said that it's enough. Is everything okay?" He seemed upset and I felt guilty for all of the mixed emotions swirling through me.

"No, no. Of course, I'm going to come home. I'm just saying that I feel guilty."

"Oh. Well, I have to go. I'll talk to you later." He got up from his bed and his expression looked almost hurt.

"Bye."

We hung up, without saying I love you and something felt different inside me—he didn't even pay attention to what I was saying. Has it always been like this? I didn't want to compare, but it didn't feel right. When I talked to Alessandro, I felt like he listened, like he wanted to help me. Was I reading too far into everything? After all, Alessandro is here, next to me, and I am just missing Josh. I convinced myself that I needed to stop over-analyzing everything and just finish taking care of the animals on the farm.

I texted Arianna later that day to go on another shopping trip to the market for new clothes. She answered back right away that she would pick me up the next day. I couldn't wait to pick her up in my Nonna's car and show her how I learned to drive it.

Later that night, as I laid in bed, the conversation with Josh came back to my head. A feeling of panic came over me. Michael hadn't mentioned anything about staying just a month, he was still adamant that it was going to be two months, but my mom kept assuring me that he had told her one month was fine. Was it normal for me to want to stay or was I being selfish? For the first time ever, I actually felt needed here. Feelings of confusion mixed with panic started to overwhelm me, so I decided to scroll through my feed, trying to busy my mind from over-thinking.

Laila posted a few photos with Irene in the Hamptons, some at the beach and some back at the house with other friends, probably partying together. Josh was in the background of one of the pics, a side profile of him with a drink in his hand, talking to another guy.

I don't want to be there. Nothing was pulling me now to be there with them. How did three weeks change me so quickly? I went from not wanting to be here for even a minute to not wanting to go back home. My stomach twisted and turned that night, unresolved feelings tormenting me to analyze every situation. Nighttime was the worst for my anxiety, and this proved to be true again as I found it difficult to sleep.

"Cristina. *Cristina.*" I felt a gentle tap on my shoulder and heard someone softly calling my name. "*Sei pronta?* Are you ready?"

I opened one eye a crack and saw Arianna hovering over me, a small smile on her face. I quickly shot up, reached for my phone, and saw it was after ten.

"I'm so sorry." I kept repeating, getting dressed in front of her, not caring what she saw.

"Cristina, it's okay! Your nonna had me come check in on you. She said it was unlike you to sleep in late."

"I'm going to wash my face and then I'll be ready." I ran to the bathroom, splashed water in my face and sighed when I saw the pillow creases lining my puffy face. Great. I quickly applied some liner and mascara and headed out with Arianna.

The market was already bustling, the usual vendors had taken their spots, yelling out what they were selling to the locals. It felt good to recognize faces and feel like I almost belonged, even if it was only for a month. I promised myself that I would make sure to come back every year, despite my mom not wanting to visit. Arianna seemed more excited than usual, helping me pick out clothes and putting them against me to see which looked nicer.

"I don't know, Cristina. This purple looks pretty on you." I took the shirt from her and stood in front of the mirror. It was cap-sleeved, fitted, and reached just past my belly-button. The lilac-color complimented my hair and eyes.

"Ten Euros?" I said, looking at the price tag. "I'm definitely buying this." I dropped it across my arm and continued sifting through other clothes.

"What about this dress for the feasts we go to?" She asked, holding up a dress she just pulled from the racks. My fingers laced between the fabric, feeling the soft material, and noticed it was a style that I had seen a lot of women wear around here. It was sleeveless and had a dark blue empire waist that was tight around the top and flowed out with a bright-patterned skirt that reached my ankles. I was surprising myself with how my tastes seemed to be changing.

"It's beautiful. Okay, I'll take it too."

We walked by Angela's after and grabbed a gelato, our bags swinging from our arms, warm sun beams on our backs.

Arianna turned to me, her eyebrows raised. "I heard you are getting driving lessons from Alessandro."

"Oh no. Has he been complaining to you about them?"

She let out a laugh. "No, he seemed happy that he was helping you. In fact, I know I keep telling you this, but he's been so much happier lately."

"Oh. Do you know why? Maybe he started seeing someone," I said.

Her eyebrows raised again, and she took another scoop of her gelato before responding.

"I haven't seen him with any girls lately. They usually break up with him, though. They always complain that he works too much and has no time for anyone in his life."

I nodded my head and felt bad. Arianna was looking over at me, studying my face, while mixing her gelato around with her spoon. "You know…. too bad you are dating someone. You two are actually perfect for each other."

I scoffed, shoved another scoop into my mouth, and waited a minute before responding. "We are complete opposites. We would never work. Besides, I think my boyfriend might propose soon." I hadn't been thinking about a wedding or a proposal at all lately. I wondered if it was because I had been too busy with work or if the time apart had somehow affected the way I thought about it.

"*That's* exciting." She smiled, but the words didn't sound sincere.

***

"Not bad so far, Cristina. But you have to put your foot quickly on the gas if you don't want to go backwards."

I'd been getting better during the next driving lesson, starting the car and driving it around, only getting reminders on when to shift the gears. But I knew that moving the car up the hill was going to be tough.

I tried again, shifting my foot quickly from the brake to the gas as I lifted my foot off the clutch, and watched in surprise as the car moved forward, not stalling or rolling back.

"I did it!" I screamed, as Alessandro took my hand and placed it back on the gear, reminding me to shift. We drove for a few minutes more before deciding to head back.

We both laughed as I pulled the car into the driveway, parking it outside of the garage.

"That was good, but don't get too excited." He said, smiling over at me.

I heard a buzzing noise and he picked my phone up, handed it over to me, but accidentally clicked accept on Josh who was FaceTiming me.

"Hey." I said softly, I didn't want to talk to him in front of Alessandro. I stepped out of the car, shutting the door behind me, and saw Alessandro do the same.

"Hey, babe. Who are you with?" I noticed a muscle in his jaw tense and his eyes narrowed. His voice was definitely icier than normal.

"Oh, just my neighbor Alessandro. There's no need to worry— he's practically my cousin. He was helping me get something." I kept rambling and stopped myself. I glanced over to Alessandro, his expression changing, and saw him turn away from me and head towards his house.

"Oh, okay. Well, I called because I wanted to say I missed you. I haven't seen you in a while and you missed some of my calls."

Had I? I knew I missed one of the calls when I was shopping with Arianna, but I didn't think any more than that.

"I'm sorry, I've been busy lately. So, tell me what's going on in the hospital." He started talking about his schedule, and what surgeries he had performed, and I kept glancing over at Alessandro walking back to his house, getting further and further away.

"So, what do you think?"

I focused back on him and blinked, not knowing what the question was.

"Um, yeah that's fine." I hoped that was a good enough answer so he wouldn't realize I wasn't paying attention.

"Is everything okay, Cristina? You seem off."

"No, I'm fine. Just tired—I didn't sleep well last night."

"Alright, I'll talk to you tomorrow."

"Bye."

Alessandro was back in his house, and I felt bad I didn't say bye to him or thank him for another lesson, so I decided to text him thank you.

I kept checking my phone all day, wondering why he wasn't texting anything back.

"Oh no." I muttered to myself. I completely forgot that I was supposed to help him collect wood with the tractor. I decided to walk over to his house instead of texting, and check to see if he needed help.

"Cosa ci fai qui?" He asked what I was doing there.

"I was supposed to help you collect the wood, remember?"

His face became unreadable, it was the same expression he had when I first arrived, and it made me nervous. "I'm busy right now."

"Is everything okay? I didn't want to take up too much of your time with driving lessons. I think I got it now anyway, so thank you."

He hesitated, his body still in the doorway with one hand gripping the frame. "You weren't taking up too much time, so don't worry about it. I just need to get back to work now." He turned around and walked back inside.

I went back home with my head hurting. Why did he all of a sudden turn cold again? I reached the farm and checked on the animals, scattering the corn feed on the ground, trying not to think of the unsettling confusion that was building up inside of me.

14

Quattordici

le emozioni - emotions

I heard the tractor drive past my house the next day and ran outside to see if I could catch Alessandro. I tried to wave at him, but the tractor was so loud my voice couldn't be heard over it. I ran up to him, finally getting his attention, but needed to stop and catch my breath since I was panting hard.

"Cristina, *cosa succede?*" Alessandro asked me what was the matter as I was leaning over, my hands pressed against my legs, trying to catch my breath.

"I—I'm...fine." I stammered between panting. "I was supposed to help you get the wood. I didn't know if you were mad at me, because you didn't respond to my text and haven't talked to me. Oh my God, why am I so out of shape! I did spinning classes back home—why didn't I realize I couldn't run?"

Alessandro's jaw relaxed and he let out a laugh. My heart lifted seeing him happy again, away from the gloomy mood that had taken over him yesterday.

"Hop on." He said, his head gesturing to the tractor. I grabbed his hand and he helped me climb up. I took a seat on top of the wheel cover, holding onto the frame of the tractor. A breeze brushed through my hair, and I started to remember how it felt to be a young girl again. Every unwanted emotion and problem I had vanished. I felt nothing—just free. I had lost this feeling, and now that I felt it again, I didn't want it to go away.

Alessandro headed down the fields, stealing a glance over at me every once in a while, and shook his head, one side of his lips curving up into a smile. I stared at him when he concentrated on the road ahead and wished I had a pencil and paper to trace his strong profile. The way his hair was pulled back from his forehead, his nose strong, but not overpowering his face, and his full lips, made me remember what it's like to kiss him.

"*Cosa?*" He asked, curious to know what I was thinking about, as he turned to me.

"*Niente.*" I replied *nothing* softly, and then turned back to stare at the cut wheat fields and the river that was getting closer. We were almost at the bottom of the valley and I saw the pile of wood.

"Wow, you are a lumberjack too?" I said, amazed at how much there was. I hopped off the tractor and stared at the pile with my hands on my hips, in awe at how much time it must have taken him to cut it all.

He gave me a grin before throwing a pair of gloves at me. "Come on, Cristina. Let's see if you can pick up wood better than you can run."

I jokingly smacked his arm as he passed and he laughed again, this time letting it escape from him with no restraint. I skipped towards him and leaned over to pick up a piece when he grabbed my arm back.

"You will break your back like that. Bend your legs." He said, mimicking how I should pick it up. I bent my legs, copying his motion slowly on purpose, and he rolled his eyes, realizing I was teasing him.

"Go ahead, make fun of me. You will thank me when your back doesn't hurt tonight."

We worked for an hour, picking up the wood and piling it in the wagon attached to his tractor. I felt the muscles in my arms ache, as if they were thanking me for using them. We fell into a rhythm where I picked up a log, walked over to the wagon, and met him on his way back. At first he would pat me on my back, motivating me to keep going as he passed, but then he moved to tugging my hair, making me laugh, and then squeezing my nose.

"Really, Alessandro? My nose is itching, and I can't even scratch it!" I said, as I had a log cradled in my arms carrying it to the wagon. I finally felt relief after I dropped the log, ripped off my glove, and scratched my nose. I looked over to see him laughing while getting another log.

"Alright, this is good for today. Let's head back."

I headed to the tractor, about to climb on, when I realized I forgot my other glove.

"Sorry." I said, bumping straight into his chest, after turning around. I was already on a step and he was still on the ground, making us face to face, and his arms were around me holding onto the tractor. I froze again, as I often did when he was so close, and couldn't breathe or think straight. A small voice inside of me was threatening to push me against his lips to just see how they would feel against mine. The voice was growing louder, but he moved back, allowing me space to go down to get my glove. We were silent on the way back, and I was about to say goodbye as I hopped off, before he stopped me.

"Do you want to have lunch with me? You helped me so much that I would feel better if I could at least offer you something."

I didn't want to stop spending time with him, but I also didn't want to leave my nonna alone. "Let me call my nonna and see if she is okay." He nodded his head, and I walked a few feet away, putting the phone next to my ear waiting for my nonna to answer.

"*Ciao*, Cristina, *tutto bene?* She asked, wondering if everything was fine.

"*Sì*, Nonna. Alessandro wanted to have lunch together, but I wanted to make sure you were okay."

"*Vai*, Cristina, go! Don't worry about me, I have been alone all of this time, I can handle lunch by myself." She let out a laugh, told me to have fun.

"So, what's for lunch?" I said after hanging up.

I sat with my legs extended in front of me, on top of the blanket Alessandro laid out under the pergola.

"Are you kidding? This is my dream lunch. Wine, bread, cheese, and sausage—all homemade."

"Except the bread, Marco made that." He said, his eyes twinkling as he handed a piece over to me.

I took it from him, put some cheese and sliced sausage on top, and bit into it, enjoying the taste and not caring if I needed to go back to the market for new clothes.

"I need to learn how to make *all* of this." I gestured to the food with one of my hands while the other now held a wine glass he'd just handed to me.

His smile grew and he filled my glass and laid down on his side, his elbow propping him up.

He took a sip of wine and then looked at me, his gaze intense again. "What makes you happy, Cristina?"

I tilted my head. I was not expecting a question like that. How should I even answer something like that? "I don't know." I deadpanned.

"See—that's what we need to find out."

We. A chill ran through my body and I wasn't sure if it was from the light breeze that was blowing through the field and rustling the grass.

"I graduated from college and got a job that I failed miserably at. It's because I didn't like it, or I just didn't want to work. I don't know. It didn't excite me."

He laid next to me listening, not interrupting.

"I quit and went to work for Michael's company but didn't take it seriously." I thought about my words for a moment. "To be honest with you, I don't think I've been taking a lot of things seriously. Sometimes I feel like I'm living someone else's life, and I just try to do the things that other people would want from me, but never really think about whether I want it or not. I never realized it until I came here and woke up every morning with a purpose."

He took another sip from his wine, and put the glass down, still not saying a word. I never voiced how I felt, or even acknowledged the part of me that felt like that, but I felt comfortable with Alessandro. It felt relieving to share this with him. "Enough about me though. What about you—what makes Alessandro happy?"

He swirled the liquid in his wine glass like the sommeliers do, and then looked up at me. "Well, I guess a few things, definitely working with my hands and creating things and also spending time in nature with the people I care about."

I looked down from his strong stare. It was creating a fire inside of me that I needed to extinguish. I felt the heat reach my cheeks and prayed that it wasn't obvious to Alessandro. I took the glass of wine, held it to my face to block as much of it as I could, and took a few sips. "I know I keep telling you this, but you need to try selling this wine. It's too delicious to not be shared with everyone."

He shook his head. "You are too generous. I don't think anyone would buy this."

I was about to protest, but noticed it was already 2:30 in the afternoon. "Oh shoot, I need to go. My poor nonna has been doing all of the chores by herself." I started to grab the glasses and plates to put away, but he placed his hand on mine to stop me.

"I got this. Go to your nonna."

I smiled, thanked him and was about to head out before he stopped me. "Cristina?" He asked, holding onto my arm.

"Yes?" I felt shivers shoot through my body.

"Tomorrow night don't make plans. I want to take you and Arianna out to a *trattoria* with some of my friends."

"Okay." I said as he let go. I headed back towards my nonna's with my heart thumping through my chest.

***

I was washing some of the vegetables I picked from the garden for lunch the next day when my phone vibrated on the counter next to me.

ARIANNA: **Soooo what are you going to wear tonight?**

I smiled, excited for our plans with Alessandro and his friends at the *trattoria* that night.

CRISTINA: **I was thinking maybe the new dress I bought at the mercato. What do you think?**

ARIANNA: **Perfect! I'm going to wear that new blouse I got!**

I took my time applying my makeup later that evening, making sure I didn't skip any steps and loaded on the mascara to make my eyes pop. I wriggled into the dress, smoothed it out, and stood in front of the mirror, happy with how I looked. I was about to take a picture to send to Arianna when my phone started buzzing.

"Hey!" I answered when I saw Josh's face appear on the screen. "I was just headed out."

"Hey, babe. Where are you going?"

"Out to eat with a bunch of friends."

"Oh, let me see what you are wearing."

I scanned the phone up and down the length of me, showing off my new dress.

"I can tell they're not giving you enough money for outfits." He said, and my face burned.

"I actually like this dress. Besides, I'm cut off, remember?" My tone was short with him, upset that he criticized my outfit without even giving me a compliment first.

"I'm kidding babe, relax. Anyway, I miss you. It's only a few more days and we can see each other."

"About that..." I was putting off telling him about this, but knew I wasn't going to be able to avoid it forever. "I was thinking about staying an extra week. I feel bad leaving already. My nonna doesn't even have her cast off yet."

I could tell he was getting upset because his nostrils flared slightly, and his mouth was pressed closed tightly. "Okay. I need to go, Cristina. I'll call you tomorrow."

He hung up, not giving me a chance to say goodbye, and I threw my phone in my bag.

15

Quindici

contento - happy/ content

I woke up smiling the next morning, reminiscing the memories of the night before.

Alessandro drove both me and Arianna, so we drank a little more wine than we should have and laughed at each other most of the night. Alessandro got a kick out of us, shaking his head at how we became silly teenagers, and his friends joined in, making the whole night fun.

I met two of his friends—one who came with his girlfriend and the other with his wife, and I tried my best to talk to them in a mix of Italian and English. By the end of the night we were laughing at how we seemed to have created our own language.

I stretched out the muscles in my arms, got out of the bed, and walked into the kitchen, taking a seat next to my nonna who was slowly sipping her espresso.

"It's nice to see you happy, Cristina—much better than when you first came here." She took a bite out of the cookie she'd dipped into her espresso cup.

"I am, Nonna. I'm sorry if I seemed upset at first. It was a big adjustment for me, but I feel much better now." I got up, poured my own cup of espresso and sat down again, taking a slice of the cherry *crostata* she had just made.

"Well, you look much healthier too. You were all sticks and bones and *adesso sei bella*." She said, finishing off in Italian that I was now beautiful. I got up, kissed her on the head, and took another sip from my espresso before heading off to the farm with the rest of the slice of pie in my hand.

"*Brava*, Cristina. Now I won't be afraid if you drive on the road anymore." Alessandro said, after another one of our driving lessons. I gave him a playful smirk before getting out of the car, ready to go back to the garden to pick more of the vegetables.

"Did Arianna text you?" I asked, turning back around to face him. "She's been talking about this singer that is going to be at the feast tonight in this town near us."

"Yeah, but I don't think I can go. I still have to trim back the vines in the vineyard because *someone* has been keeping me busy all day with driving lessons." He said, his eyes playful with mine.

"Oh okay. I'll let you know how good they are. I wouldn't want you to miss out on time in your vineyards, especially since I know how good your wine tastes." I smiled back at him and he looked down. I swore I saw his cheeks flush.

We walked together towards his property, talking about what I could do with the *zucchine* that was running rampant through the garden. I promised I would try to make his favorite dish and take pictures after it was done.

That night, I had made my nonna dinner, chopping up some

of the fresh tomatoes and creating a light sauce. The directions I followed were from Alessandro who had texted me and explained what to do during our driving lesson.

I took a picture of the *zucchine* dish, as promised, and sent it to Alessandro. He responded quickly, saying that it looked exactly like how he made it, even though I knew for a fact it didn't. I got dressed and waited for Arianna to pick me up for the feast.

"So, this singer performs only classics. He does mostly folk songs—traditional ones that my parents and grandparents grew up listening to."

Even though Arianna had lived here her entire life, the classic songs he would be performing tonight were also a part of my culture. My mom and my dad's parents were both born here, and I wanted to explore that part of my heritage. I put my arm through Arianna's, and we headed towards the main piazza, where the stage was set up.

"This is so much fun!" I said, twirling Arianna. An accordion player was moving his fingers over the keys, pushing and pulling the bellows, creating a beautiful rhythm and a singer belted out the song in dialect, the same that my nonna used to talk to my mom. I knew the words were Italian, but not the same ones taught in school. Arianna grabbed my hand and we swung each other around, laughing and feeling free.

"Let's get a drink!" She shouted over the music and I nodded after realizing my throat was dry from all of the dancing.

"You know, Cristina, a lot of people said you were a snob since your family has a lot of money—and I mean a lot. But they don't know you, because you are far from it. I could tell by your eyes, when I first met you, that you aren't like that. Deep down, you are a good person that just *happens* to have a lot of money."

I gave her a small smile but couldn't pretend what she said didn't bother me. People thought I was a snob. A rich girl, who thought she was better than all of them because they worked on the farm and her step dad had money. A haunting thought shoved its way through my head. Did I think that? Did I ever think that way? I took a sip of my *aranciata* and thought about what my life was like before my parents got divorced. I was happy. Besides my parents fighting, I was genuinely happy. I played outside, got my hands dirty, and had no worries. I had good friends who didn't care about what I wore or how I looked—we only cared about having fun.

As soon as Laila and the new school entered my life, I started having worries that I wouldn't be good enough. I was someone who was constantly stressed and wondering if they would realize I wasn't one of them. Laila had shown me how to dress—but was it because she was embarrassed about what I'd wear? Was I helpless and she just took me under her wing and made me idolize her? Lately, she only responded with one line when I texted her, saying she was on her way somewhere and couldn't talk. Even though I was unsure about how Laila felt about me in the beginning, I always thought Blake was there for me. I remember one shopping trip where she rolled her eyes whenever Laila called one of the dresses in the store 'ugly' or 'insulting'. The more I thought about my friends at home, the more my mind kept settling on my relationship with Josh. Were my eyes truly opened with him? Were we meant to be together? He felt like someone I *should* be with. The person my parents and friends expected me to marry.

My life was full of expectations. I had never really sat down and thought about what truly made me happy. I loved working with my hands, my hair tied up, and watching the garden come to life. I was happy with how full the vegetables were getting, most ready to be picked, and how the string beans wouldn't stop growing. I shivered thinking how claustrophobic the city sometimes felt with skyscrapers blocking all of the beautiful views like the ones here.

Here, I could see other towns perched on the rolling hills, and at nighttime, the lights sparkled from each village creating a breathtaking view that would be ingrained as a memory once I left.

I brought my mind back to where I actually was, a little bar just off the center of the town, and instantly found it hard to breathe. We finished up our drinks and I only half listened to Arianna as she told me about something she had seen on TV. As soon as she finished, she grabbed my hand, and we headed back to the piazza, near the stage to dance more. Dancing forced all of those thoughts away before they suffocated me.

Arianna twirled me more, and we both got back into the rhythm of the music before I felt a tap on my shoulder. I turned around and I felt as if something had hit me and taken the wind from me. His hair was gelled back away from his face, he wore a tight-fitted shirt showing off his tan, strong arms, and there was a hint of amusement dancing on his face, probably from watching us.

"*Che cosa fai qui?*" I asked Alessandro what he was doing here. I was surprised Italian came out instead of English, and I noticed his head jerk back too in surprise.

"*Ho finito di lavorare e così posso fare qualcosa di divertente.*" He explained he had finished working and wanted to do something fun.

"*Posso?*" He said, asking Arianna if it was okay that he'd intervened, and she looked at him with a puzzled expression and gesturing yes, Alessandro turned to me before saying, "Arianna is an okay teacher, but I am going to really teach you these dances." He took my hand and placed his other on my waist, gripping and pulling me a little closer to him. My heart felt like it was stuck in my throat. I made sure to follow his lead, as he turned me to the rhythm.

"Not bad, Cristina." He said, smiling down at me. The music slowed down, as did the chatter and noise around us. I felt like we were the only two people in the town. His hand that was gripping mine moved down to my waist and stayed there as we continued staring at each other. His eyes moved from my eyes to my lips and I slowly closed my eyes as he pulled me in a little closer to him.

"Alessandro." I said, my eyes still closed, but starting to feel the panic rise up within me. "I can't. I mean, it's late and I should go home. I'm going to find Arianna." Words tumbled out of me, trying to create an excuse that he would understand. I felt his grip lessened on my waist before he let go, stepping back.

"*Va bene.*" He said, letting out a breath and relaxing his shoulders. He put his hand on my elbow and held it there as he guided me through the crowd, looking for Arianna.

"*Vuole andare a casa.*" Alessandro said to Arianna that I wanted to go home. Arianna looked at me, her eyebrows pulled down, but then agreed to take me. I turned and waved bye to Alessandro, my body still recovering from our dance. Arianna and I walked to her car, and I turned around one more time to look at the feast and get one last glimpse of Alessandro.

"So, I'm kind of sure, no, actually definitely really sure that Alessandro likes you more than a friend." Arianna turned the key in the ignition of the car. "I *told* you he has been happy lately—but the way he looks at you, the way he is happy when he sees you, I know him enough to know he likes you."

"I don't think he likes me like that. We are friends and are just helping each other. And Arianna, nothing can happen. I have a boy-friend at home, remember?" I tried to convey this as convincingly as possible as I pulled the seatbelt across me, but from the way my voice sounded, I didn't even know if I was convinced.

Arianna played with the radio until she found a song she liked and blasted it while I leaned my elbow against the window and stared into the dark sky. There were barely any streetlights on the narrow road that took us back to the house, making the stars visible. I spotted the Little Dipper and searched the sky for a shooting star to wish for my headache to go away.

16

Sedici

all'improvviso - all of a sudden

The rooster crowed and the cicadas let out their high-pitched buzz in the distance as I opened the kitchen window the next morning. I held my breath when I saw Alessandro driving his tractor and stayed inside, not wanting to see him after last night. I let it out in one big huff and turned back to the stove to turn the sauce.

I took my phone out to check the time and see if Josh was awake. I pressed the camera button next to his name and willed myself to relax when he answered.

"Good morning." I said to him, seeing that he was still laying in bed.

"Hey." He answered in a groggy voice. "I haven't seen your face in a while. I missed you."

The usual pang of guilt hit me, making me feel horrible that I hadn't FaceTimed him recently. "I'm sorry. I'm embarrassed to call you when my hair isn't done or when I come back from working in the garden."

"I can't wait until you are finished with all of this and *my* Cristina comes back home, not this farmer version of her."

I wanted to tell him that his words hurt me, but was scared to ask him what he would think if this version was the real me—would he still love me? I decided to let it go and asked him about work and the hospital. He talked to me the next five minutes about what surgeries he had lined up and how he got stellar reviews from some of his patients.

When we hung up, I started analyzing the phone call, as I had been doing with everything in my life lately. All he does is talk about himself. Maybe it's my fault and all I do is ask about him and never offer anything about myself. I started thinking about this while I drained the pasta, put some sauce on it, and took out the *zucchine* and string beans I had made. Cooking was becoming a relaxing pastime of mine. I enjoyed making new things and surprising my nonna. She met me a few minutes later, kissing my cheek, before sitting down.

We ate together and I told her that I had learned the *tarantella* last night at the feast which made her laugh and reach down to hold her belly. I knew that she was still in pain.

"Nonna, does it hurt again?" I asked, putting my hand on her shoulder.

"*Un po',*" she said, "a little." I texted Arianna discreetly if she could make a doctor's appointment and she responded back ten minutes later that the doctor could stop by this afternoon.

I was clearing the table when I noticed my nonna didn't go back outside. I went to her room to check on her and saw her laying down on the bed.

"Nonna, *il dottore arriva dopo.*" I said, explaining how the doctor was coming, so she wouldn't feel ambushed when he showed up later.

She nodded her head, and closed her eyes again, her hands under her pillow. My heart broke for her—I was so used to seeing her working outside that the minute she showed some type of weakness, it made me feel completely helpless. I wanted her to be strong again, to make sure she was as healthy as she always had been.

The doctor came about an hour later and Arianna pulled up right after him. I held the door open, and she squeezed my arm as she walked past me.

"Has she been okay?"

"No, she has been in bed since lunch."

The doctor walked into Nonna's bedroom, and we both followed behind, not saying a word.

"*Buongiorno, Signora Filomena, come sta?*" At the sight of the doctor, she sat up, her feet now dangling off the bed.

"*È sempre la pancia, Dottor Imbriano.*" She answered, pointing to her belly.

They talked back and forth, and I looked over at Arianna who made a gesture with her hand that she would tell me everything after. After the doctor checked her, he got up, said bye to my nonna and then smiled at me, before telling me in his best English what he had explained.

"Your nonna is a stubborn woman. She needs medicine for her condition, but she doesn't want it. Can you make her take it?"

"I will try my best." I said to the doctor in a reassuring tone.

"Her arm is healing nicely. She told me you are helping her, so thank you." He dipped his head and began walking back outside.

Arianna said she was going to head back to her house, and I gave her a hug goodbye, thanking her for being there for me. I walked back inside and headed to my nonna's room to talk to her.

"Nonna, what do you have?" I asked, picking up the brush from her side table and brushing her hair back gently.

"It's *colite*. I don't know what it translates to, but I don't want to take any medicine for it. I never took medicine, why do I have to take it now?"

"Nonna, sometimes medicine helps. I know you are a strong woman, but it's okay to take it if it makes you feel better. You're in bed and can't do anything, if you took the medicine you would be able to keep working." Her face became pensive as I continued to brush her hair. She suddenly turned around to face me with her eyes narrowed.

"Enough of this. Tell me about you and Alessandro. Are you together? You know he likes you, right?" I stopped brushing mid stroke, and those feelings that I had managed to put aside came right back.

"Nonna, I have a boyfriend back at home. Remember?"

"So? I had a boyfriend before I met your nonno. But then I met your nonno, *ah, come si dice*, yes—there were sparks. I knew he was the one. The other boyfriend was nice, but it wasn't natural. With your nonno, we didn't need to talk all of the time—we could sit down and stare at the stars and be just as happy."

I continued brushing her hair and smiled at the story, never having heard it before. My nonno died the year after I was born, so I had only known him through pictures and stories my mom and nonna had told. I imagined the two of them sitting in front of this house, with the amazing view in front of them, holding hands and looking at each other lovingly.

"Nonna, I can help you with the medicine. Let me know what you need, and I can go get it at the pharmacy and remind you to take it."

I heard her take a deep breath and watched as her chest rose and fell before she nodded her head yes. Relief flooded over me. I made a mental note to call the doctor and find out what medicine she needed.

Nonna shooed me away then, telling me she wanted to rest, so I headed outside and sat down in the shade under the cherry tree.

Colite in English. I typed into Google, and *Colitis* showed up. I remember hearing a lot of commercials back home about medicine for it and how it could be a debilitating disease. I researched as much as I could about it, in between taking care of the animals and picking more of the vegetables that were ready, and then headed back with at least a plan of action.

I headed back to the house but stopped in front of the grain house that was no longer in use. I had never gone in it before and was curious to check it out. It resembled a small house from the outside, roughly the same size as Nonna's with the same colors of stucco around the exterior as well. I walked through the door and my mouth dropped when I saw that it was a beautiful open space, just needing to be finished. I walked through the rooms, saw some grain piled up in the corner and onions and garlic hanging from the ceiling, being dried out. There were stairs that led to a barren second floor loft.

My head spun with all of the possibilities this little space held. I felt a sudden rush of excitement flowing through me as I pictured a set up similar to one that I had seen in a Hallmark movie.

I stepped back in the house, checked in on my nonna, and saw that she was sitting at the kitchen table, sipping on some tea.

"Nonna, that grain house you have—you don't really use it anymore, right?"

"I used to, but now I have someone cut and take the grain away quickly, so there's no need to store it anywhere. *Perché?*" She responded, asking why.

"I'm not sure, I was over there earlier admiring it. It looks like you had plans to do something with it."

"Actually, we thought that your mother would want to stay here with us in the summer so we were in the process of converting it into another house for all of you."

"Why doesn't she ever visit?"

"Your mother always hated this life. She always acted like she was better than this. When she met your dad, she was in love at first, but I knew they wouldn't stay together because he was too nice to her and didn't make a lot of money. Your mom likes feeling like a princess." She said, shaking her head.

I wondered if my nonna was upset with the way my mother turned out. I never had any doubts about her growing up. She always did her best to make sure I was dressed nicely for school, well fed, and loved. But I understood how my nonna felt, she just wanted to share this life with her daughter.

I heard the tractor stop in front of the house and immediately went outside, forgetting that I was supposed to be avoiding Alessandro.

"*Ciao.*" He said, turning the tractor off and smiling at me. "I texted you before. You didn't want driving lessons today?"

"I'm sorry, I forgot to answer. The doctor came to visit my nonna because she wasn't feeling well."

"How is she?" He asked, stepping down from the tractor, and running a hand through his hair.

"She has *colite*, but after some begging, I convinced her to take the medicine she needs for it."

"Okay, good. I'm glad you're here."

Blush crept up my cheeks again.

"I appreciate that, I'm going to head back inside, though." I needed to put some distance between us before I did something stupid

"Okay Cristina, please don't hesitate if you need help with

anything." He climbed back on the tractor, starting the engine back up. *"Ciao,"* he said with a smile.

I was mad with myself and my jumbled emotions. I knew the right thing to do was to respect my relationship with Josh and stop talking to Alessandro altogether, but I couldn't get myself to sever the tie again.

I trudged back inside, moving the beaded curtain aside that covered the door frame, and headed towards my room. I sunk into my bed, laying on my back with my legs crossed, and held the phone above me scrolling through my feeds. My heart stumbled through its usual syncopations when I saw a picture of Josh talking to two girls at a beach house in the Hamptons. I was instantly led to believe the worst. Was he cheating on me?

I was about to put the phone down when I saw him calling me.

"Hey." I said, still laying in bed with the phone positioned above me.

"Everyone, say hi to Cristina." I sat up as he angled the phone around the room fast enough so everything was a blur. "She is working on a farm in Italy." His speech was slurred, and a glazed expression covered his face. I could barely hear him over the music blaring and groups of people talking in the background.

"Josh, if now's not a good time I can talk to you later." I shouted over the thumping of the bass.

"Are you going out with your new friends, Cristina? Is that why you don't want to talk to me right now?" His voice sounded like he was trying to test me.

"No, Josh it's you. I don't want to talk to you while you're drunk at a party. Call me when you actually have time for a conversation" I slammed down my phone on the bed. I started feeling second-hand embarrassment for him. He was 29 years old and a surgeon, but still getting day-drunk to the point of non comprehension at some random person's beach house. I put the phone back on my nightstand and tried to force the anger out of my mind.

17

Diciassette

uno scherzo - a joke/ trick

I was in the garden the next morning, picking a head of lettuce for lunch, when I felt my phone vibrating.

"Hey, Alessandro—is everything okay?"

"Cristina, can you run here quickly? I need some help."

"Where are you?"

"In my house. The door is open, just come right in, and hurry!"

I put the phone in my pocket, dropped the lettuce, and sprinted across the field to his house.

"Alessandro?"

I stood another minute in the doorway, trying to catch my breath, before I walked through the house and into the kitchen.

"What happened?" He was standing with his hands submerged in a bowl of milky-white water.

"Nothing happened to me, I'm fine, but I needed to get you here quickly because the mozzarella is fresh—and you *have* to see this."

"Really, Alessandro? You yelled at me to come over here so I could see how you make fresh mozzarella?" I said, narrowing my eyes and smacking him across his arm.

"Ahia!" He said, his hands were still in the water, as he brought the shoulder I smacked up to his ear.

"Ay-ah? What is that? A karate move?"

"Ahia. That's the noise you make when someone hurts you. Why? You don't say that?"

"No, in America we say *ow.*" I said, laughing. "So, you mean to tell me I have to even translate the noise I make when something hurts me?"

He chuckled and shook his head. "Yes. Now go wash your hands —you need to feel this."

I walked over to the sink, washed my hands, and moved next to him, a tingle traveling through my body.

"Put your hands in the water and feel the mozzarella. See how much you can pull it to see if it's ready. Go ahead, try." I took a piece from the water and pulled it with my hands. "That's ready. Now we can put the pieces together." He grabbed the pieces, taking my hands with his to show me the steps, and formed a braid.

"I'm probably going to need to record how you formed that braid. It didn't look like the way I make it in my hair."

He let out a laugh and went over to the table, sliced some bread and a type of meat before handing it to me.

"I'm just going to wait until the mozzarella cools to try it but have this for now."

"What type of meat is this? I remember having this when I was younger." It resembled a dried sausage, but the shape was flatter.

"This is *soppressata.*"

I took a bite and closed my eyes. The crunchiness of the bread and the saltiness of the *soppressata* combined created a symphony of tastes that I could only imagine existing in heaven.

"Oh my God Alessandro. If you handed me a glass of your wine with this I think I would pass out from the taste."

Immediately, Alessandro shot up from the chair, got two glasses, and pulled a bottle of wine from the cabinet.

"I didn't mean for you to *actually* get some." I said, laughing at him and taking one of the glasses.

"No, you meant it. I could see it in your face." He said, giving me a subtle wink as he flashed a smile.

I took a sip, relaxing back in the chair, and stared at Alessandro, wanting to know more about him.

"Do you get lonely in this house all by yourself? I know your sister lives down the road with your mom, but it must be lonely at night."

He played with his wine glass with one hand, while his other drummed the table lightly.

"I never thought about it. I'm so busy the whole day that when it's night, I just collapse into bed immediately." A flash of sadness crossed his face before he took another sip of wine.

"Is it hard to work all day like this? Do you want to do something else sometimes?"

"No. This makes me feel alive—even though I can do other things though. My friend taught me how to run wires and work with electricity. I also worked a while building houses with one of my cousins too—but I didn't feel anything. It didn't make me want to get out of bed in the morning. I don't make a lot of money doing this, but I am happy, and I have enough money to enjoy the life I want."

He was the exact opposite from the people I surround myself with at home.

"It isn't *that* hard, though," he continued. "My sister and her husband help as much as they can, but they work a lot in a factory nearby, so they are pretty busy. I'm teaching my nephew how to ride the tractor, so maybe this life might be for him, or maybe he will want to be a lawyer. Whatever he wants." He shrugged his shoulders before taking another sip of wine.

"I wish it were that easy. Back at home, everyone just expects me to do something that will make a lot of money. The only thing that has been making them happy lately is the fact that I started working for Michael."

"How is Michael by the way? I remember meeting him that one summer. Are you happy he is part of your family?"

"He's wonderful. I can't say anything bad about him at all. My mom is happier, too. I just feel bad for my dad. He was more simple than she is. He would be fine with taking me to the park, dressed in shorts and a t-shirt, and playing all day." Alessandro listened, not saying anything, just focused on me as I kept talking. "But enough about that." I said, wanting to steer the conversation back towards him. "We need to start selling all of this stuff you are making."

"There you go again—it must be your business degree that makes you like this." His eyes were now gleaming. He got up from the table and sliced the mozzarella.

"No, seriously. I know you don't care about the money—but a lot of people are missing out on this amazing food. It's not fair for them." I said, taking the slice of mozzarella he handed over to me. "You see? I said, my mouth full. "This is what I mean!"

He was laughing more now, which made my heart dip further in my chest.

"I should head back and see how my nonna is."

"I'll give you a ride on the tractor—I have to pass by there anyway."

"Well, that's pretty hard to say no to. You know how much I love tractor rides." I said, raising my eyebrows.

He laughed and placed one of his hands on my back. "Let's go."

We pulled up to the house and I noticed Arianna leaning against her car, her arms crossed in front of her, and her eyebrows were pulled together.

"So, your nonna tells me you two spent the whole day together." She said walking towards us. "How interesting." Her mouth curved into a small smile.

I stepped off the tractor, looked at Alessandro and smiled before turning back to Arianna. "Well, this one," I said, pointing with my thumb backward to where he was still sitting, "calls me frantically this morning telling me that he needs help and to rush over, but it turns out he just wanted to show me how he makes mozzarella."

"Really, Alessandro?" Arianna let out a laugh and shook her head.

"I mean, yes but I didn't ask you *frantically*." Alessandro said, rolling his eyes.

"You said to *hurry!* I thought your house was on fire!" I rebutted, with a smile.

Alessandro was about to answer back but Arianna cut him off. "Alright, you two, enough bickering," she said, with a smile on her face and arms still crossed. "I was going to talk to you both about the feast tonight and see if you want to go."

"I'll go, but only if I drive both of you." Alessandro said.

"Okay, I'll go too," I said. I wanted to get out and do some dancing anyway. "Do you want to meet here first? We can get ready together."

"Yes!" Arianna said, her face lighting up. "Alright, I'm going to go. I'll see you both later."

I waved to both of them, my eyes locking with Alessandro's for a second before I went back into the house to see how my nonna was.

"So, you and Alessandro were together for a long time." My nonna said with a smirk as soon as I walked in.

"Nonna, it's not like that. He is a friend, that's all. How are you today?"

"I'm better."

"So, I was reading about what you have. We shouldn't make anything fried or greasy for you for a while. It says you should eat bland foods, like toast, bananas, eggs. You need to stay away from anything that is hard to digest, even some vegetables that aren't cooked. I'll help you make dinner tonight, Nonna. We can grill some chicken and I'll make some vegetables that are easy for your stomach. Oh, and no wine and limited coffee."

"*Gah*," she said as she let out a deep breath. "This is why I don't listen to doctors. Nothing I eat is bad for me."

"Nonna, I'll do it with you. Come on, let's make dinner together."

***

"*Vai*, Cristina. *Non ti preoccupare di me*. Have fun." My nonna was ushering me to leave and saying not to worry about her after Arianna pulled up. Arianna came in the house, greeted my nonna, and ran to my room.

"I was thinking of wearing this dress tonight. What do you think?" I said, holding up a fitted light blue dress.

"I love it!"

I looked through some of the outfits I had bought to see if I had anything to offer Arianna.

"Here, try this on. It doesn't fit me, but it would look so nice on you." I handed her a designer mini-dress I had bought a year ago, for a Hamptons party. It was a black and white tweed strapless dress that reached halfway up my thighs, showing just the right amount of leg.

"No no, Cristina. This is too expensive, I can't. I'll spill wine on it and then ruin it and then it will take my whole month's salary to make it up to you."

I let out a laugh and pushed it to her, telling her not to worry about it. She hesitated but slipped it on anyway. My jaw dropped when I saw how perfect it fit her.

"Arianna, you better watch out. Guys are going to be all over you tonight." I gave her a playful wink.

"I don't know. It's beautiful, but I'm nervous. Isn't it too much?"

"Are you kidding? What do you have to hide? You are a gorgeous girl, but you need to show it. Be proud of how beautiful you are."

She stood up taller and tilted her head up. "Okay, maybe just for tonight."

"Awesome." I said, smiling back.

Alessandro picked us up twenty minutes later and I let Arianna sit in the passenger seat. He stared at me through the rearview mirror and squinted his eyes at me before turning his attention back to the road. I was mad that something as small as that could still make my stomach twist into a tiny knot.

When we reached the town, I pulled the two of them towards the stand that was selling sandwiches with provolone and *prosciutto cotto*, the Italian version of ham.

"Sorry, guys—but this will always be our first stop. I need to try this before we go dancing or do anything else." They both laughed as I took a bite of the sandwich and moaned quietly, pulling the melted provolone until it broke.

"I'm just going to say hi to my friends, so I'll see you guys later. Have fun with your sandwiches." Alessandro walked off to meet two other guys and I turned to Arianna, who had almost finished her sandwich.

"Arianna—that guy is checking you out over there. He has a green shirt and light brown hair. Take a look!" I patted her arm and whispered loudly to her. He kept sneaking a glance over, his light eyes darting up towards her.

"Who, Marco? He owns a bakery in the town next to us. He's the one who delivers the bread on your street."

"That's why he looks familiar! He's cute though and seems nice—right? Maybe we can go talk to him?"

I saw her hesitate a moment before she shook her head. "No, don't worry, Cristina. It just doesn't feel right."

I paused for a moment before speaking. "You know what I was thinking, Arianna? I did this one time back home and it went so well I think it would work here too, especially since there are so many feasts at night. What if we did something to honor Giovanni? We could raise money to help find more effective treatment options for the type of leukemia he had. We can have a stand at one of the feasts and ask people to donate some food products to sell. Then we can donate that money to the charity or organization that you want to honor Giovanni."

She nodded her head while I spoke, almost as if she was calculating exactly how to do it. "We would need to get permission to have a stand at the feast. That could take a while."

"It doesn't need to happen tomorrow. How about I do it? I'll handle all of it." I offered.

"You know..." She said, nodding her head, "I think that is something Giovanni would have loved."

I gave her a hug promising that we would try to make this happen as I felt my phone vibrating in my pocket. "Sorry, I have to take this. I'll just be over there." I pointed at a bench and walked away from her.

"Hey." I said, holding the phone in front of me.

"You missed two of my calls today." Josh said, with no introduction. "What's going on, Cristina? Is the farm taking up that much time that you couldn't answer my calls?"

"I'm sorry. It's just been crazy lately."

"Crazy? Cristina, there is nothing for you to do. That's just play time over there. You mean to tell me you can't even answer a phone?" His voice grew louder and the muscles in his jaw twitched.

"I said I'm sorry, Josh."

"Well, have fun wherever you are." He said and hung up the phone.

I clenched my fists to my sides and felt blood rushing through my body. He thinks what I'm doing is a joke. I held the phone in my hand a minute longer before throwing it back in my bag and headed over to Arianna, who was now talking to Alessandro. I took a deep breath in, held it, before I blew out slowly, not wanting to carry my anger through the rest of the night.

"I just told Alessandro about your idea, and he wants to donate mozzarella, dried sausage and wine. This is going to be amazing, Cristina. Thank you!" She gave me and Alessandro both a hug. "I'm going to tell Giovanni's parents—I called them, and they said they were here."

Arianna's enthusiasm lifted me right out of my foul mood I was in.

"That was a really nice idea you had, Cristina." He said, and somehow I felt a soft warmth fill me, completely replacing whatever anger I had before. "I think that is what she needs. You have been a really good friend to her, and she is lucky to have you." That warm feeling grew, and I appreciated how Alessandro complimented me.

He stared at me, looking at each of my eyes, before he spoke again.

"You are getting prettier every day you are here."

My eyes widened and my cheeks began to burn. There was no hiding it from him.

"Follow me, I have to show you something." He said, grabbing my hand.

I nodded and he led me away from the piazza and the music, towards a higher part of town, and through a small park. He held my hand as we made our way through the trees to a bench. I walked towards it and saw that there was a drop after it, leading to a valley with little twinkling lights from the houses down below. The stars were bright against the night sky and my body relaxed into the back of the bench.

"This is beautiful." I said, staring straight ahead at all of the lights against the darkness. I began to wonder how anyone could be angry while staring at a view like this. It felt like a part of me—something I was always meant to see.

"You know," he said, looking over at me. "You can see our houses from here." I tried to figure out which were ours, but they all looked similar.

"Look." He said, motioning for me to come closer. "You see those three lights close to each other over there? That one is yours, and the one above that is mine." I leaned in closer to him, trying to figure out which ones they were.

"Oh, I think I found them. Is there a yellow light to the left of mine?" I asked, turning to him. I hadn't realized we were so close to each other, because when I turned to face him, his lips were only a few inches from mine. I was sure that I had stopped breathing. I looked at the outline of his face from the soft light of the moon. His hard jawline and eyes swimming in mine made me realize I wanted him even closer. My body felt frozen though, and I wasn't sure what would happen next. His eyes stilled on mine, full of confidence and strength, making me want to learn more from him. They bored into mine as if he was searching for something. His gaze shifted down to my hand. I felt a gentle touch, his fingers reaching out over mine, slowly grazing them, and his thumb brushing softly against mine, creating small bursts of electricity that traveled straight up to my lips. He looked back up at me and I leaned closer to him, listening to this voice inside of me that said to get closer, stop hesitating. He leaned forward too, and I closed my eyes, closing the space between us. I didn't understand where I was or what was happening.

My body felt like it was bursting, every fiber of my being shouting that this was the absolute right thing to do. The gentle kiss became intense as I turned myself towards him, one of my legs crossing over his. His hand was now behind my neck, pulling me closer to him, and his other one gently rested on my leg. He pulled away from me, his forehead resting against mine, and we stood there silent for a few moments.

"We should find Arianna." He said, his voice low and his breathing a little heavy. I couldn't say anything, so I just nodded my head and got up with him. He took my hand, lacing his fingers between mine, and smiled at me, making my heart jump again. We walked through the park alone. As we approached the feast, I let go of his hand before Arianna would see us.

"There you are!" Arianna said bye to her friends and then ran over to us, smiling.

"I have been looking for you two—where were you?"

I was still dizzy and trying to come up with a response, when thankfully Alessandro did.

"I wanted to show her the view of our houses. She finally figured out which one was hers." He turned to me.

"Should we go home?" I asked, since my emotions were tied so tightly around my heart that I didn't know what else I could say or do.

"Yes, let's go." Alessandro said, and we walked towards his car.

Arianna mentioned different ideas for fundraising on the ride back, but Alessandro and I remained quiet, just nodding our heads and smiling at her. Arianna sat next to him in the passenger seat, and I took a seat in the back, stealing glances of Alessandro through the rear-view mirror. His eyes met mine every once in a while, and my emotions rippled through my body.

"*Buona notte.*" He said to both of us after he dropped us off at my house. Arianna got out and hugged me goodnight before she drove her car the rest of the way home.

"*Buona notte*, Alessandro." I said, turning around again before I walked into the house. I saw him take a deep breath, nod once, before he turned his car back on and went home.

Diciotto

una sorpresa - a surprise

I was dreaming of kissing Alessandro the whole night. For some reason, I didn't feel guilty and knew that I would break up with Josh the next time we spoke. I didn't want to seem that desperate, so I decided to stay inside most of the morning, catching up on some chores around the house. I blasted my playlist while cleaning the bathroom, humming to myself as I pushed the mop across the floor.

After lunch, I checked my hair, put it in a high ponytail, and applied lip gloss. I stepped outside and saw Alessandro's tractor coming towards the house. I waved hi to him as he approached and I felt flutters in my belly, thinking again about that kiss. He had almost reached my house when a jet-black Porsche pulled into the driveway and stopped.

The car looked so out of place it took me a few seconds to adjust to the sight. When the door opened, Josh stepped out—dressed in slacks, a button-down shirt with the sleeves rolled up, and sunglasses on. I was too stunned to move that I didn't even feel his hug as he squeezed me after walking over.

"I missed you, Cristina. I had to see you—I got a few days off this week. I booked a flight last night."

Alessandro's tractor stopped in front of my house, and I saw a look of confusion take over his face. He stepped off of it, his eyebrows scrunched as he looked at Josh then back at me.

"I wasn't expecting to see you at all." I finally said back to him. I glanced over and noticed Alessandro had his hand behind his neck, looking like he wanted to leave.

"Alessandro, this is Josh. He just flew in." I said, stumbling over my words. Alessandro nodded his head towards him but offered him his hand. Josh shook it and wrapped a hand around my waist. I froze next to him and squeezed my eyes shut for a second, an emptiness now taking over me.

"I missed my girlfriend. She was supposed to come home, but I came here to bring her back instead." He turned to me and said, "Michael said you could fly back with me. I'm leaving in three days."

I forced a smile back at him, but I felt as if my body would crumble beneath his hands, nothing giving me support to stand up. How could they decide when I was supposed to leave? I know Michael wanted to prove a point, but he doesn't get to play around with my life like this. This is not like him at all.

I looked at Alessandro and saw hurt in his eyes. I wanted to tell him that I wasn't expecting any of this, especially after that kiss we shared.

"So, are you going to show me around?" Josh said, cutting the awkward tension that was building up between Alessandro and I. My eyes pleaded with Alessandro to forgive me, trying to make him understand how I felt without words, but he just turned back, and climbed on his tractor.

"Wow, does he talk?" Josh said.

I stared at Alessandro, getting smaller in the distance, and almost had the idea of running straight to him. My body felt as if it were pulling in all directions, but all I could do was just stay put. I looked back at Josh, his eyebrows pulled together, and answered. "Yes, but I think he didn't want to speak in English." I said as an excuse. The confusion started to melt away and clarity hit me as I looked back at Josh standing next to me. "Why didn't you tell me you were coming?"

"Are you happy that I am here?"

"Of course I am." I said, plastering a smile on my face as he hugged me again. He leaned over to kiss me, and my initial reaction was to pull away, but I forced myself to kiss him back, even though it didn't feel right.

"So I was thinking—the Amalfi Coast is only an hour away. We can stay here for a while, then drive there and stay for a day or two before we head home."

I felt flustered with the plans he made without consulting with me first. I rolled my lips between my teeth and waited a few seconds before responding. "I'm not sure if I can leave my nonna so quickly. She just started new medicine and I wanted to help her until her arm heals."

"Listen, Cristina. She will be fine. She has been alone all of this time, I'm sure she won't mind a little more alone time. Come on, take me inside so I can meet her."

He grabbed my hand and we both walked inside, finding my nonna in the garage with a shocked expression on her face when she saw us.

"Nonna, this is Josh. He surprised me and flew in." I saw my nonna's face become skeptical as she took his outstretched hand and shook it.

"Nice to meet you Josh." She said, her eyebrows still pulled down.

"You too. This is quite the setup you have here." He said, gesturing around him. "The land around the house and the view is beautiful."

"Thank you." She said, wiping her hands on her apron. "Are you hungry?"

"Actually, I am. Thank you. Or should I say *Grazi*."

"Grazie." My nonna responded back, reminding him the last *e* is pronounced.

"That's right. *Grazie*." He said, repeating it the right way but without even attempting to softly roll the *r*.

She walked to the kitchen, slower than normal, and opened the fridge to take out some leftovers we made.

I reached for the bread and started slicing it, placing it on the table in front of him.

"Wow, Cristina, no wonder you put on some weight—this is what you have been eating?" He said, whispering to me while my nonna was getting more food out.

I narrowed my eyes and slammed the plate in front of him, watching him jerk back. I could feel my fingers tense up and almost clench into a fist.

"I didn't mean it in a bad way—you look good. I'm sorry, babe. It's been a long flight. Please sit near me and eat too."

My emotions still felt tightly wound around my heart from his surprise arrival and now his unsolicited comment, but I stretched out my fingers, trying to loosen up my emotions, and decided to sit down anyway. I took a piece of bread and provolone and listened to him ask my nonna questions about the farm and what I had been doing. I studied his face as he seemed sincere and every once in a while he looked back at me, his eyes slightly crinkled at the sides. My nonna started opening up to him, explaining how I had helped her grow more vegetables than she ever had in all of her years here and I saw a glimmer in her eyes as she looked over at me. Josh reached under the table and squeezed my knee and smiled at me too, the first normal gesture he had done since arriving. I looked over at him, watched his eyes soften and his lips still pressed into a proud smile, and thought that maybe I was being too hard on him. He did fly across the ocean to be with me.

We chatted a little more, talking about the weather and other things you would normally talk about when meeting for the first time, and then my nonna got up to clear the table, refusing any of my help.

"You two talk more. I have this." She said, waving at me to sit down.

"Well, *Signora,* I was thinking that I would take Cristina with me for the next two days to the Amalfi Coast. Would that be fine with you?"

"Cristina is a grown woman. She can make her own choices." She said, her words having a slight bitter edge to them.

"What do you think?" He turned towards me holding both of my hands in his. "Come with me—it'll be fun, I promise." I looked over at my nonna and she turned away, purposefully avoiding any eye contact with me.

"Okay." I answered meekly, not sure I was doing the right thing.

"Alright, you go pack and I'm going to check out this place. I'll be outside waiting for you." He said, giving me a quick kiss on my lips before getting up from the table. I reluctantly walked over to my room and stared at my clothes. A feeling of emptiness and anxiety was consuming me, and I couldn't believe how in less than 24 hours I went from being overjoyed to having no emotion at all. I turned around to see my nonna enter the room, a sad look across her face.

"Cristina, *non è più per te.* You are a different woman now than you were when you came here." I nodded my head as I understood my nonna telling me he wasn't for me. I gave her a hug and told her I would figure it all out.

An hour later we were on a narrow, winding road along the sea, my heart in my throat whenever a bus would pass us, making me feel like we would run off the road. I kept checking my phone to see if Alessandro texted me.

"I promise this will be fun." Josh said, as he took his right hand and squeezed mine. I noticed he had rented an automatic car and then my heart tugged missing the driving lessons I had with Alessandro. This is it. The end of staying here. I'm going home in a few days and that's it. I bit the inside of my cheeks and dug my nails into my palm so I wouldn't cry, trying to stop thinking of anything that would tempt a tear to fall down my cheek.

I took a deep breath and willed myself to calm down. I saw Josh look over at me again and he took my hand in his, holding it gently. I looked down at both of our hands and my heart hurt for us. We were in love—I was in love with him. I owe it to him to try to get back the connection we had. I was away from home and got a crush. I need to get over it.

It was that moment that I made up my mind and decided I was going to enjoy my time with Josh and remember why we had fallen in love in the first place. I turned to him, touched his cheek, and he smiled back at me, making a part of my heart wake up.

"Come here. You need to see this view!" He said, pulling my hand towards the beach after he parked the car. We turned around and my mouth dropped at the view. Houses upon houses lined the prominent hills in front of us, creating a beautiful wave of colored blocks jutting out of the hills. Restaurants lined the bottom of the hills where they met the beach, with people enjoying the same view seated at tables outside. He squeezed my hand again and then turned to me, a gentle kiss becoming more passionate as he placed his hand behind my hair. He pulled away slightly, his breath still tangled with mine, and shook his head.

"I missed you so much, Cristina."

I kissed him again, realizing I had missed him too.

We spent an hour on the beach, sitting next to each other and watching the waves slowly roll in. I felt the connection grow again and started feeling happy, but guilty at the same time. It definitely wasn't the right time to confess anything to him and figured that would be something to talk about back home, even though the guilt still rattled my mind. My thoughts were interrupted when my belly started growling and I looked at my phone, realizing it was already 7:30.

"We need to eat—let's find a place." I said, pulling him up by his hand.

"The jet lag is killing me still." He said, laughing and following me. We settled on a restaurant that was near the beach, taking two seats outside.

"Wait, did you book a place to stay?" I asked.

"Yes—remember Dr. Hasselman? He is good friends with one of the hotel owners here, in Positano, and booked us a night here and another night in Capri—he paid for it. He had told me he was impressed with how I had handled a surgery and wanted to show his appreciation in some way."

"Wow, Josh. That's amazing! You *have* done really well this past month."

He took my hand between his, caressing my fingers. "I missed you though. I'm sorry if I was short with you on the phone. I think all of the stress lately from trying to do my best has made me lose my temper a lot more easily." He took a deep breath and set my hands down. "Lately it feels like everything has been overwhelming. I barely have time to breathe in between surgeries or do anything for me."

"At least it looked like you had fun in the Hamptons." I said in an assuring way.

He looked at me confused, and then a flash of clarity came across him. "Yeah, at least that. They had invited me to a lot more, but I just couldn't. Plus, it didn't feel right without you."

I smiled at him and looked at the menu the waiter had given us. Yes, seafood! I made a mental note to order *calamari fritti,* or fried calamari, and *spaghetti allo scoglio,* a sauce with seafood in it.

When the waiter came, I placed my order and was surprised that Josh had ordered a grilled local fish.

"That's all you're ordering? Josh, you're in Italy. Order something more!"

"No, I don't want to put on weight. It's been hard trying to maintain my weight while working those crazy hours. We're not all on vacation, you know."

I recognized that it was a jab towards me, but I didn't want to say anything and have it lead to an argument.

Once the food arrived, I dug into the calamari, making sure to enjoy each bite. Josh started talking about his coworkers while I twirled the spaghetti in front of me, grabbing some clams and mussels onto my fork before I took a bite. I stopped chewing when I saw Josh's face move back in shock.

"Wow, Cristina. I am not used to seeing you eat like this." He looked at me up and down, making me feel self-conscious. "You really *have* changed over the past month."

I finished chewing the spaghetti and thought about what he meant. Did I change in a good way? I swallowed the spaghetti down, my throat seeming a little more constricted, and then patted my mouth with a napkin before I answered. "I feel different. Before, back at home, I'd been afraid to eat anything like this at all. But I was missing out. Have you ever tasted fresh mozzarella? Like, a few minutes after someone makes it? Or even better, fresh mozzarella on warm bread?"

He laughed and took a sip of his wine, and then shook his head. "No, I guess I'm not that lucky."

"When we go back, you have to try Alessandro's. He makes his own wine too. It's probably the best I've ever had."

He took another sip of his wine and put it down, his face hardening. "So, Alessandro—are you guys friends or something?"

"No. I mean, yes, we are friends. But like I said, he is more like a cousin to me. He just helps my nonna a lot and..." All of a sudden my throat dried up. "I need to just drink for a second." I took a sip of my sparkling water to coat my throat. "That's all though."

He looked at me skeptically, but then went on about another resident back at the hospital that reminded him of Alessandro. I felt relieved that I didn't have to tell him about the kiss.

After dinner, we walked around the town, holding hands, and decided to find our hotel since it was getting late. Josh got our bags out of the car and met me in front.

"This is beautiful, Josh. You really need to thank Dr. Hasselman for getting this for you." The blues and whites in the room gave it a beachy vibe, while the fixtures around it added a modern elegance. I walked over to the balcony and leaned against the railing, admiring the view of the sea. There was a little table with two chairs and where I pictured having breakfast with a view.

"You're beautiful." He said, coming up behind me and wrapping his arms around my waist. My heart softened and I turned around, still wrapped in his arms. He kissed me gently on my lips, then led me back into the room, towards the bed. I was afraid of how I would feel to be more intimate with him, after all of this time, but the kiss we shared proved that there were still feelings between us. Our kiss turned more passionate as we reached the bed, Josh slowly taking off my shirt, breaking our kiss for only a moment, and then laying me down on the bed. He stared into my eyes a few moments, then pulled the cover over us, our bodies connecting once again.

The next morning, I picked on a croissant with apricot jam sitting at the small table on the balcony while Josh sipped on a cappuccino. Our next stop was Capri and sightsee there before heading back to my nonna's the next day. I wanted Josh to understand that I wasn't ready to leave yet and that he should go home without me for a little while, but I didn't want to ruin the good mood he was in. I made a mental note to wait until after dinner.

We reached Capri by ferry, took a taxi up to the top of the hill, and explored the town. If I were to close my eyes and try to picture Capri again, my mind would be filled with yellow lemons and green leaves against a white background. It was such an elegant town, rivaling the beauty of nearby Positano, and luxurious stores lined the cobbled streets.

After grabbing a quick bite to eat, Josh turned to me, excitement filling his eyes. "So here is what we are going to do. You are going to get your hair and nails done, I already made an appointment. Then, go shopping and get yourself an elegant dress for dinner tonight—any you want. I'm going to wait for you at our hotel right here—Gatto Bianco. Here is my card."

Surprised, but grateful to have the time to myself, I figured it would be the perfect time to process the last 24 hours.

I walked into the salon first, noticing it was more posh than the one Arianna had brought me to. The hairdresser ushered me into a chair and took time blowing my hair out, section by section. Another woman took my hand and started applying nail polish at the same time. It had been a while since I had my nails done and it definitely felt nice.

I admired myself in the mirror when I was finished, loving how soft and smooth my hair had felt, and walked over to the nearby stores to find a dress. Various boutiques lined the streets and I admired all of the window displays before walking into one.

"Good afternoon." The shopkeeper instantly greeted me in English, assuming that most people were tourists. I wondered how she would feel if someone broke out in perfect Italian right back to her and I wished I could've been the one to do that. "Can I help you?"

"Yes, I'm looking for a dress, something to wear out to dinner."

She raised her eyebrows, giving me a look up and down. "Are you a size 40?"

"Actually, maybe a size 42."

I followed her through the store as she pulled out various dresses and outfits, and finally settled on a few before I tried them on. I went over to the changing room and admired the way it hugged my curves, curves that hadn't been there a month ago.

"*Questo.*" I said, handing her the dress that I had decided on. It was a halter dress, long and flowy, and a mix between a jade and emerald green, something bright enough for Capri during the day, but elegant enough for a formal dinner. When I handed her Josh's credit card, a sudden wave of nausea came over me. I have no problems using his money. This is a lot of money—more than I had spent my whole time here for just one dress.

I continued smiling at the shop assistant as she pushed the card into the reader so I could mask the doubt that was growing inside of me. I couldn't believe how quickly I converted back into my old self. My heart thumped against my chest.

She handed me the dress and card. I tried to smile as I took it, not wanting to show her the onslaught of the emotional conflict that started brewing inside of me. I headed out of the store, my bag in hand, and walked back to the hotel to meet Josh.

"Wow, look at you. *Bella,* as the Italians would say." Josh said as he spun me around, admiring my hair. "Let me see the dress." I pulled out the dress and his head pulled back as a smile formed on his face. "Now this is the Cristina I can't wait to see at dinner. We have a reservation at 7 at Aurora—it took a lot of calls to make this happen." He grabbed my waist, pulling me close to him, and I closed my eyes, trying to calm down and appreciate what he tried to do for me. I opened my eyes and saw him staring at me. "I love you, Cristina."

I leaned in to kiss him gently on his lips and then stayed still close to him. "Alright, we have a half of an hour. Get dressed and we'll start heading there."

I stepped into the bathroom, stared at myself in front of the mirror, and shook my head. You lied, Cristina. You lied to Josh. You lied to Alessandro. And now, you are lying to yourself. You think you know what you are doing—but you don't. I held my breath enough to expand my chest fully. I wanted to breathe out and expel all of the negative thoughts that were building up inside of me. What did I want? "I don't know." I said softly. I splashed water in my face and clenched my teeth. "I'm not good enough to deserve any of this." The muscles in my jaw were still tight, but my eyes were void of any emotion and I tried to understand who I was looking at in the mirror, but I didn't even recognize myself.

"Cristina, are you done?" Josh called from behind the door.

"Yes, one minute. Sorry, I wanted to freshen up my makeup too." I took a deep breath, splashed more water on my face, and then re-applied some bronzer and blush. I slipped into the dress and then stared at myself one more time. I prayed that I would figure out what the person staring back at me actually wanted.

We were seated at the back of the restaurant, in a cozy section and Josh had ordered a variety of food for us. He seemed flustered and was a little short with the waiter who didn't understand his pronunciation of the Italian wines he picked.

"Is everything okay?" I asked, surprised.

"Yes—I don't know why they insisted on folding the napkins this way." He fumbled with the napkin and finally unfolded it and placed it across his lap. "So, are you having fun here?" He said, taking my hand.

The uneasy feeling I had crept back up, and as much as I tried to push it down, it seemed to stay there, the knot twisting tighter around my stomach.

"Yes. It's beautiful. I do miss my nonna though." I started, hoping this would be a good moment to mention that I wasn't going back home with him in two days.

"I know, I know." He said, interrupting me. "Listen, there was something I have been meaning to ask you."

Everything in the room froze, like it was suspended in midair. I was sure that if all of the geologists in the world got together and compared notes, they would've realized that was true. I saw him slowly get up from his seat, not standing fully upright, and then drop down on one knee. I looked around, saw some people turn to us, pointing, with their expressions wide in shock and happiness. I felt my heart slow down, the beats taking over any other sound in the room. He reached into the pocket of his tan slacks and pulled out a box, opening it like a clamshell so that I could see what was inside. A four-carat radiant diamond, in a white gold setting, was placed delicately inside of it—waiting for the answer to the question that scared me more than anything in the world.

I couldn't hear what he was saying. His mouth was moving, but I only heard mumbles—two years and love, you make me happy, and I've missed you. When his mouth stopped moving, I knew he had done it—asked the question I'd been anticipating for months back home. I broke away from his face and looked at the other people watching us around the room.

No. Both my brain and body screamed inside of me. I was sure that I would regret everything if I said no. His eyes begged for a response, a yes. I nodded my head yes slowly a few times before I pushed a smile onto my face and then told him yes out loud. He jumped up, grabbed me in a hug, and swung me around, the onlookers cheering. The waiter filled our glasses with champagne, and we toasted to each other before I saw him take out his phone.

"My parents begged me to FaceTime them as soon as I asked. Obviously we will wait to have the wedding when I finish my residency, but I couldn't wait any longer to ask you. You need to call your parents too."

"They knew?"

"Yes, that's why Michael agreed that you could come home earlier. I told him what I was going to do, and he knew that when you said yes, you would want to come back home with me."

I knew it was odd for Michael to force a decision like that on me. I needed more time. I heard him talking to his mom, turning the camera to me so that she could congratulate me. I thanked her and then took out my phone, ready to face my parents.

"Let me see!" My mom squealed as soon as she answered the call. "That is impressive. Michael, did you see that? Look at that ring!" Michael walked over, put on his glasses, and leaned forward trying to examine the ring.

"That is a beauty. Congrats, Cristina. We are excited for the both of you."

"Thanks. Listen, I wanted to talk to you." I said, moving slightly away from Josh. "I'm not ready to go back in two days. I was thinking maybe I could stay an extra week and help Nonna get used to her diet and the medicine she needs to take."

"Cristina, Nonna is fine. Just come home, it's been long enough." My mom said, her expression serious.

I saw Michael put a hand on my mom's shoulder and let out a quick huff. "No, Cristina. You take all of the time you need. I know Josh decided this very last minute and then wanted to surprise you when he called us, but I warned him you would need more time before you come back home." I saw my mom look at Michael, but he shook his head, almost as if they would talk about it later.

Michael understood what I was going through. He wasn't pressuring me or telling me I would be fine to leave. My own mother instead was the one who looked at me if I was crazy for wanting to stay. I talked to them both a few minutes more and hung up, the confusion settling as I knew one thing for certain—I was going to stay here longer than two more days.

When we returned to our hotel that night, I couldn't sleep. I told Josh my head was pounding from all of the excitement of the day, and I needed to just sleep it off, so I headed straight to bed, tucking myself in. He wasn't ready to go to bed, so he kissed me on my forehead and said he was going to post pictures of the ring and announce our engagement. I turned my phone to silent when I saw him go outside on the balcony. I didn't want to talk to anyone from home, especially after he posted the pictures.

I woke up the next morning and looked over to see Josh in bed next to me. I hadn't heard him come back. I looked at my phone to check the time and saw 32 missed messages.

"*Ugghhh...*" I let out a grunt, slipped on my shoes, and grabbed the ring off of the nightstand. I headed to the balcony, hoping that the view would calm my nerves. Slipping the ring onto my finger and looking at it alone for the first time felt uncomfortable. It looked too big and showy. I twisted it around and heard Josh call me from inside.

"*Buongiorno.*" He said, sitting up in bed and stretching his arms above him.

"Hey." I said, sitting on the edge of the bed. "I was thinking we could head back to my nonna's house earlier. It would be nice to have lunch with her."

He squinted his eyes and his eyebrows drew down as he looked at me. "Anything for my *fiancée*." He said, pulling me in for a kiss.

19

Diciannove

la confusione- confusion

We were on the road an hour later, driving through the winding roads with cliffs dropping off into the sea, my heart skipping beats every time Josh took the turns hastily. As we began to approach my nonna's house, the sight of the rolling hills and familiar landscape of the town comforted me.

Before heading inside, I sat motionless in the passenger's seat. "Josh, I need to tell you something." I reached over and grabbed his arm covered in a freshly pressed light-blue button up shirt. "I can't leave tomorrow. I know you want me to come back with you, but I have a few more things to do around here before I can say goodbye."

I saw a flash of anger cross his eyes before he took a breath and responded. "That's fine. It'll give my parents time to plan an engagement party for us when you get back. Listen, though. I can't stay here tonight. I'm going to head back to a hotel closer to the airport so I can catch the flight early."

"Okay." I said softly, looking down at my ring. It contrasted so blatantly against my nonna's rustic house. I played with it, took it off, and handed it to Josh. "I don't want to accidentally lose this here. Would you mind taking it back with you? That way it'll be safe until I come home to show it off."

He didn't hesitate and grabbed it from my hand. "That's actually a good idea. I didn't even get a chance to insure it yet." He leaned over, gave me a quick kiss, and opened his car door. We walked inside and my nonna greeted us both with a hug.

Josh took a seat at the table while I pulled out provolone from the fridge and sliced some bread. Nonna asked us about Positano and Capri and I did most of the talking.

"Josh, are you okay?" He was resting his head against his hand on the table but got up as soon as I called his name.

"What? Yeah, I'm fine. I'm sorry. I think I'm going to head out earlier and find the hotel close enough so I don't miss the flight. I have to go back to work right away and I'm probably going to sleep as soon as I get to the hotel."

"Oh, okay. I'll walk you to the car then."

He gave my nonna a hug and we walked out, towards his car.

"I'm sorry I'm not coming with you, but it'll only be a week." I said, stopping right in front of the car door.

"It's okay, I understand." He laced his fingers through mine. "I'll miss you though."

"I'll miss you too." He leaned in and gave me a gentle kiss.

I felt a wave of relief as soon as he started backing out onto the road.

"Cristina, come here. I can see you are not okay." My nonna walked up behind me as I stood outside, watching his car drive further and further away. She pulled me in for a hug, and my tears fell on my cheek, and onto her shoulder. I didn't try to stop them as she squeezed me tighter.

"Don't worry, Cristina. You have a lot of things to think about. *Solo tu puoi capire.*" Only you can understand.

I busied myself gardening and feeding the animals, not mentioning the engagement to my nonna. I saw Alessandro but he didn't stop by or even look my way. He was right to hate me and there was nothing I could do about it because I understood. I wasn't sure about anything anymore.

Arianna stopped by later that night, excited I was finally back, and wanted to hear how the Amalfi Coast was.

"Cristina, it's one of my favorite places in all of Italy and it's so close. Was it magical? Did your boyfriend love it?"

"Yes, it was beautiful. I've never seen anything like it. But I missed it here. He wanted me to go back with him, but I told him I had to stay another week. Besides, we need to plan for the fundraiser." I didn't want to tell her about the engagement. My problems were nothing compared to the loss she had faced.

"Yes! That's great! We need to call the *Municipio* first."

"*Municipio?*" I said, not sure what that word was.

"Oh, um...the place in the town that has records...the Town Hall."

"Let me help, Arianna. I can be on the call with you so we can make sure everything is covered."

We decided on a few dates we thought would gather the most money, with all of them being after I left. I tried to hide my sadness of not being able to be there when the fundraiser actually took place.

"Okay, we have enough. Come over tomorrow and we will call the *Municipio.*" I said, taking my time to pronounce the new word. I missed Arianna those past few days. In this small time, she had become someone I felt comfortable to be around. She gave me a hug and headed back to her house.

"Versa, Nonna. *Versa."* I told my nonna to continue pouring the espresso into my mug. I needed caffeine. I only had six days here and wanted to make sure I could help my nonna as much as I could and make sure Arianna was set to go for the fundraiser.

Alessandro's name kept bouncing around my mind. I needed to see if he was still going to donate some of his products to the booth, but I couldn't face him yet.

I decided I needed air, so I walked out to the garden to get my hands dirty again.

The tomatoes were turning a bright red and the peppers nice and plump. I would miss this. I wanted to be here the whole summer and see all of the vegetables get harvested. I grabbed the basket I brought with me from the house and started picking the tomatoes one by one. I tasted some of the cherry tomatoes, my cheeks tingling after biting into them, enjoying the warm, sunkissed taste. I made my nonna promise me to start jarring some of the tomatoes while I was still there, so I could learn before I left.

I was about to reach for the eggplants, when I felt my phone vibrate.

"Dad? Hey, how are you?"

"Well, I heard congratulations are in order." My stomach instantly sank. I'd completely forgotten to tell him.

"Thanks, Dad. I was going to call, but everything was so sudden and crazy. I wasn't expecting it at all though."

"Are you okay? You seem down."

"Actually, Mom wanted me to go home with Josh after he proposed, but I didn't even know he was coming."

"Honey, I'm sorry. You were right to stay. Your mom is funny like that though. I could see her wanting to hug you right away and congratulate you."

"Dad, she doesn't realize that Nonna needs help. She can't be here by herself. She brushed it off like it's not a big deal."

"Do you want me to talk to her?"

"No. I guess I will. I don't know, Dad. A lot is changing all at once." I pulled in my lower lip under my teeth and felt a tear well up in the corner of my eye. I haven't cried to my dad since the day he moved out. My mom had been mad at my dad for being weak and I was always afraid to be just like him.

"You know, Cristina. You don't have to have all of the answers right away. Sometimes you need time to let things figure themselves out on their own. I'm not saying Josh isn't a nice guy, but you might have more things you want to figure out before you completely commit."

He was right. I needed time. I needed time here, then at home. How do I tell Josh? He already told everyone I said yes. Maybe if we have a longer engagement and then in a few years I will feel ready to marry him.

We talked a little more before we hung up—and this time I wanted him to know how much I loved him and missed him. I also promised him I would go and visit him as soon as I got back.

I walked back to the house, clutching the phone closer to me. I felt guilty for how I had treated him. Listening to my mom complaining about him all of the time made me look at him differently. I knew it wasn't right and I wanted to make it up to him somehow.

As I approached the house, I saw my nonna talking to Alessandro outside. I never had a chance to speak to him after our kiss. I clenched my jaw shut, forced myself to face him, and walked up to them, a soft hello escaping my mouth.

He whipped around to face me, and I could see the shock quickly being replaced by an indifference. My nonna looked back and forth between us, and I swore there was a hint of a smile on her face.

"Scusate, ragazzi. Devo dare da mangiare agli animali." She excused herself telling us she had to feed the animals. I stood next to Alessandro, still not sure what I should say, but knew I had to at least talk to him about the fundraiser for Giovanni.

"So, I..."

"Cristina..."

We both started talking at the same time which made me laugh and he cracked a smile. His expression softened, and he gestured for me to talk.

"I wanted to talk about the fundraiser. I was going to meet Arianna tomorrow to call the *Municipio*." He raised his eyebrows slightly as I pronounced *Municipio* in the best Italian I could.

"Yes, I can still donate anything you need. Just let me know when it is." He took a few steps back.

"Okay, I will." I replied, and he nodded his head, his face expressionless again, and he headed back towards his property, away from me.

I wanted to open up to him and explain everything I'd been feeling and how confused I'd been over the past few days, but I worried that it would only hurt him more. I figured the best thing to spare his heart would be to just leave and help him get back to his life before this summer.

Arianna stopped by mid-morning the next day which immediately put me in a good mood. There was a new spark in her as she planned the fundraiser for her fiancé she had lost forever. I was awestruck at how she worked, motivated and fulfilled. Seeing her like this and helping her accomplish something so meaningful helped me put my problems on the backburner.

"So, I talked to Alessandro, and he still wants to donate some food and wine." I said, as soon as we sat down on the steps, enjoying the warm, dry heat.

"Wait," Arianna turned towards me, shielding her eyes from the sun. "You talked to Alessandro?"

"Yeah, why?"

"No, nothing. Thanks for asking him." I could see her getting flustered and wondered if she wanted to change the subject on purpose.

"No problem," I said. I could feel an unspoken tension between me and Arianna that I didn't want to address. "You should call the *Municipio* now and I will listen in."

Arianna did all of the talking and I was surprised that I was able to pick up more Italian than I expected to. She decided on a date a little over a week from now, and I could feel the emptiness in my heart opening up, wishing I could be here for it.

"So..." She said, after she hung up the phone. "We are all set. There were no issues, and they even asked if we needed help setting anything up." She looked at me and her expression became heavy. "Wait—are you even going to be here next Thursday?"

"No, I'm leaving four days from now."

"Four! Cristina, you can't. What am I going to do without you?"

"Arianna, you have done all of this by yourself. I was just here to guide you along." I thought about Alessandro. Sometimes we need help, a guide to direct us the right way—that person that will help us see what the right way is and lead us along it. Those people are special, they are the ones that want to see you succeed, that want to see you smile.

I worked hard in the garden that day, making sure my nonna wouldn't have much to do after I left.

"Mom, you don't understand," I said to her later on the phone, "I know Nonna can do it, but she is pushing herself and it's too much for her."

I could hear Stella and Samantha fighting in the background and my mom was trying to shush them.

"Okay. I will hire help for her. Someone at least to come and clean up the house and help her prepare her meals. I was talking to Josh's parents, and we had decided to do something on Saturday to celebrate the engagement."

I squeezed my eyes shut and rubbed my hand over them. "That's fine, Mom."

"Honey, let me go and see what these girls are up to. I'll talk to you later. Love you."

"Love you too."

I did *not* want a party. My mom had already taken it upon herself again to plan things for me. If she was already planning the engagement party without my say, who knows what would happen for the actual wedding. A knot caught in my throat. I needed to digest the fact that I was going to marry Josh, and there was nothing that I could do about it except to start warming up to it. I texted Josh throughout the day like I used to when I was home. I just needed time to reignite my feelings that used to burn so strongly inside me for him.

My nonna had been working in the garden and I decided to head over to help with the animals. The baby lamb had grown in the past few weeks and started venturing closer to me as I brought it food. The turkeys started accepting my presence, noticing me as a regular and ignoring me as I scattered the ground corn on the floor. I headed towards the bunnies, wanting to rake up their pen.

"Ugh...Where did I put it last?" I said out loud to myself as I searched the rest of the fenced area for the rake. I looked around, and then bumped my leg into a piece of fence that was sticking out, making me trip.

"Oww..." I grunted, grabbing my leg. I looked down, praying not to see blood, but luckily saw it was just a small scrape. A figure then came up to me and I squinted my eyes and tried to block the sun with my hands to see who it was. Alessandro was holding out his hand to help me up.

"*Ahia.*" I said, looking up at him while grabbing my leg, a smile forming on my face. I saw the corner of his lips tug up. He let out a laugh and shook his head.

"Did I do it right? It's *ahia*, right?" Wait, so does it just work with *ow*? What other noises are different?" I looked around trying to think of other noises that could be different and then remembered the animals. "Like the rooster," I said, pointing at it. "It says *cock-a-doodle-doo?*"

Now his shoulders moved, and he was laughing even more. "No, we say *chicchirichi.*"

"Wait, key-kee-ree-key?" I said, pronouncing each syllable.

His whole expression changed, and I felt that connection again, not as strong as before I left, but an inkling there saying we could be friends—that he didn't hate me completely.

"What about a dog?" I asked, now curious too to hear the other differences.

"We say *bau bau.*"

"Hmm...I can see that. We say *woof.* Alright, what about baby chicks, *i pulcini.*"

"*Pio pio.*"

"*Pee-o pee-o?*" I said, now laughing. "We say *peep.*"

"*Peep? Ma, no! Non può essere!*" He exclaimed, saying it couldn't be that.

"Wait, what about a frog? We say *ribbit.*"

"*Basta, Cristina. Ma non puoi dire ribbit.* A frog cannot say ribbit. Do you hear ribbit? No, it says *cra, cra.*"

At this point, I had tears in my eyes trying to mimic all of the animal noises he had taught me so far. I knew that this was a game that could go on forever, so I changed the subject. "Thank you, by the way, for helping Arianna."

He nodded his head and dug his hands into his pockets. "I need to thank you, Cristina. You have been a really good friend to Arianna, someone she's needed lately." In just a few days I had forgotten his gaze, that strength of his eyes as he stared into mine, daring me to look away, but I couldn't. There was so much behind that gaze that I wanted to know and figure out.

"You don't need to thank me. That's what friends do for each other."

He nodded again, and his shoulders came up slightly, his hands still in his pockets. He opened his mouth and hesitated. He looked to the side, then back at me again before asking, "Are you free tomorrow? We are all going to the beach right before lunch and bringing sandwiches with us. It's me, a bunch of my friends and some of their girlfriends, and I think Arianna said she was coming too. I can drive you both if you want."

I didn't even hesitate for a moment. "Yes. I'd love that. I'll text Arianna. Maybe I can even drive and pick her up so she doesn't need to bring her car here."

"As long as you are careful, Cristina." He said, narrowing his eyes with a smile.

"I will be. I'll remember to shift the gears this time," I said. We said goodbye and I watched him head back over to his house, content that I had this moment with him before I left, knowing we were friends again.

CRISTINA. **Get ready—I am going to pick you up tomorrow before the beach to truly perfect my driving. Alessandro invited me earlier and said you are going.**

I texted Arianna as soon as I got back to the house later that night.

ARIANNA: **Oddio, are you sure? You are leaving soon—you need to be careful!**

CRISTINA: **I got it, Arianna! Don't worry! :-)**

I wanted to do this one thing before I left. I needed to prove that I could drive a manual car, so I could impress my family when I got back.

I had received a text from Laila congratulating me and I never responded back. I didn't want to lie and say it didn't hurt me that she hadn't really kept in touch this whole time I was here, but I knew we would pick right back up where we left off when I returned. I started to type out a message.

CRISTINA: **Thanks, Laila. I know I said I expected it—but it definitely was still a surprise.**

I waited a few minutes, waiting for a quick reply, but then threw my phone on the bed knowing she wouldn't text back. As soon as it bounced on the bed, it lit up.

LAILA: **Oh come on. You knew. Now you can go live your happily married full-of-bliss life.**

I chewed on my bottom lip not knowing what she meant by that. That's one thing I hated about texting, you could come across as a bitch or the sweetest person ever with the same message to two different people depending on how they read it.

I let it be and figured I'd see her in a few days and know then.

She was never one to be tied down anyway, so she probably did mean it in a playful, mocking way—but either way, I wasn't going to let it bother me.

I sent a message to Josh too. I hadn't FaceTimed him since he left, but since I was going to see him again in a few days, I didn't think it was necessary. I was about to put down my phone again, but this time I got an email notification from my mom with my flight information. I read through it and took note of the date and time.

2 O

Venti

la spiaggia- beach

Okay, foot on the clutch. Start the engine. Wait, make sure you're in first gear—okay, good. I can do this. I was lucky Arianna lived about ten minutes down the road so I wouldn't have to worry about turns or remembering how to get there—all I needed to do was concentrate on driving.

ALESSANDRO: **Please text me if you need help or if you want me to come with you.**

That was the first text I received from Alessandro since that night at the feast. I smiled and texted right back that I would be fine, and he should relax. I was secretly happy that he cared enough to text me, remembering that I was trying to drive by myself.

Here we go. I did a quick sign of the cross, something I always saw my nonna do anytime she was about to do something scary, or right before she made the provolone, praying it would come out right. I started the engine, took my foot off the clutch, and pressed the gas slowly, my eyes widening when I noticed the car going forward and not stopping.

"I did it!" I said out loud to myself. I headed on the road, past Alessandro's house, and beeped the horn twice at him as he waved to me from his porch.

"*Oddio*, Cristina, you made it!" Arianna said as I wiped away the beads of sweat on my forehead with the back of one hand while my other one was still tight around the steering wheel.

"No celebrating yet, we still need to make it back." I let out a deep breath, waited for Arianna to buckle up, and then turned around, heading home.

"*Please, please, please.*" I softly prayed to myself as we approached the first hill. I made sure to shift down one gear to get more speed so the car wouldn't stall. "*Come on, come on.*" When the car made it over the hill to a flat road, I celebrated a silent victory in my head.

"Cristina, I'm really proud of you." Arianna said to me as we slowly approached my nonna's house. "Can you believe you did it? You made it without stopping once. Come here." She took me in for a big hug and I relaxed myself on her shoulder, not realizing that I had tensed every muscle in my body during the car ride.

I was proud of myself—I couldn't wait to tell my dad what I had done. I wanted to make him feel as special to me as I could. I checked the time, saw it was 11am and knew he would be up already since it was 5 in the morning there. I took a selfie in the car, smiling widely, and writing underneath *Look who learned to drive manual.* He wrote back right away, telling me he was so proud of me and knew that I could do anything I put my mind to.

"Girls, do you have everything? Bathing suits? Towels? Change of clothes in case?" Alessandro said as we walked towards his car, swinging our beach bags.

"Yes, yes. Don't worry about us." I smiled as I scooched into the backseat. I saw one eyebrow raise from the rearview mirror and then he shook his head.

"Oh, I worry. Especially now that you can drive here."

I rolled my eyes at him, and I took a picture of the three of us before he started driving. I needed to remember these moments with them.

We reached the beach a little over an hour later and I tried to read the sign of the town.

"*Ca-stell...*"

"*Castellabate.*" Alessandro said, standing next to me as I tried to pronounce it. "*Santa Maria di Castellabate.*"

"*Cah-stell-ah-bah-teh.*" I said slowly. I loved how each letter had a distinct sound—each vowel was pronounced, not blended with others to make a new sound like it was in English. Each vowel and consonant were important enough to be pronounced on its own— it stood out and begged to be recognized, and I loved the Italian language for it.

"This is amazing." I took a breath as I absorbed the view around me. The beach was dark sand that felt soft and cool under my feet and the sound of the rolling waves crashing on the shore lulled my body to relax. The waves were small compared to the ones out on Long Island where if you weren't paying attention, they would knock you right down. These were enough to mimic the white noise sounds you would hear when you needed that extra help going to sleep at night. I looked over to my right and saw people sunbathing on these massive rocks that ran perpendicular from the road to the beach and then noticed some restaurants with outdoor seating along the road. Alessandro had mentioned we were going to go out tonight to eat and I imagined it was at one of those restaurants.

I walked next to Arianna, placed my beach bag next to hers, and laid out a towel on the sand. The view was not as striking as it had been in Positano, but for some reason I felt better here—relaxed and more at home with Arianna, Alessandro, and their friends.

"So, what did you bring?" I asked Arianna, as she opened her bag and pulled out something wrapped up.

"Just a sandwich. What about you?"

"Yeah, me too. My nonna packed it for me though, which I thought was sweet." I opened mine up and was delighted to find pickled eggplants, mozzarella, roasted peppers with grilled chicken on soft bread—something I had been making for her too since it was lighter for her stomach. I bit into it, enjoying every bite, and pictured my nonna's face as she handed it to me. *Ecco, Cristina. Have fun today—you deserve to have fun. I love you.*

"You're eating already?" I looked up to see Alessandro with his hands on his hips, one arm also holding a soccer ball. "Now you have to wait to go in the water."

"*Ho fame.*" I said, telling him I was hungry. "Besides, Arianna started eating first." I laughed and pointed my thumb at her while she was mid bite.

She covered her mouth, finished chewing, and then smiled back at me "Sure, blame me, Cristina. Anyway, you guys have fun and play soccer together, we'll start getting tan here."

Alessandro shook his head while smiling and walked away, kicking the soccer ball with another friend.

"Is it true that you can't go in the water after you eat? My nonna would scare me about that to the point that I wouldn't eat before swimming in my friends' pools."

Arianna laughed and then shook her head. "Listen, a lot of the *nonni* here will scare you into thinking many things—like if you point at the moon, you will get warts. Or if you drop olive oil on the floor, you will get really bad luck." We both laughed and finished our sandwiches, looking over at the guys playing soccer.

"Arianna, that's Marco, the baker—right? He keeps looking over at you."

I saw Arianna make eye contact with Marco. He had on bathing shorts and a white t-shirt with his company's logo on the back. His brown hair was cut short and styled neatly back and his light blue eyes had a playful look to them. I noticed he was a little shorter than Alessandro, and not as fit, but his whole demeanor made him seem warm and kind. He smiled back at Arianna, and she blushed and looked down. His friends then yelled at him to pay attention since he missed the ball and now had to run across the beach to get it.

"You should talk to him. He seems nice and he's good looking."

"Okay, okay. I promise I will, but not right now. I want to lay down and just tan for now."

I stood up, took off my tank top and slipped out of my shorts, feeling vulnerable since I filled out my white, ruched bikini a lot more than I used to. I quickly sat back down on the towel, not wanting to bring any attention to myself, and applied sunscreen before I laid down.

"Look at you, Cristina." Arianna said, staring at me with her eyebrows raised. "Too bad you have a boyfriend because I just saw all of those guys checking you out."

"*Uggghhh...*" I grunted, feeling my cheeks turning the darkest shade of crimson. "I'm going to wrap myself in a towel."

"No! I didn't mean it like that. I meant it in a good way. You should be proud of yourself, like you told me."

I smiled at her and nodded my head. I let the sun warm my body, making it tingle as I laid next to Arianna, happy to have this moment with her.

"Will you come back and visit more often now?" She asked, turning sideways and blocking the sun with her hand.

The question caught me by surprise. "Yeah, I was thinking of coming back for Christmas. Maybe spend it here."

"That would be amazing, Cristina! I know it's not Christmas in New York, but we still do traditional things here too."

I smiled and listened as she described how the town decorates a huge Christmas Tree in the middle of the piazza and how they organize a festival to honor it. I felt a part of this town too now, and I wanted to see all of the seasons here, not just summer. We talked more, when all of a sudden the soccer ball rolled between us.

"Dai, ragazze—per piacere!" I heard someone calling out. I looked and saw one of Alessandro's friends beckoning for us to throw them back the ball. I stood up, held it in my hands, ready to throw it, but I noticed another guy had his arm raised too, so I looked over and then stopped. I felt a rush come over me, my fingers were now becoming clammy, as I stared at Alessandro, shirtless, waiting for me to throw the ball at him too—but I couldn't even think straight.

My body had completely stopped, and I prayed my mouth wasn't open, revealing how shocked I was. If he was good looking with a shirt on, then I didn't know how to describe him with his shirt off. He was perfectly defined, whatever work he was doing around his property was paying off. I knew I needed to do something and getting rid of this ball and sitting back down was the first thing, but I became flustered and embarrassed to throw it.

Somehow, Alessandro mistook whatever look I had as a playful one and started running over to me, telling me he was going to take it from my hands. When he reached me, I pulled the ball away from him, now having the confidence to tease him, but the brush of his arm against my stomach made me shudder, as he tried again to reach for the ball.

He shook his head, quickly got the ball from me, and then told his friends in Italian that he was going to throw me and Arianna in the water. I started running away from him, laughing.

"You can run now, Cristina, but I promise you I will get you later." He said, teasing me with his eyes. He ran into the water, his other friends following him too. The fire had started slowly burning again, and I knew it was a dangerous feeling to have, but for some reason, I didn't want to stop it.

"We will see about that."

I took Arianna and we both ran into the water near the guys.

"Just because you are in the water, doesn't mean you are safe." Alessandro said to me as he waded closer.

"Maybe you should be careful, too." I said, staring right back at him.

He let out a laugh, then turned to his friends who were playing volleyball waist-high in the water. His whole presence seemed strong, from the defined features on his face, to the way his shoulders spanned when he jumped to hit the ball. I had to stop staring, so I looked over to Arianna, who wasn't doing any better than me since she was staring hard at Marco.

"Alright, that's it. You need to talk to him." I said, nudging her elbow. She looked down, a blush creeping over her cheeks, before dropping deeper into the water.

"I will, I will. Okay, we need to talk about how Alessandro can't stop staring at you though, too. I know you two are just friends and you have a boyfriend, but he really cannot stop looking at you."

My heart fluttered a few beats and my body started feeling warmer, almost as if the sun's rays turned up to a higher level. I should feel guilty—I didn't have a boyfriend, I had a *fiancé.*

"He isn't, Arianna. He is just looking for a way to splash water on me or do something else when I'm not looking."

"Yeah, I'm not so sure. The way you look in that bikini, that's not all he is thinking."

I playfully smacked her arm and dipped my body under the water like she had, becoming more self-conscious. I carefully turned towards him and caught his gaze, before he quickly turned away and caught the ball.

We spent most of the afternoon in and out of the water, some of the boys teasing us while the others were with their girlfriends, spending most of their time together. I chatted with two of the girl-friends, talking about differences between New York and Italy and they asked me which I liked more.

"It's hard to compare. They are two completely different places for me. I was born there, so a part of my heart will always search for that home. But this is a different type of home for me. One that took me in quickly, never questioning, and made me feel like I belonged, too."

Arianna squeezed my arm as I said that, and the other two girls smiled.

"Last time to go in the water before we head to dinner!" Alessandro shouted to us as he ran past, hitting my shoulder to get my attention. I looked up and saw him jump straight into the water, so I excused myself and chased after him, enjoying the last time in the water while in Italy.

"Alessandro!" I said, shouting his name as I reached him. When I saw him turn to me, I splashed him with water and watched him try to dodge it by jumping back.

"Oh, no. That's it—get over here!" He said, chasing me. I treaded away from him, as fast as I could, but he quickly caught up to me, his arm wrapping around my waist under the water, bringing my back against his stomach. I was surprised by how he grabbed me, but he kept laughing, throwing me back in the water. I went under, my hair getting wet, and stood up and smacked him on his arm.

"Ow!" He said, his smile still wide and using English this time to express he got hurt.

"Ow? You were the one who threw me in the water!" I matched his smile, my hands on my hips.

He dipped his whole body under the water, his hair dripping wet as he stood back up. I watched the drops of water trickle down his chest and abs and then quickly caught myself since I was obviously staring at him too long. A corner of his lip pulled up when my eyes met his, and he quickly splashed me with water before I could say anything. I was about to splash him back when a few friends called out to us telling us they were going to go to eat.

"Just wait until later." I said, my lips pressed closed into a tight smile. He let out a laugh and placed his hand on my back leading me out of the water. His touch made me feel something that I couldn't quite place. We walked back towards the group, his hand had dropped from my back once we were out of the water, and I got my towel, trying to dry myself as best as I could. I pulled out a sundress from my bag and slipped it on over my bikini. I towel dried my hair and sprayed a little leave-in conditioner, hoping it wouldn't become a frizzy mess once it dried into curls.

We sat at a long table outside of the restaurant and all ordered individual pizzas with beers. The boys teased each other, having us all laughing out loud, and I closed my eyes, thanking God to have this day with them. This was better than the Hamptons. The amount of alcohol we had here was nothing compared to what everyone consumed back home, and I never remember laughing this much. My cheeks were actually hurting, and I had to beg them to stop making me laugh, which of course made them joke even more. Every once in a while, I stole glances at Alessandro, who would lock eyes with me and smile.

"*Limoncello per tutti!*" The waiter said, sharing in the excitement with the table and offering us all a glass of liquor. We all took our glasses and lifted them up, yelling out *cin*, before drinking it all at once.

"Wow, that's strong!" I said, releasing a shudder. I turned to Arianna but noticed she was talking to Marco who was sitting across from her. Her legs were crossed, facing him and she had both of her elbows on the table, her head resting on one of her hands, as she leaned towards him. Everything about her body language said she was interested in him, and I didn't want to interrupt whatever they were talking about. I looked over at Alessandro and made a slight nod with my head towards Arianna, so he could see what was going on. He looked over, then turned back at me, his eyebrows raised and a smile forming on his face.

The bill came and we divided it between us, Alessandro graciously paid for me and Arianna because he knew I would be leaving soon, and this was his way of saying goodbye. I thanked him and felt reality hit again that I was leaving but promised myself I wouldn't let it ruin the rest of the night we still had.

I noticed that some people had gotten up to walk around. Marco had moved closer to Arianna, and they were still talking to each other. I didn't want to bother her and looked up to see Alessandro motioning with his head to move away so we could leave them alone. I got up quietly, not wanting to interrupt them, and headed over to the other side of the table with Alessandro.

"I don't know about you, but I need to walk that pizza and beer off." I said, patting my stomach. He laughed and agreed so we headed to the beach. The air was still warm, but the sun had just dipped below the horizon, creating a haze of reds and pinks across the sky. We walked next to each other back onto the beach, and I took off my shoes, wanting to feel the sand between my toes.

He turned to me and took a deep breath, before looking back towards the sea. "So, you're leaving in three days." He said, kicking a tiny bit of sand up with his left foot. "I'm going to miss you, Cristina. Your nonna is fun and everything, but it was nice to have you around."

I promised myself I wouldn't get sad even though I felt the emotions simmering below the surface. I didn't want to see Alessandro or Arianna sad either, so I knew what I had to do to change the mood.

"Follow me." I said, leading him closer to the water. His eyebrows pulled together, but he obeyed. I was hoping this would work.

As we reached the water, I lifted my hand above my eyes, creating a sort of visor, and pretended to spot something out in the sea.

"Alessandro, wait. Look at that! Do you see that shiny object in the sea over there?"

He pulled his head back and looked where I pointed, but still was puzzled.

"Come here, closer. Look, you can see it over there. Maybe duck your head a little this way so you can see it from my level." He was following everything I said, now ducking his head, and when he reached lower to me, I quickly shot down, scooped a bunch of water and splashed it right on him. He froze for a second, in shock, and then I saw his eyes widen as he looked at me, now shaking his head.

"Oh that's it, get over here!" He picked me up, threw me over his shoulders, and I protested, laughing and kicking my legs at the same time. His arm held strongly around my thighs as he took me further into the water. I kept shouting for him to put me down, in Italian—*mettimi giù*, between laughing as he continued carrying me out.

"*Va bene.*" He said, agreeing, pulling me down from his shoulders, holding onto my waist, and dipping me in enough that my whole bottom half was wet, including the sundress I had put on. I glared at him as he laughed. His presence so close to me was intoxicating, but I saw in his eyes that he knew it would be best to start backing away from me. A voice in my head shouted out that I could not let that happen.

"Alessandro!" I yelled out, as he backed away. "Don't you run away!" He wasn't going that fast, almost as if he was trying to taunt me, so I ran up behind him, put my hands on his shoulders, and tried to stop him. He easily kept walking, despite all of the strength I put into stopping him, so I swung my arms around his neck, pulled myself up on his back, and wrapped my legs around his stomach to slow him down. He started slowing down, his breathing getting heavier, as he trudged towards the shore. He finally stopped, kneeled down in the water, making me go up to my stomach in it as well.

"I got you now!" I shouted as soon as he stopped. I unwrapped my arms and legs and he turned around, facing me, now shaking his head. He grabbed my waist, as if he was going to throw me back in, but his hands stood there, strong against me. Something in his face changed—his expression was now serious. My body let out a tremble from a breeze that touched my neck and his grip tightened around my waist, pulling me closer to him.

Everything changed at that moment. I had no doubts, no worries, no questions. I had him in front of me. His rough hands, the ones that had created so many beautiful things, were around my waist. I had his strong body in front of mine, but I needed it closer. For the first time in a long time, I knew what I wanted, and it was right in front of me. I wasn't thinking of right or wrong, should or shouldn't, I was only thinking of moving inches closer so I could feel him against me. I took my arms, wrapped them around his neck and felt his hands move up higher on my waist. I pulled him closer to me, but felt him hesitate. There were no questions about the future, there was only now. I pulled him closer to me even more, finally feeling his stomach and chest against mine, through our wet clothes. My breathing hitched, and I pulled his neck towards me, needing to feel his lips again on mine. When our lips finally touched, the kiss was gentle, a reminder of the last time we had shared it. His fingers gripped my waist tighter, and the kiss quickly turned intense, with both of us needing to feel more of each other. I wrapped my legs around him, both of us still submerged under water, and one of his hands moved to my thigh while the other still gripped my waist. My hands threaded through his hair, pulling him even closer to me, but it still wasn't enough. We broke apart, both panting as I stared at his red lips, trying to pull in as much air as I could, before we kissed again. He pulled back, a few moments later, and let go of my waist and leg, letting me stand up in the water.

"We should get out before it gets too cold." He said, still looking into my eyes.

"Okay." I managed, still stuck in the moment, but following him out of the water, walking alongside him. I took off my dress, toweled myself dry, and saw him stare at me, his eyes widening even more. I put on the shorts and shirt I came with, and he quickly changed his shirt.

"There you two are!" Arianna jogged toward us. "Did you guys go swimming?" I saw her expression go from happy to confused to shocked, her eyes widening as her eyes darted between the two of us. "Anyway," she said after we didn't answer. I felt my cheeks heat up because she had to know what we'd been up to. "I'm going to get a ride home with Antonella and her boyfriend. They live next door to me, so it makes sense."

"*Sei sicura?*" Alessandro asked if she was sure.

She answered him back in Italian, too fast for me to understand, and he nodded his head silently.

We continued walking, the tension building up again, especially since we had a whole car ride home alone with each other.

"Do you want to head back home?" I asked him softly.

He hesitated, looking straight at me and nodded his head the slightest bit. He took out his phone, explaining he was going to text everyone that he was leaving, and then headed towards his car, opening the door for me to go in.

I had never sat in the passenger side in his car, always wanting Arianna to sit next to him. We drove quietly back to the house, the ride lasting a little more than an hour. I pulled my legs up onto the seat and looked out the window, watching the fields and small towns as they passed against the night sky. He stopped the car once we reached his house and looked over at me.

"Do you want to come in?"

"Okay."

He pulled the car into his driveway, and then turned it off, but waited a few more seconds before stepping out. He reached over to me, pushed a strand of my hair behind my ear, making a small quiver travel through my body.

"Your hair is beautiful like this when it naturally curls." His voice was a touch louder than a whisper. His hand brushed my cheek gently before he dropped it down. I could see he was hesitant to leave the car, so I opened my door, walked over to his side of the car, and took his hand to gently pull him out. I held onto his hand as we reached the door, and he unlocked it, letting me inside. We both stopped in the doorway, looked at each other, before we both took each other in, our lips pressing against each other's, continuing the kiss from the beach. His hands wrapped around my waist, and I was on my tip-toes kissing him. He pulled me up, lifting my feet off the ground, and I wrapped my legs around him, our kiss intensifying more. He walked me towards his bedroom, laid me down on the bed, and then began to kiss me down along my neck, making every part of my body come alive. My legs were still wrapped around his waist, trying to keep him as close to me as I could, and I didn't care about anything else going on—I just needed to be with him. I unhooked my legs and sat up, now pulling his shirt over his head. I took off my shirt too and then he moved his lips further down, kissing the hollow of my neck, then along the edge of my bikini top. A quick shudder came over me and I placed my fingers on his back, trying to pull him even closer. Every part of me was tingling, burning, and craving even more all at the same time. I undid my top, threw it on the floor, and he stopped, just staring at me.

"Do you know how long I have wanted to be with you?" He said, looking at me directly in my eyes.

I shook my head no, not even able to find the word for it.

"For a long time, Cristina. It has always been you. It has *only* been you."

I took off everything he was wearing while he did the same to me until both of us stood, looking at each other completely bare. He wrapped his arm around my back and laid me down in bed while resting his elbow next to me, both of us now delicately exploring every part of each other. I didn't want to know the time or anything else going on—I just wanted this moment to last forever.

We laid in bed after, his hand threaded through mine, and he nuzzled into my neck. I never had these moments with Josh, just laying next to each other after we were intimate. He would usually get up, make something to eat, or take a shower.

"Stay tonight." He whispered in my ear. I turned to kiss him back, and he wrapped his arms around me, holding me close to him. He started kissing near my ear, down my neck, sending racing shivers down my spine. We spent most of the night with each other until we were exhausted, finally falling asleep.

My eyes shot open the next morning, the trickles of sunlight coming through the slats on the shutters. I looked next to me at Alessandro, not my fiancé. Panic consumed me as I realized what I had done. I removed Alessandro's arm, still wrapped around my stomach. How could I have been so sure of something the night before and now regret everything immediately the next day? I was leaving in two days. Just two days and I have completely upended my whole life. And, on top of everything, this was all completely unfair to Josh, and I now felt like the worst person in the world.

"Alessandro?" I whispered, trying to lift his arm off of me. "Alessandro?"

He moved and opened his eyes slowly, his lips turning slowly into a smile.

My shoulders dropped—I felt something for him. Last night was perfect, probably the most memorable night I have ever had. What would I do with him now that I was leaving? I couldn't live here—this wasn't my life. My life was back home.

"Are you okay?" Alessandro got up on his elbow, analyzing my face. His eyebrows narrowed when I pulled the blanket over me, covering most of my body.

"Alessandro—last night… It was a mistake. I'm sorry. I'm leaving in two days and my parents are having an engagement party for me next week, and…"

"Wait—what? An engagement party?" He sat up straight in bed and moved away from me. "You are *engaged?*" His eyes shifted down to my left hand, as if he were searching for a ring.

I grabbed my left hand, squeezing it. "Yes." I couldn't look him in the eyes when I admitted it.

He got up, his fists clenched by his sides and his eyes turned cold. "Cristina, why didn't you tell me this? Are you kidding?"

"I'm sorry. It's just that I was confused. I mean, I am confused. I didn't know…"

"No, no excuses Cristina! You cannot be confused with some-thing like this. You are getting *married.* You cannot be confused with what we did last night. You can't have both!" He grabbed his clothes and threw them on hastily. "What is it you want from me? Was I just someone to make you feel better about yourself? Someone's feelings you could play with? *A cosa stavi pensando,* Cristina? *Dimmi!*"

His voice got louder and his face got redder, especially when he switched into Italian, probably so he could get the words out faster, asking me what I was thinking, and to tell him.

"Non lo so. I don't know. I wasn't thinking. It just felt right." I said meekly. I wanted to close my eyes and disappear. I hurt him.

I watched him walk around the room, searching for something, avoiding eye contact with me. He picked up sneakers, sat down on a chair, and rushed to get them on.

"I'm sorry." I said again, hoping he would look up at me. He continued lacing his sneakers and looking down, his lips pressed tightly together.

"Is he even right for you? Does he make you happy? Does he actually make you a better person? Does he love all of you?" His voice was getting louder as he asked each question, not even giving me a chance to respond. "You know—what does it matter anyway? I should have known I wasn't enough for you. I am sorry that I don't make a lot of money like your rich boyfriend or have an expensive car. I am sorry I live a simple life here and don't wear expensive outfits like everyone you know. Go ahead, go have a happy life back in New York." He was looking at me now, his nostrils flaring and his eyes darker. "And here I thought you changed from the 15 year old girl you were. It was all a lie, wasn't it."

I squeezed my eyes closed, tears escaping anyway, falling down my cheeks. He was right. I didn't change. I thought something had woken me up here and made me realize what I really wanted, but instead I hurt someone I really cared about, maybe even thought I loved. I wanted to tell him it wasn't true what he was saying, but I didn't even know myself, so I just stood there, not responding, my eyes tightly shut, praying I would have an answer.

He left the room and slammed the outside door shut, leaving me inside with an emptiness that rivaled any other horrible feeling I had felt. For some reason, this was just as bad as the day my dad left —when I knew everything would be different after that moment.

I finally pushed myself off the bed, not wanting to leave, but also realizing I couldn't stay in his house. I grabbed my clothes and quickly threw them on, swung my bag over my arm, and ran back to my house, fighting back tears.

"Cristina, what is the matter?" My nonna said, pulling me into a hug. My chest heaved as I continued sobbing onto her shoulder, reliving all of what happened while I was here. She pressed a hand against the back of my head, her other broken arm was carefully placed on my back, holding me close.

"I don't know, Nonna. I don't know what I want anymore or who I even am. Why did I even come here for so long? Why did I try to be a different person here? It's not me—I don't even know who I am or what I like." I rambled on, hiccuping between sobs, burying my face in her shoulder. She continued patting my back, softly shushing me to quiet down, and I felt the tears drop from my face onto her shoulder.

She pulled back, placed a hand on the side of my cheek, and looked into my eyes.

"I know who you are and so do you. You are the girl that wants to be happy—that wants to live life. You want to be free and feel important to yourself and to others. Those days that you were happy and smiling—that is the Cristina I remember and know. Never apologize to anyone for who you are. You are not the girl who came here a month ago—no, you are a woman. One that is strong, confident, and happy."

I stood there listening quietly and nodding my head. My nonna's eyes looked straight into mine, with a fierceness that showed she believed everything she said. I just needed to believe what she was saying too.

I stayed to myself all day, trying to work through what I had done. Arianna stopped by that night, her forehead creased and her mouth downturned and I wondered if she already knew.

"Hi, I just wanted to spend time with you before you left."

"Thanks, Arianna. Let's go to my room." I led her down the hallway, looking for a place to talk in private.

"Cristina. What happened last night with Alessandro? His friends are telling me that he is different today—angry."

Tears were welling up in my eyes again, I drew a deep breath to stop them, but it wasn't working. I dug my nails into my palm.

"It's bad, Arianna. I don't know anymore." I started, feeling as if my body was a dam threatening to burst. "We kissed yesterday at the beach..."

"I knew it!" She gasped, but there was a hint of a smile on her face as well.

"No...I mean, yes, we did. But then we went back to his house...and..."

Tears were fully flowing now, impossible to stop, my shoulders heaving and the dam bursting, letting all of the emotions through. She reached over to me, grabbed me in a hug, and let me stay there until I could compose myself again.

"Cristina, I feel like there is only one question that needs to be answered—do you love him?"

"Love who?"

She looked at me, her expression puzzled. "Your boyfriend."

"Well, he is *actually* my fiancé and..."

"Oh...now I understand everything." She shook her head, connecting all the dots. Suddenly I felt more tears coming, but saw her shake her head, her hand gripping mine. "No, I didn't mean it that way. I understand why it's hard for you and how Alessandro is feeling too."

I imagined she'd talked to him and that was why she was here. Her hand was still gripping mine and there was sorrow in her eyes. I wanted to tell her that she should be mad at me—not feel sorry for me. I was the one who cheated on her fiancé. I deserved nothing. I deserved to go home alone. I definitely did not deserve Arianna's sympathy.

"I'm not a good person, Arianna. Who does something like this? It felt so right in the moment, but I know it was wrong. It's almost like I couldn't stop myself. You can hate me—I would completely understand."

"Cristina—I don't hate you! In fact, this is what love is. It's this complicated, confusing thing that will make you do anything, and completely lose your mind. I am sure you were listening to your heart—and you are a good person—you didn't intend to hurt anyone."

I listened to her talk, but her words just rebounded right off of me. I slept with her good friend, and she still didn't hate me, but instead was comforting me. I knew I would miss her. My mind kept comparing the conversation to what Laila would say to me. She was never one to allow me to get tied up in my emotions and explain how I felt.

"Arianna, thank you for being such a good friend, but if I keep thinking about this, I'm actually going to lose my mind. I'm so confused and thinking about it makes it worse. Can we talk about what happened last night with Marco instead?"

"Oh, Marco..." She said, a smile hinting at her lips. "Well, we talked a lot last night, and he is really nice. It's just, you know. I don't know if I am ready."

I nodded my head, not wanting to make her feel any pressure with him. I was the last person to make decisions on that. "You will know when you are." I said, squeezing her hand. "Well, how about the fundraiser? It's next week, right?" A feeling of emptiness came over me when I realized I wouldn't be there to see it after I asked her.

"Yes. Everything is good—we have a stand and Alessandro will help set it up..." Her voice then trailed when she mentioned his name. She probably saw it from my expression that it hurt to even hear him being mentioned.

"That's good." I forced myself to say. I knew she could tell I was being fake but was nice enough to just not say anything else. "I really want to be there."

"I really want you to be there too! But don't worry—we will be fine. And, I have to keep thanking you because Giovanni's parents are so excited about this too. His mom wants to make some cakes to donate." She seemed so excited about it, that I wished I could change my tickets and somehow stay another week.

After Arianna left, I spent the night next to my nonna, needing comfort. She didn't ask me about how I was feeling or pry, instead we worked side-by-side making some provolone together. I made sure to watch everything she did so I could make it myself when I went back home. This was a part of me—and I didn't want to forget it.

"Nonna, I'm coming back for Christmas, but I need you to promise to listen to the lady that comes to help you. I love you so much." There were tears in both of our eyes as we said goodbye, hugging each other, and the car service was already waiting outside to bring me to the airport. "Please be careful with what you eat and take care of yourself." I continued. "And make sure you take your medicine. Oh, and tell me when you are picking the olives—Arianna will come down and FaceTime me so I can see it." It was bothering me that I wouldn't be there to harvest all of the vegetables once they were ripe.

"Cristina, I've done it before—I can do this. Don't worry about me." A tear escaped her eye as she hugged me tighter. "And, this comes off in a few days." She lifted up her cast and a small smile came through on her face. I felt bad that I wouldn't be able to receive a hug from her with both of her arms.

I took my bags, headed towards the car, and waved bye to my nonna before ducking inside. I stared out the window and wanted to memorize the house, the lands surrounding it, the farm down the path, and the garden next to it.

The driver pulled out of the driveway and headed down the road past Alessandro's house. He was outside, a shovel in his hand, staring at the car, holding the top of the shovel's handle as the blade buried itself slightly in the ground. He looked away as the car went past and took the shovel back in his hands, moving dirt into the wheelbarrow. A part of me was screaming from the inside to stop the car, run to him, take his face in my hands and kiss him—but that was the same part of me that caused all of this. That same part that was used to having whatever I wanted and getting it any time I could. The part that was spoiled, thought I was better than a farm boy, and deserved more.

I took my phone in my hands, texted Josh I was on my way home, put it back in my bag and leaned into the seat, closing my eyes. It was too hard to watch the landscape as we drove to the airport, getting further from my freedom. I let out a sigh, felt my chest heave as tears threatened to fall again, and shut my eyes, hoping to sleep for the rest of the ride.

"Signora. Signora DeRosa? Siamo arrivati."

I quickly opened my eyes as the driver nudged me awake and realized we were already at Capodichino, the airport in Naples. I opened my phone and went to the email my mom sent me and saw that it was only a direct flight, straight to JFK.

After nine hours on the flight, the back wheels of the plane bounced a few times on the tarmac before it lowered the front down, slowing down to turn into the gates. I looked out the window and saw skyscrapers lining the horizon making me feel like a stranger in my own home.

We all stood up as soon as the seatbelt light turned off, and I went to grab my handbag. Josh had said he wasn't able to take off to pick me up, but he would see me tonight, at my apartment. I hadn't really talked to him much this past week, but I knew I would have to tell him what happened with Alessandro. I was prepared that he would want to break up with me, and I couldn't blame him. But I also knew that if he didn't, I couldn't stay engaged to him.

The crowd moved together slowly towards customs, following an invisible tether that brought us exactly to the right lines, waiting to be called. I saw families with kids waiting in line, couples holding hands, and some stealing kisses. I was in limbo, between a place that was home the past month and a half and a place that had been my home since I was born.

"Cristina!" I heard two identical shouts as I passed the sliding doors after getting my luggage. I looked over and spotted Samantha and Stella, their tight curls bouncing up and down with them as they shouted my name. My heart welled up as I took in their faces. I missed their sass, their indifference at times. Hearing them shouting my name and seeing them smiling made me want to squeeze them tight. My mom was right behind them, her lips pressed into a tight smile, but her eyes warm and glimmering in the corner of them. I went over to them, hugged them all tight as a few tears fell down.

"You look beautiful. That air must have been good for you there." My mom said, after kissing me on my head and letting me go. "Come on, let's go. Michael is getting off early and should be home by now."

We headed outside, the stifling, muggy New York City air entered my lungs, welcoming me back. I heard my phone ping with a message.

ARIANNA: **Are you home? I miss you!**

I looked at the time and noticed it was 6:15 pm which meant it was past midnight in Italy.

CRISTINA: **Almost. It is definitely not the same being back home. I promise I'll visit for Christmas.**

I didn't tell anyone yet what my plans were, but I knew I had to go back. It didn't matter what happened with Alessandro, I was sure that with time he would maybe become my friend again, or at least not hate me as much as he did now. I didn't want to wait as long as I did last time before returning.

We made it back to my mom and Michael's apartment, Stella and Samantha ran inside to their rooms, leaving me there with Michael and my mom.

"We are really proud of you, Cristina." Michael said, taking me in for a hug. "Your nonna couldn't stop talking about all of the amazing things you did with the farm and garden and how much you helped her. Here, sit down. I couldn't wait to show you this."

I wasn't saying much to them, mostly since I was still on Italian time, already used to being in bed by now, but also because I wasn't sure of anything anymore. I felt like I didn't belong anywhere. Maybe when I went back to my apartment I would feel more like myself.

I sat down around the table next to my mom and Michael was across from us

"So, we wanted to do a lot for you, Cristina. You deserve this and more. You really proved yourself while you were there." He got up, grabbed a folder, and went back to the table. I could see him glancing at my mom, a wordless conversation floating between. "We got you new credit cards, to replace the old ones, and I paid off your lease for the apartment for the next year." He opened the folder and handed it to me. "We wanted to help you start on the right foot when you start working again. You are welcome back anytime you want—I know you probably need a week to settle in, celebrate with Josh, but after that, I'd love to have you work at my company again."

I could see a sort of pride in the way he handed the folder over and looked at me. It was a different Michael from the one I left at the airport before the trip. I didn't want to let him down again—but had I actually changed for the better? Josh was probably about to break up with me, there would be no engagement, Alessandro couldn't stand me. Did I deserve what Michael was giving me? Did I even want it?

I got up and thanked him, giving him another hug, and walked over to do the same to my mom. I still felt uncomfortable about relying on his money but knew that for now there was nothing else I could do. I didn't have any of my own money saved. His name was on my apartment lease, my car lease, and now even on my credit cards.

My phone started ringing, and I looked down to see Josh FaceTiming me. I wasn't ready to face him, but I willed my finger to press the green button.

"Hey babe. How was the plane? You're at your mom's?"

"Yeah, I just got here. It was good. I'm really tired though and jet lagged."

"Well, hopefully not too tired enough to go out. I'm on my way to pick you up. Be outside in five minutes."

I hung up and felt dread come over me. I didn't want to go out. I wanted to go back to my apartment, curl in bed, and be by myself.

A car pulled up in front of the building and Josh rolled down the window from the backseat.

"Hop on in, babe," he said. I walked to the other side and slid in next to him.

He told the driver directions and then looked over at me.

"You're finally home." He leaned over and kissed me firmly on my lips, but I pulled away after a few seconds. He must have sensed something was different from the look on his face, but didn't question me, instead he took my hand in his, and interlocked our fingers together.

"I reserved a place near here to go out. I was thinking that you could stop by my apartment after."

"I'm sorry Josh, maybe I could just go back to my apartment? I didn't even shower yet and I don't know how much longer I will be up for. Right now, I just want to sleep." A muscle in his jaw twitched, but he nodded his head, letting go of my hand and grabbing his phone. I didn't mean for it to come out the way it did, but being here with him, knowing what I needed to tell him, I couldn't relax.

We reached the restaurant ten minutes later, driving through the congested Manhattan streets—something I hadn't missed. I hadn't realized this was not normal, that this wasn't something that I even wanted to accept. I missed the soft greens and yellows, not the harsh grays and silvers I saw here.

We were quiet most of the way there, and as we got out of the car and walked towards the restaurant. He reached out to hold my hand, and I took his, feeling bad that I wasn't happier to be here with him. He didn't deserve this, and I didn't think I had the heart to even tell him about Alessandro tonight. It would be too much for me to even take, I just needed one more day. I decided to try and enjoy one more night together, before I lit a match on our relationship.

"This is known for being the best Italian restaurant in this area. I figured since you just came back and probably still miss being there, it might make you feel better." He said, squeezing my hand. I looked over to him, my lips turning upwards into a smile and silently thanking him with my eyes.

We sat down at a table far from the door and I saw him take the ring box out of his jacket. "You can put this back on again, Cristina. I got it insured and everything." He opened the box, took the ring out, and placed it on my finger for the second time, making my stomach twist into a knot.

I stretched my fingers apart, looking at the ring, and for some reason it didn't stand out as much as it had in Italy. Here it almost felt like it fit in—almost as if this is where it should've been all along. Of course I knew I would have to give it back, but not tonight.

"So your fiancé here is quite the big guy on campus." He said, taking a sip of the red wine the waiter had poured.

"That's great! I really am proud of you!" I tried to sound as supportive as much as I could, but at the same time stifled a yawn. I went to take a sip of wine but as soon as the wine touched my tongue, it felt wrong. I missed the wine that Alessandro made or the one that we had in Italy from other people from the town. I forced myself to take another sip.

"Oh, and our parents are organizing something for us on Saturday. We are going to have it at my parents' house in Connecticut. I think your mom already sent the invites out and it's all pretty much planned."

I took a bigger sip of wine, then placed the glass down, forcing myself to smile. "That's so nice. I feel bad that I didn't help."

"You know our moms live for these things." He said, giving me a wink. I took a deep breath in, praying that filling my lungs with oxygen would help me clear my mind.

He continued talking about his residency, what surgeries he was performing, and how he was convinced that he would get the fellowship. "It's almost as if Dr. Lettino is dying to tell me- but can't." He said, biting into the ossobuco he ordered.

I nodded and listened as I twirled my spaghetti on my fork.

The waiter came by with dessert, but I looked at Josh pleadingly that I needed to get home. He agreed, called a car, and then we walked outside still holding hands.

"I know you're exhausted. Do you want to get together tomorrow?" He said, his hand still holding mine.

"That would be great. I'm sorry—I just need to rest first."

He nodded his head and kissed me gently on my lips as soon as the car pulled up. "You take this car, I'll call another one."

"Thank you."

"Goodnight."

"Goodnight, Josh." I sat in the backseat of my car, told the driver the address, and watched as the city whirled past my window.

My apartment was exactly how I left it, but even cleaner. My mom had texted me while I was at dinner that she would have Maria drop off the luggage and dust before I got home. I was so used to cleaning this past month that I felt guilty that Maria did it for me. I took off my shoes, happy to be barefoot, and got undressed as quickly as I could and walked into the shower.

Thoughts churned in my head of what tomorrow would look as I laid in bed and what I would say to Josh. My stomach twisted when I realized that I hadn't talked to Laila in a few weeks either, and wondered if we would just go back to what we were like before. Then an image of my dad came into my head and I knew I needed to go see him. I owed that to him.

I woke up expecting to hear the birds chirping through the window and the smell of espresso seeping into my room, but then remembered where I was. It was only 4:30 in the morning, still dark outside, but I couldn't go back to sleep.

I got up with more energy than I would've expected and went to make an espresso, but suddenly remembered I didn't have anything for it.

I opened Amazon, typed in "Italian espresso maker", and ordered the one that looked almost identical to the one my nonna had. I walked to the cupboards, looking for something to eat since my stomach was really grumbling, but only found some Paleo-friendly bars that were a few months old. I grudgingly opened the wrapper, took a bite, and made another note to stop by the store later and pick up a different type of breakfast.

I spent the next hour unpacking my luggage, putting some clothes away and making sure to wash others. I felt weird in my apartment, alone, with views of glass and brick surrounding me. I took a seat on the couch and decided to call my nonna.

"*Ciao*, Cristina! *Come stai?*" She was so excited to hear from me.

"*Ciao*, Nonna! I'm a little sad, but okay. Did the new lady come to help you?"

"Yes, but she doesn't know what she is doing! It is a waste of money!"

"Nonna, please be patient with her. Remember how I was when I first came? She can really help you. How's your stomach? Are you following the diet?"

"*Sì! Mamma mia, non ti preoccupare!*" She laughed after telling me not to worry. We continued chatting about the garden and farm, and she laughed telling me that the baby lamb almost escaped again, but she caught it on time. When we hung up, my heart still hurt, and I knew it would take a while before I could feel okay again. I just hoped it wouldn't take so long.

Around 10 am, I decided to text Laila, asking to meet up at our usual cafe for something to eat. I needed to clear the air between us and get things back on track. I was still surprised though when she texted ten minutes later, saying she would meet me.

"So, not gluten-free? Are you sure?" Laila asked, watching me take a bite into the croissant. I laughed a little and made sure I enjoyed it while she picked at her gluten-free one. I made a new vow to enjoy all of the food I ate in the way it tasted best. I wouldn't overdo it, but I wouldn't feel ashamed either for eating what I wanted.

"So, what'd I miss? I saw you having fun at your house in the Hamptons a lot." I said, taking a sip of the cappuccino I ordered.

"Yeah, it was okay. Josh was there almost every weekend and I practically had to kick him out." She took a sip of her drink and I flinched back, remembering that Josh said he hadn't gone that much.

"Oh, that's funny." I said, trying to normalize my voice the best I could. Why did he feel the need to lie to me? It's not like I would've been mad, but he made it seem like he didn't want to go. I brushed those thoughts aside and took another bite of my croissant. "So, is there a new guy? Or is it still Pablo? Or is Jeff coming back in the picture?"

She choked a little on her drink, before answering. "Oh no, Pablo is out of the picture. I haven't really been seeing anyone. You know me—I will never be serious."

We talked a little more and I realized she avoided saying Irene's name in front of me, even though I knew she'd been spending time with her. I wanted to tell her I talked to Blake, but something stopped me.

"Wait, I need to see the ring!" I had put it back on before I got here, not wanting to create more drama by not wearing it in case she asked. She took my hand in hers, twisted my hand slightly sideways making the stone catch and reflect the light, and nodded her head before saying anything. "This is gorgeous. Josh knows a good diamond." There was a slight sadness in her eyes that I couldn't quite place, making me question if she really did want to settle down.

We gave each other quick hugs goodbye and I spent the next hour walking around Central Park, enjoying as much green as I could before I went back home.

JOSH: **Hey babe—back to back surgery until tonight. Can we see each other tomorrow? I'm so sorry—good thing we have our whole lives to be together so there is no rush.**

I felt relieved. I still needed another day to think about what I would say. I decided to head back to my mom and Michael's apartment and spend some time with her and the girls.

"Stella—make sure you finish your art project—you need to hand it in tomorrow!" My mom yelled out, but I was sure Stella didn't hear anything. "These summer enrichment classes are more work for me than her lately." She said jokingly, pouring some hot water into her teacup.

"Do they like the classes?"

"They don't like anything except playing on their iPad and talking to their friends or making stupid dance videos." She said, laughing into her cup. "So, how is Nonna *really* doing?"

The question caught me by surprise. She was insistent that Nonna was fine while I was there. "I don't know, Mom. I mean, I am worried about her doing too much. She couldn't even get out of bed some days how badly her stomach hurt."

She nodded her head before taking a sip from her cup and then placing it back down. "I never understood her. I know she thinks I'm weak and that I'm a princess or something."

My eyebrows shot up since those were exactly the words she had used, *a princess* while I was there. "I know she thinks it was my fault that things ended with dad. But we were two different people. I really don't think we were ever in love. Everyone expected me to marry him because our families came from nearby towns and knew each other and he spoke Italian. But we both wanted different things. He wanted to settle and didn't really care about going ahead in life. It was like he was stuck in a place he didn't want to get out of. I wanted to see the world, go out with him, do different things— but he hated it. He would rather stay home and watch TV. I knew we wouldn't work out, and so did he. But we tried to stay together until I realized I wasn't living life."

All of these years and my mom had never revealed this much to me. She shook her head, took another sip, before she spoke again. "Anyway, it doesn't matter anymore. We have you, and that made our relationship together worth it in the end. And now that I'm with Michael, I feel *alive.* I know you might think I married him for money, but when I first met him, I had no idea how much money he had. We were both at a bar, waiting for our dates to show up, and when they didn't, we laughed about it and just connected. For a few months, we would just meet up at cafes and restaurants, just talking about our life plans and what we wanted to do. He was humble, gentle, but strong at the same time—I don't even know how to explain it. He wanted to do the same things as me and when he first kissed me—there was a connection that I could not explain—like I knew he was the absolute one."

I thought I should have felt sad that she was talking about someone that wasn't my dad in that way, but I didn't. I understood how she felt, because I felt that way with Alessandro. Those kisses we shared were indescribable. They made me feel emotions that I'd never felt with Josh but didn't want to admit. I was about to tell my mom I understood and explain to her how I had felt this month, before she interrupted me.

"I know Nonna didn't approve of Michael at first because he wasn't Italian, almost as if she thought I would lose everything Italian about me. She had always been like that though. Always making sure that I spoke Italian to her, used my Italian name, and ate Italian food. She pushed it so much that I think I started hating it. I didn't want to even hear my name in Italian anymore." I had never seen her this vulnerable. It made me want to confide in her too.

"But, in the end, Cristina, you are lucky. You have Josh and he adores you. I was talking to his mom before about Saturday and they kept saying how lucky we all are that you both have each other." My shoulders slumped and a hard knot appeared in my throat. I had wanted to tell her everything that happened in Italy, from Alessandro to Josh, but after she mentioned how I was lucky with him, I was afraid she wouldn't understand.

"Yes, I am." I said meekly, upset with myself that I wasn't letting her know the truth. She continued on about the engagement party, what Josh's mom had planned to serve and who was invited. I tried to listen but kept thinking of how the conversation with Josh would go when we talked tomorrow. My mom was so happy now, describing all of the different cookies they were getting for dessert and how they would place them on tiered serving dishes in the middle of the tables. I nodded my head, agreeing with everything she was saying, and kept thinking about what I needed to do.

I needed to see my dad. I didn't want him to feel left out of my life anymore. It's not fair for him. After a few more minutes of listening to my mom go on about centerpieces, I quickly excused myself to the bathroom so I could call my dad without my mom hearing.

"Hey, how are you, beautiful?" My dad said, as soon as he picked up. "How was the flight?"

"It was good. I missed you though. I was wondering, are you free tomorrow? Can I come out and see you?"

"Oh...um...yeah, sure!" I could tell he wasn't expecting me to ask him, but he was pleasantly surprised. "I'll be home from work after 2pm—is that okay?"

"That's perfect! I'll see you tomorrow." I knew I needed to do something else too, and the fact that I now had time, made it all work out.

CRISTINA: **Blake—are you free tomorrow around 11? I would love to get together!**

Less than 5 seconds later, she texted back.

BLAKE: **Yes!!!! I moved in with Matt, did you want to come out and visit us? I would looove it if you did!**

CRISTINA: **That would be perfect! Text me the info and I will see you tomorrow!**

The next morning, I took my car out of the parking garage and felt strange sitting on the leather seats. After more than a month away from it, it suddenly seemed massive and much too showy. Did I really need a car this big? What family did I have to drive around in it? Where was I going to need a car like this? I pressed the button to start the ignition and my left foot went looking for the clutch before I remembered it was an automatic car.

"Come on, Cristina. Get a grip. It's just a car." I told myself out loud, not allowing any other sad thoughts overtake me. I had time before I would meet Josh and tell him everything, and I wanted this time with Blake and my dad to be without any other negative thoughts.

I looked at the cityscape in the rearview mirror as I exited out of the tunnel, heading on to the 495, and felt a sense of relief. Even though the traffic was horrendous, the idea of going towards more greenery and smaller buildings made me feel like I could breathe again.

About a half hour later, I followed the directions on GPS and pulled into a driveway in front of a Cape Cod red-bricked house with dormer windows sticking out of a gray-shingled roof. There was a little patch of grass in the front, a hedge along the front of the house, with some yellow lilies blooming in front of it. I felt comfortable in front of this house, like I wanted to go inside, make dinner, and invite friends over. I could see why Blake was so happy here.

"Look at you, Cristina! You look so good!" Blake ran out of the house, a Golden Retriever following her right behind. She took me in a hug and held tight, swaying slightly saying she was so happy to see me. It felt good to see her again. I'd barely gotten a hug from Laila when I saw her yesterday, but here Blake was squeezing the breath out of me.

"So, you moved in?" I asked after she had finally let me go. "What is it like?"

"I love it. I know it's a small house and Laila is probably rolling her eyes at me that I made this move, but I honestly don't care—I am really happy with him. Plus, I work from home, so it's nice to at least have a yard where I can sit outside and get some sun."

I could see she was genuinely happy from the way she moved to the way she spoke. Everything seemed alive about her, and it made me jealous. I remembered how I would skip to Alessandro's house or to the farm to tend to the animals.

She took me inside, explained that Matt was working at a restaurant in the city and wouldn't be back until later that night. "We need to plan another time where we are all together." She exclaimed, sitting on the couch and the dog jumping on her lap. This was a completely different Blake I was used to seeing but I realized this was probably who she had been trying to be all along. She never was one to follow what the trendiest clothes were or what parties to attend. She had always known what she liked and wanted, and never strayed far from that. I had never even noticed it—instead I almost pitied her at one time, thinking she was the lost one. Here she was, the only one of us that had everything figured out and I was jealous, but happy for her.

"So, tell me all about Italy! I'm sure the food was *amazing*." The dog's head lifted up as she was talking, and she scratched its ear.

"I *actually* miss it. It was hard to come back home, which was not something I was expecting at all. I know I was only there for a little over a month so I shouldn't really feel different, but..." I trailed my words, not wanting to get choked up. Blake suddenly shifted her position on the couch, causing her dog to jump off her lap as she leaned forward towards me.

"Cristina—I know that look on your face. What happened? Who is he?" Her face lit up as she asked me, and it made me panic that it was that obvious. Was it obvious then to Josh?

"No, he was no one. I mean, obviously no one since I am engaged..."

"That's right! I saw the post! And you said yes?" Her face scrunched up.

"I did, but..." I wanted to tell her everything. We were best friends at one point and it killed me that I couldn't tell anyone else how I felt. I knew I needed to at least tell her. "I don't know Blake. I don't know if I should marry Josh. On paper, everything seems perfect between us, but I don't know if I am ready."

She looked at me for a few seconds, before leaning back into the couch and responding. "Cris—I'd never tell you what to do or how to live your life, but I think if you genuinely listened to what your heart was telling you, I wouldn't have to." I thought about it for a moment. Trying to unravel what she meant. I felt the words of a friend who knew me long enough to use my nickname. It was as if we were back to our high school selves, when dating advice was much simpler and we did what felt right. I found myself back in Michael's apartment, Blake sitting next to me on the couch watching *Mean Girls* after I got bullied for my Walmart shoes.

"Blake, I *did* meet someone in Italy. I felt happy, alive—kind of how you look now when I see you." A small smile grew on her face and she nodded her head, waving her hand for me to continue. "With Josh, well, I don't feel like myself. I think that it's who everyone expects me to be with. I didn't even want to say yes when he proposed." Tears welled up in the corners of my eyes, but I didn't try to wipe them away. "I haven't told him yet. Our mothers have a party planned for us on Saturday..." I tried to stay articulate and cover all my points, but it was hard with my feelings welling up inside of me. Blake uncrossed her legs and scooched to the end of the couch, extending her arms for me to hug her.

"Cris, I know you think you need to feel guilty, but in reality, it's Josh who doesn't deserve *you*. I knew it from the first day I met you. You have such a good heart, but I don't think you ever fully trusted it. I never wanted to tell you anything, because, well, I thought your heart chose him and you were in love."

I thought about her words and compared how I felt with Alessandro to how I felt with Josh. I felt slightly clearer—as if my brain was finally admitting what my heart was telling me—that it wasn't love. It was convenience, expectations, not love.

"Tell me about the *Italian*."

I told her all about Alessandro, about how we met when I was eight and how every time I visited my Nonna we'd spend the whole summer together. I told her how he was my first kiss and how we hung out together again when I went back at 15 years old, but then stopped seeing him after Laila texted me not to date him.

"Ugghhh...and you listened to her? Cris—you know how she is. I'm sorry, I know you're friends with her, but I am happy I'm not talking to her anymore. Remember Keira, my friend from college that hung out with us a few times? Well, turns out Laila hooked up with her boyfriend—while they were still dating! She is the last person you should listen to."

My mouth dropped. I knew she wasn't the type to be serious with anyone, but I didn't think she would do that. Blake saw my expression change but waved on for me to continue.

I told her about how he hated me at first, but how we got close, our driving lessons, how he taught me how to cook, then about Arianna, and all of the feasts. I told her about our kiss, and then Blake jumped up on the couch, excited for me, but her expression changed when I told her about Josh surprising me. I finally told her about the day at the beach, what happened that night, and when I finished, I let out a huge breath venting all of the tension and stress out of my body like a balloon.

"Cris—I don't even know what to say. That sounds like a love story."

"I know, I know, but Blake, he lives across an *Ocean*-—on the *literal* other side of the world! I'm pretty sure it's love, but what do I do now? He hates me—I could see it in his eyes that he truly hates me after what I've done to him. I'm breaking up with Josh tonight, no matter what, but I need this time to be alone. Figure out what I really want."

She leaned over and gave me another hug. In my ear she whispered ever so faintly, "I think you know what you want." She excused herself for a moment to grab something for us to eat.

"I'm sorry it's just a sandwich and salad. If Matt were here, I would have had him make you paella— it's amazing!" She said, handing me a plate, and setting the food down on the table. We chatted for another hour, catching up on everything that's happened in the past year.

"Blake—I am sorry I haven't kept in touch with you and..."

"Don't say anything Cris. Listen, I know how Laila is, and I know how you are. You will always be my friend, and I will always be here for you."

I closed my eyes and silently thanked her. I was so lucky to have two friends in my life that forgave me when I wasn't my best self and believed in my character. A weight had fallen off my shoulders—I was ready to face Josh tonight.

I headed back on the 495, driving further out east, reaching Suffolk County, to see my dad. I stopped in front of a small ranch and pulled into the driveway, narrowly avoiding the empty garbage can. The houses on the block all looked like they had the same architect and builder, the variety was the colors of the siding to give some personality to each house.

I took a moment to take in my dad's house. In all of this time I had never even come out here to see it. Shame built up inside of me as I began to realize how I had treated him, and how he had never made me feel guilty of it.

I looked for the doorbell and ended up just knocking on the door, loud enough so he would hear.

The door slowly opened to reveal my dad, a stocky but fit man in his 50s, wearing a faded red T-shirt and tan cargo shorts. "Wow! Cristina, you look beautiful! It's good to see you. Look at what a month in Italy does to you!" He exclaimed, swooping in for a big hug. I hugged him back, wanting to say more than just hello with that hug. I wanted to tell him I was sorry for how I had treated him.

"It's good to see you too, Dad." He ushered me inside to the den, took off a newspaper that was on the couch and motioned me to sit down.

"Lisa, come here! Cristina's here!" He shouted over his shoulder but turned to me still with a smile splayed across his face. "You're going to love this place. It's only five minutes from the bay and lots of times we just go out at night, walking along the beach, and enjoying the view." Lisa had just come in with beverages on a tray and nodded her head while setting it down in front of us.

"So good to see you!" She said, her blonde hair moving in front of her shoulder as she leaned in to give me a hug. I'd met her a few times and she had always been shy, but nice—never really adding more to the conversation other than if she was directly asked. "Your dad has been telling me about your trip to Italy, it sounds exciting! I keep telling him I want to go." She said, her head gesturing quickly to my dad.

"Yeah, I loved it. It was hard at first, but I learned so much about farming and taking care of the garden. I kind of feel lost right now—I miss it."

"That sounds wonderful." She said, handing me a glass of lemonade. I looked over at my dad who had a gleam in his eye as he looked at me. We continued talking about what it was like in Italy, and I asked about what they liked to do together and any vacations they had planned. Lisa continued to joke to my dad that she wanted to visit Italy and my dad let out a laugh and promised it would happen soon.

We went outside and decided to walk along the beach, while Lisa said she was going to stay back and prepare something for us to eat.

"Cristina, is everything okay? The last time we talked in Italy I remember you weren't sure about some things. Do you want to talk?"

"Actually, I do, Dad. I'm breaking up with Josh tonight. I don't think I'm really in love with him."

He let out a sigh of relief, picked up a shell from the sand, and handed it to me—reminding me of our times at the beach when I was little and he would always find the most beautiful seashells for me. "I think you are doing the right thing."

"Why do you say that?" I asked.

"You are a good person, Cristina. You aren't like some of those people you hang out with that are so full of themselves and their money. I always liked that one girl, Blake—but the others, not so much." He picked up another shell and handed it over to me. "And, whenever he was with you—he never looked at you like you were his world. He wanted to be the world for you and for everyone else. And you made him feel like that—but did he ever make you feel special?"

That's exactly what I didn't feel with him. It was always about him—about his surgeries, his position, where he likes to eat—and I just followed along, as if I were just a spectator in his life.

"You're right, Dad. I never even thought about it that way, but I started to realize something was different, especially after being near Alessandro."

"Alessandro? The boy that lives next door to Nonna?"

"Yeah, but he isn't really a boy anymore, Dad." I said, letting out a laugh. "We spent a lot of time together this past month. He taught me how to cook different meals, drive a manual car, and he made me feel like a better person."

His eyebrows raised up and his eyes slightly widened. "Your

nonna told me his family helped them out a lot when she moved back. He seemed like a really nice boy when you were younger." His phone pinged with a message and he stopped walking to take out his glasses and read it. "Lisa just texted and said to start heading back. Oh, and just pretend you like whatever she makes. I know it's nothing like what your nonna makes, but she's trying." He said, a small smile forming on his face.

"Dad, I never asked you—but are you happy with her? I know we are talking about me and what I'm feeling, but I worry for you too."

"I love her. She makes me happy. But I loved your mom too—you know that, right? It was just different with her. Our parents sort of pushed us together, saying we would make the perfect couple since we were both from the same part of Italy. We were in love at first, but we both knew there was something missing, something we couldn't fix. I don't regret a single moment of anything because I have you. Now, with Lisa, well she makes me want to come home from work, not hang out with the guys, drinking a beer at the bar. I just want to come home to her, watch a movie together, go for a walk on the beach, or just sit outside on the bench next to each other. I guess that's as good as it'll get for me." He added, letting out a chuckle.

We reached the house and Lisa greeted us at the door, ushering us to come inside quickly before the food got cold.

"I hope you like it. I got the recipe off of Food Network. It's chicken scampi pasta." We sat down at the table, and she scooped some spaghetti into a bowl for us. I thanked her graciously and twirled a forkful with a piece of chicken and bit into it.

"Lisa, this is delicious. You'll need to send me the recipe!" I exclaimed, after swallowing a bite, savoring the hint of lemon in the dish.

"Oh, really? Thanks! I...umm...don't have your number, but I can have your dad send it."

"Wait, just give me yours and I will text you so you have mine."

"Great!" I could hear the happiness in her voice as she told me her number and I felt my dad smiling at me while I was programming her contact information in my phone. We then continued chatting until dinner was over. It was a little past five and I had to head back to see Josh.

"I promise I'll come out and visit more." I said to my dad as I gave him a hug.

"And I'll keep reminding you how proud I am of you." He said back, giving me a kiss on my forehead.

"Thanks Lisa for the delicious meal. Anytime you find a good recipe, send it my way. I'll do the same with you." She took me in for a strong hug, and I saw the corner of her eyes a little damp.

"Thanks, Cristina. It was so good seeing you." She said as she stepped back. I headed towards my car and waved at them one last time before I pulled out of their driveway and headed back home.

I pressed the call button on my steering wheel to connect to Josh.

"Hey, babe." He quickly answered after the first ring. "I was going to call you to make sure we were still good for tonight."

For some reason now, the fact that he kept calling me *babe* bothered me. I had never paid that much attention to it, thinking it was just a cute nickname he gave me, but now it just didn't fit me.

"Hey. Yeah, we are. Is it okay if we stop by your place? I don't feel like going out anywhere really."

"Yeah, that's fine. We can order food if you want."

"No, I ate by my dad's place. We can just stay together and talk."

"Your dad's place? Since when do you go visit him? Did he even have room for you?"

I clenched my jaw and gripped the steering wheel tight before I responded. I wanted to yell at him for saying that.

"There was room. And I promised him I would visit more often. I'm driving home now—I can stop directly at your apartment in about an hour."

"Yeah, that's fine. I'll see you then."

I spent the hour thinking about all of the time we had spent together and it made my blood boil even more. I thought about how he knew I didn't like fancy food but took me to those restaurants anyway. He never made me feel important at any job I had but always had to mention how much he was doing at his. Even when I tried to show him my garden that I had taken care of, he basically laughed at me. I was done—officially done not being an equal in his life. I wanted more—and I was going to get it.

I pulled into the parking garage closest to his apartment and played with the ring box in my bag. I hadn't worn the ring the whole day. I walked determinedly to his apartment building, took the elevator to his floor, and walked through the sandy-colored hallway straight to his door. My nerves were catching up to the rest of my body and I could see my hands shake as I knocked on his door. I took a deep breath and reminded myself I was doing the right thing and I was strong enough to face my feelings.

"Hey" He said, pulling the door open enough to let me in. He wrapped his arms around me, but I gently pressed my hands against his chest. His eyes narrowed as he took a step back and looked at me with tight lips. "What's wrong?"

"Josh, we need to talk. Can we sit?" I needed more space and I wanted to make sure I said everything I had been thinking.

"Yeah, but Cristina, what's wrong? Wait, sit here." He said, moving a pillow from the heather-gray loveseat that was in the middle of the living room. I took a seat and he sat next to me, our bodies shifted towards each other, one of my legs resting higher on the couch. Although I had been in his apartment many times before, this time the blaring white walls and the minimalist design created an uncomfortable feeling in my stomach. I leaned over to get the ring box out of my bag and handed it to him. He looked at me confused and didn't say anything until he opened it up and saw the ring was there.

"I need to tell you something. Well, a lot of things. But first—I don't think we should be engaged anymore."

"Wait, you're breaking up with me?"

"Yes, I don't think we are right for each other..."

The stark look of confusion drained the color from his face. "What happened, Cristina? What changed you?"

"I don't know. All I know is that I left this island and *found* myself in Italy. It's not something I know how to explain."

He shot up from the couch and flinched back. "You slept with him. That guy, Alessandro, right? I knew it." He said tightly as his nose slightly twitched. He then turned his body away from me and placed both of his hands on his hips as he stared up to the ceiling. I could see his shoulders rising and falling from his deep breaths as he was probably thinking of what to say next. I had gone through different scenarios in my head of what would happen and what I would say, but at that moment my mind went blank. I didn't know how to respond.

I decided to stand up, hoping this position would help me explain to him how I felt. "I know it was a mistake and I am sorry. It shouldn't have happened. I didn't want to hurt you..."

He twisted his head around to the side and I caught what I thought was a fleeting smirk on his face. "No. It's fine. Don't worry —because you weren't the only one having fun." He fully faced me.

His expression changed and there was something I could not quite place in his eyes.

"I'm sorry, I don't know what happened." I continued but stopped when I realized what he had just said. "Wait—what do you mean by that?"

His eyes had a cold and calculated look as he continued to talk, and a small shiver traveled up my body. "You know what I mean. You weren't the only one sleeping with other people."

"People?"

"Well, how do I know? But tell your friend Laila that I will meet her again tonight. She can't seem to keep her hands off of me."

"What?" I prayed I didn't hear him correctly. The room started spinning and there was a ringing in my ears that kept getting louder. I wanted to run out of the room, but I needed to face him and hear what he had to say.

"That day you almost caught us when you FaceTimed me—that was her bag, she was over. You thought you were the only one, didn't you? No, Cristina. You weren't."

My throat was closing up. Laila? She was with him all of this time? My fists closed and my nails dug into my palm. Why was Josh smirking like this? Was he happy to let me know?

"How long has this been going on?"

"Well, let's see, Cristina. Way longer than you and Alessandro have been having your fun in Italy." I had never seen him like this before. It was as if he had been putting on a show the whole time we were together and now I was seeing the real Josh.

"Why? I didn't *want* to hurt you. Why didn't you just break up with me?" I could barely get the words out. My stomach twisted and everything I had eaten threatened to come up.

"I don't know. Maybe because I thought we were good together. Maybe because I did see us together in a house, with kids."

"But why would you cheat on me, then?"

His eyes drifted down and he no longer had the odd expression from before. Now he just looked defeated. He sat back down and rubbed his eyes with his palms and stood there a few seconds more before responding.

"I don't know. I felt like there was something missing and I can't explain it. I don't know if it's the stress from work or maybe I liked the idea of us together, but maybe we weren't right in the end."

"You should've told me! When were you planning on telling me? After we were married?" My voice started rising after I realized that he may have never told me if I hadn't gone this summer. If he was telling me that they were hooking up before I had left for Italy, then that means if I had never gone, they would've still kept seeing each other. I covered my mouth with my hand and took a deep breath through my nose, forcing myself not to get sick as I felt the bile rise. Out of all of the scenarios that had run through my head, I never pictured this one.

He leaned forward on the couch, his palms now resting against his forehead, and he kept shaking his head. I didn't know what else to say to him. I needed to get fresh air and process everything that happened, but I still needed to finish talking to him. We had spent two years together and I wasn't going to leave until I felt resolved.

"It doesn't matter anymore. We weren't right for each other and we are lucky we figured it out before it was too late. I'm sorry for what I did to you. I never meant to hurt you, but you were right. We both were trying to fill something that was missing. I don't want it to end badly and look back at this time with just hatred. I don't have the energy to do that. I just want you to find what it is you really want and I know I'm going to do the same."

He lifted his head up from his palms and looked at me, his eyes jumping between mine. He opened his mouth to speak, hesitated, and then opened it again.

"I'm sorry."

"So am I, Josh."

I picked up my bag and walked past him, finally feeling a sense of closure. I wanted to get out of that apartment now that we were officially done. I was with all of the wrong people this whole time.

As I exited his building, I walked outside to a sky filled with orange hues from the sun that just dropped below the horizon. I looked at the street, the cars' horns blaring, the bikes swerving between them, when all of a sudden it hit me.

I walked towards the garage and waited for the attendant to pull up my car. Excitement started building up inside of me after I knew exactly what I needed to do. My phone vibrated with a message and I looked down to read the text.

LAILA: **Josh told me he told you.**

CRISTINA: **Yep. It's fine. You can have him!**

A huge smile splayed across my face as my car pulled up. I jumped in, put it in drive, and headed back to my apartment, my fingers now drumming on the steering wheel. I turned the volume up and sang along to the radio and felt like for the first time, I knew the path I was meant to follow.

21

Ventuno

superare - to overcome

I tapped my foot nervously, waiting for the announcement of my flight. I had checked my phone five times in the past two minutes, making sure that the time didn't miraculously change and I wouldn't be late.

I can do this. My nerves are making me pat my hand against my jeans. I couldn't sit still. Just 24 hours before I had broken up with Josh and now I was at JFK with a ticket back to Naples. My mom had said she wasn't going to speak to me if I went, saying I was making a big mistake—but it didn't matter. In time, I was sure she was going to understand, just like how she had felt when she was younger married to my dad. Speaking of my dad, he had given me his blessings when I told him, and said I was doing the right thing since it made me happy. I kept watching the flight attendants behind the desk and silently prayed that they would board us in the next few minutes. Somehow just being on that plane meant I would be closer to Italy, closer to where my heart felt full, and closer to where there were people that made me want to be a better version of myself. I didn't have anything planned, I knew I just needed to make it on time for the feast the next day.

Okay, I'll land in Munich at 12 pm, then wait three hours, take another flight at 3pm to Naples, get there by 5, drive to my nonna's house by 7 after I get my bags. That'll leave me time to get ready for the feast. I looked over the flight schedule and mapped out what I needed to do in order to get to the feast on time. This was the only flight that was available, and I wanted to make sure I got there by the next night so I wouldn't miss Arianna's fundraiser for Giovanni. I was meant to be there to help her and now I would.

"Lufthansa flight 411 with service to Munich now boarding section D." I grabbed my carry-on and headed to the gate after I heard the announcement. I stood in line, my ticket and passport flipped to the page where my picture was. I kept nervously fidgeting, silently pushing the passengers ahead in my mind so I could board the plane. Once I reached the attendant, I handed her my ticket and practically ran to my seat.

The gravel crunched under the wheels of the van as it pulled in front of my nonna's house. It was already past 8:30 pm, and I was glad to have made it after almost losing my luggage. I was ready to leave the airport without it when it miraculously showed up, alone, on the conveyor belt. The driver opened the door for me, helped me get out and then walked to the trunk to get my bags.

"Cristina?" My nonna cried out as soon as she stepped out of the front door and spotted me. I ran over to her, took her in a hug, and she hugged me back with both arms, now without a cast. Tears fell down as I pulled away from her and saw she had tears in her eyes too. "*Ma cosa fai qui?*" She asked, wanting to know what I was doing there.

"Nonna, I know what I want now. I knew it all along but was afraid to admit it. I was afraid of what others would think of me and I wasn't strong enough to realize what was right for me."

"I am proud of you, Cristina. Always follow your heart. I made that same mistake with your mother. Sometimes, we think we know what is good for our children—but they are the ones that end up teaching us some lessons too."

"Thank you. So, I need to run to the feast before it's too late but I'm going to wash up quickly first."

"Yes! Go! Do you want me to drive you?"

"No, Nonna. I am going to drive there. I need to." I smiled at her, hugged her again, and ran to the bathroom, trying to freshen up with a quick shower as fast as I could.

Twenty minutes later, a new outfit on, I was in the driver's seat, ready to drive. I saw my nonna do a quick sign of the cross and then wave to me as I turned on the ignition.

I can do this. I silently prayed too as I lifted my left foot off the clutch as my right foot shifted to the gas pedal. When the car didn't stop, I let out a gasp, quickly waved to my nonna, and headed to the road.

I had made it past the first hill without the car stopping, but I had forgotten to down-shift. I was approaching the second hill, but didn't down-shift enough and the car stalled before I reached the top of it.

"Oh no!" I said out loud to myself in the car. There were no houses around in this part of town and there would be no one to help me. Sweat beads broke onto my forehead and my hands became clammier. I pulled the emergency brake and tried to remember what Alessandro had taught me the last time it happened to me. "Okay, it's in first." I said out loud, trying to focus all of my nerves on making it over the hill. "If I pull down the emergency brake and switch to the gas, it might work." It gave me comfort to say the steps out loud, almost as if I had become Alessandro and I was now my own teacher.

I pushed the emergency brake down, shifted to the gas pedal, but the car stalled. One more time. I thought, taking a deep breath in and focusing all of my nerves and worrying into getting it right. I pushed the emergency brake down again, shifted faster to the gas, and let out a huge squeal as I made it over the hill.

"I did it!" I screamed in the car. I wiped my forehead with the back of my arm and concentrated on getting to the feast.

It was almost 9:20 when I got there, and I parked the car in the first spot I found, far from the feast. I hurried out, practically jogging to the piazza, hoping to find everyone still there. The smell of the sandwiches hit me first, reminding me of the other times I had gone with Arianna, and I absorbed the view around me as I reached the piazza. People were mingling, speaking in dialect, surrounding the stage, listening to a band singing some pop songs. There were more people there tonight than ever and I hoped that it was helping their fundraiser. I looked around the perimeter of the piazza, trying to spot Arianna, and saw her behind a stand with a big smile on her face as she was talking to some people. I jogged over and stood behind the people that were talking to her and waited to say hi.

"*Grazie!*" She said to them as they gave her a hug and walked away. She had turned her back to me, not noticing I was there, but when she turned back, she stared at me with her mouth slightly agape, and it looked like the blood was drawn from her face.

"Cristina!" She yelled, pulling my body against hers and hugging me tightly. "What are you doing here?"

"I couldn't stay there. Nothing was right when I went back home. This is my home, for now."

"Really? Wow—I thought I was happy with how well the fundraiser was going, but this is even better! I was so sad when you left, and I honestly thought I would never see you again!" She hugged me again, even tighter than before. "You won't believe how much we've made! And we practically sold out of everything the first hour."

"Arianna—have you seen Alessandro? I need to talk to him."

Her eyebrows drew down as she nodded her head slightly. "He was around here before, but I haven't seen him in the last half hour."

"I'll be right back. I'm going to find him." I gave her another hug and walked towards the stage, hoping to catch a glimpse of him. I stood on my tiptoes, looked around for him, but still couldn't find him. I walked towards the bar we were at last time, peered in, but didn't see him there either. Please don't tell me he already went back home. I really wanted to talk to him now and I couldn't wait another second. I went back out to the piazza, tried to walk to the other side, and checked around to see if I could find him. I felt somewhat defeated when I still hadn't found him, but then I thought there would be one last place to try. I made it to the top of the piazza, away from the crowds, and walked through the park, past some trees. I recognized the silhouette on the bench and felt the syncopations of my heart quicken.

I took a few steps closer and he turned around, quickly standing up after he saw it was me. His head pulled back in shock and we both didn't say anything as we looked at each other for a few moments.

"Cristina? What are you doing here?"

This was it. I had traveled across half of the world to let him know how I felt. I closed my eyes, filled my lungs with the crisp night air, and slowly let out my breath as I opened my eyes to meet his. "I left my heart here, Alessandro." I tried to read his eyes, but all I saw was more confusion crossing his face. I continued, hoping he would understand me fully. "I made a mistake."

"You told me already, Cristina. You came back to tell me again?" A flash of anger crossed his face, and I got mad at myself that I hadn't rehearsed any of this before.

"No, that wasn't a mistake. The only mistake I made was not listening to my heart all of this time. It was you all of this time, too. You were the only one who had ever made me feel alive. I knew it, but I was afraid to admit it. I hid behind expensive clothes, fake friends, and a cold boyfriend thinking that was what I really wanted. I was never happy. This view, the farm, the garden...you. You make me happy."

"But what about your fiancé?"

"I broke up with him. I couldn't be with him—I wasn't in love with him. He didn't know the real me—the one that loves tractor rides, going on adventures around the farm, or taking care of the garden. Plus, he never looked at me the way you do. I love you, Alessandro."

He took a deep breath, but hesitated. I closed my eyes, a tear dropping from under my lid, and prayed that he would answer me with something. I hadn't planned any of this at all, and I was afraid of what he would say at that moment. I didn't know if my heart could handle him rejecting me.

"You came back to just tell me this?"

"Yes, but I'm also planning to stay for a while. I wasn't finished here—I feel like I just started."

He nodded his head and took a few steps closer to me, his expression still unreadable.

"You really hurt me, Cristina." I felt the depth of his gaze boring into mine.

"I'm sorry." I whispered, hoping he would say more. I swallowed a knot in my throat and my breath became shallow. I wanted to hug him, apologize for what I had done, but he was right. I hurt him twice and I didn't know if he could forgive me.

He stepped closer, only a few feet away from me now, and I wanted to reach out to him, needing to feel him after all of this time apart.

"I don't know. My heart can only take so much. I'm sorry." He looked down and took a step back. I nodded my head. I understood how he felt, so I squeezed my eyes shut, hoping that the tears wouldn't cascade down. I didn't want this ending, but knew it was a possibility, and I would still have to live with it if it had come true—which it now did.

"You're right. I'm going to go and help Arianna." I said meekly, a slight break in my voice betraying the fact that I was on the verge of crying. I turned away, walked towards the trees, when I felt him grab my arm.

I turned around, he opened his mouth to say something, but quickly closed it and shook his head. He smiled, his eyes looking into mine, before he spoke.

"I'm not letting you go. I can't. Just promise me you won't break my heart again."

I tried to talk, but couldn't, so I just shook my head no, not breaking his stare.

"I thought I lost you forever and that hurt more than you breaking my heart. I hope you didn't just come back to me for the tractor rides though." He smiled down at me and pulled me closer to him.

That smile was everything for me. I would make sure I lived the rest of my life just trying to get that smile from him. He wrapped both of his arms around me, and I wrapped mine around his neck.

"So you love me?" He said, that smile growing even wider.

I laughed, dreaming that this would've happened, nodded my head and pulled his face towards mine. When our lips touched, all of the tension drifted away from me, leaving me with this fire that now took over. Our kiss was gentle, we knew we had all of the time in the world. His hands cupped my cheeks, then moved to the back of my neck as he pulled me closer to him. My lips parted, his tongue sliding over mine, as electricity flowed through me, making every part of me come back alive. We both pulled apart, our foreheads resting against each other's, as he looked me in my eyes.

"I love you. I always have. You were the American girl that always had my heart." With that I kissed him again. I didn't remember where I was—all I knew was that I was with Alessandro, and I was in love. Real love. The kind that makes you want to be a better person. The kind that makes you want to do everything in life, with that person always next to you.

"We should see how Arianna is doing." I said, my voice barely louder than a whisper as our foreheads still touched and our breath was still connected.

He kissed me gently on the lips again, pulled me against his chest, and hugged me. I felt safe with him. He grabbed my hand and we walked past the trees, through the park, and down to the piazza. We didn't let go, instead when we made it to the piazza, he pulled me close to him again and kissed me in front of everyone. We pulled apart, still smiling at each other, and made our way to Arianna. Out of all of the scenarios that had gone through my head, this was my favorite version of all.

22

Epilogue

Un anno dopo... A year later...

"Nonna—the architect is coming in a half hour! I think he's coming with the final plans and he said he had good news after talking to the *Municipio* about the building permits!" One of my dreams was actually coming to life—thanks to Michael who had invested in it after listening to my proposal when he and my mom came to visit over Christmas. She had been upset when I returned to Italy, refusing to talk to me for a few weeks, saying I was making the biggest mistake. But she realized I was truly happy, more than I had ever been, and we started talking again after she explained how she finally understood. We were in a much better place than before and she was even different with my nonna when they spent Christmas together, actually laughing while making struffoli and all of the typical dishes that they normally serve. My dad had visited too for Christmas, finally bringing Lisa with him, and we all celebrated together, for the first time ever.

I stood in front of the grain house, the one that was meant to always be a second home and tried to envision the *agriturismo* that would be here instead. A farm-to-table sort of hotel and restaurant. I remember coming up with a presentation about how we would convert the top half of the building to bedrooms to house the guests and the bottom half would be a restaurant and wine tasting area. Each day we would host either a cheese or pasta-making class for the tourists and then bring them out to tour the farm and work first-hand on it. Michael loved the idea and wanted to help in any way he could. He insisted on just giving me the money for it, but I wanted to pay him back—I needed to do this on my own, but knew that I needed his help to start, so I only accepted his money if he promised that he would let me pay all of it back to him. My business degree was finally being put to use, and I came up with a way that I would advertise on different websites that catered to Europeans and Americans.

I heard someone coming up behind me and smiled. "How is the wine?" I asked Alessandro as I turned around and wrapped my arms around him and gave him a kiss.

A year had passed. I thought about all of the different things we had done together. At the end of October, I had helped Alessandro with harvesting the grapes and making the wine. He had pushed me to do the *agriturismo* when I first talked to him about it, excited about the ideas I had, while we were pressing the grapes. *"Only if I can sell all of the things you make there."* I had teased, but really hoped he would agree. After the fundraiser, the town was buzzing about Alessandro's wine, with everyone begging to buy it from him. It made him a little more confident than he was before about it, but he still wasn't convinced. After begging him the next few days to let me sell it, insisting that I would only open the *agriturismo* if he would be involved, he finally caved and agreed to sell his products. I had convinced my nonna to help me find people that wanted to teach tourists how to make the different local products, and we had already lined up a list of people who were going to give everything from classes on making provolone to pappardelle by scratch. My nonna was excited to teach some of those classes too and I could see a new energy in her after we started organizing the space to host it.

"So, have you decided on the date yet? You can't keep me waiting forever you know." He said, smiling at me and brushing his fingers under my chin to lift my face up for another kiss. I looked down at my left hand, my ring finger holding now one of my favorite possessions, a yellow gold ring with a small square cut diamond in the center and two smaller diamonds on each side—Alessandro telling me they each represented the times I came to Italy and stole his heart. It was only a month since he had given it to me, but I think we both knew right away that this would happen. After I came back last year, we have been inseparable since, doing every chore together and helping each other out. I hadn't heard from Laila or Josh since last year and felt better they were out of my life since I never had been myself with them. I still kept in touch with Blake, who had got married four months ago and just shared with me that she was pregnant. When I told her I decided to go back to Italy, she had been nothing but supportive and wanted to know every little detail about what happened. I was so happy to have her back in my life.

I was lucky to have Arianna, too. She started seeing Marco a month after the fundraiser and laughed when she told us she had to give him a chance especially since he bought 200 Euros worth of food to support it. We sometimes go out together as couples or just invite them over for a quiet, but fun dinner.

"As soon as the *agriturismo* opens, we are going to celebrate it with a wedding." I said, taking his face in my hands and kissing him gently.

"It will be the biggest wedding." He said, kissing me back.

"We will have the best food and wine." I said, now letting out a small laugh.

"Really? And who will bring the food and wine?"

"Oh, I don't know. I heard Marco's wine is pretty good now too."

"Oh?" He said, now smiling against my mouth as he placed another kiss on it. "Well, at least I still have my tractor, right?"

"At least that," I said. This was me, this land, this farm, this view, and all of it with the people I love. I had no doubts, no worries, no anxiety—I was exactly where I needed to be.

"*Ti amo, Alessandro.*"

"*E io ti amerò per sempre.*"

This story was inspired by my childhood working on my grandparents' farm in a town called Sant'Angelo dei Lombardi in Avellino, Italy. My family and I would often spend the summers there, where my grandparents taught me how to plant vegetables and take care of all the animals, a big contrast from our summers on Long Island spent in our neighbor's pool or in our backyard. I learned to appreciate the simplicity of nature.

Maria D.- my editor- You have made editing something I actually look forward to! I absolutely love working with you and I am lucky to have someone like you that is talented and can understand my vision for this book! Thank you!

A big thank you to my beta readers- Denise T., Laura C., Nicole D., Kelly K., Noreen F., Elise R., Chris C., Maria T.- Your support has meant so much to me! Also, a big thank you to Nicola L. for all of your help and support through all of this!

Antonella- Thank you for always being like a sister to me. We have had some amazing memories in Italy, and we even made promises we actually kept! Lylas always!

To my grandmothers- These were women that would work tirelessly in the fields all day, manage to make a complete homemade meal for lunch and dinner, and then still take care of the house and family. You taught me what it means to be a strong Italian woman and I love and admire you! Vi voglio bene! I miss you, Grandma Filomena, but know you are watching down on us.

To my grandfathers- Thank you for patiently teaching me how to drive a manual car and how to take care of the land. I still remember my Nonno Rocco explaining how to clip back the vines so the grapes would grow the best. And still, no one makes better wine than he does. And the image of my Nonno Rocco and Grandpa Filippo being best friends and playing cards together will be something that I will always remember!

To my brother- a lot of our crazy adventures inspired some of the scenes- like you getting the car stuck in the ditch, getting water from the river for the plants, and working on Nonna and Nonno's farm! Love you!

To Jacopo- I will forever remember you taking the manuscript with you on the train rides and coming home each night excited to talk about the scenes you read. Thank you for always being my biggest fan and for supporting me from day one on this. You will always be my life and I love you so much!

Arianna and Matteo- Love you more than words will ever express! One day I might be the cool mom that wrote some books, but for now, I'll stay the crazy mom that sometimes embarrasses you! Always stay sweet and silly like you are!

My parents- It was not easy moving to another country and adjusting to a new way of life, and I can only understand that now! You both continue to make sacrifices for your kids and grandchildren, and I can only pray to be as half as good as you are! I love you both so much!

And, to all of my readers who have supported me, through texts, messages, online, and in person- this is for you! Thank you!

Le Ricette:

La crostata

This recipe came from a cousin in Italy, and it is my children's favorite dessert! I kept it in the original grams measurement since it always comes out perfect every time!

200 gr sugar
150 gr butter
400 gr flour
2 eggs
A pinch of salt
1 envelope of *Pane degli Angeli* (or substitute with 1 TB of baking powder and a teaspoon of vanilla extract)
3 to 4 tablespoons of jelly (I normally use cherry!)

Mix all of the ingredients except for the jelly together. Press the dough into the base of a pie dish and leave a little dough to the side to create lattice strips on top.

Spread jelly over dough, then create a lattice pattern with remaining dough.

Bake in a 360 degree oven for 30 minutes and enjoy!

Zucchine

A simple, yet delicious recipe to enjoy zucchini. This was my husband's favorite growing up! The zucchini becomes soft and can almost be used as a spread on bread.

4 zucchinis
¼ onion
¼ tsp salt
2 cloves garlic
Oil
Parsley

Cut zucchini lengthwise, then cut in ½" pieces. Add to pot.
Chop the onions and garlic and add them to the pot. Sprinkle a ¼ teaspoon of salt on them.
Add 2 TB of oil, then cover the pot and let cook slowly on medium-low heat, turning every 5 minutes.
After 20 minutes, uncover and let cook for an additional 10 minutes. (Add more salt if needed!)

Bruschetta

This versatile side can be a fun stand-alone with crunchy Italian bread at your next barbecue or a topping to many dishes! Let your creativity run with this recipe!

4 Campari tomatoes (or tomatoes on the vine)
1 TB of fresh basil, chopped
1 tsp fresh parsley, chopped
½ tsp of dried oregano
2 TB minced red onion
1 clove of garlic (pressed)
¼ tsp salt
1 cup of mini mozzarella pearls (optional)
2 TB extra virgin olive oil
1 TB balsamic vinegar

Dice tomatoes in tiny cubes (I cut it lengthwise first, then halve that before dicing them).

Place into a bowl and add salt, garlic, basil, red onion, parsley, and oregano. Add mini mozzarella if using. Combine all together.

Add oil and vinegar. Combine well.

Can be served with toasted bread or used as a topping on a chicken or fish dish!

www.ingramcontent.com/pod-product-compliance
Lightning Source LLC
Chambersburg PA
CBHW070452300726
48975CB00007B/2142